The Third Reel West

The Third Reel West

EDITED BY BILL PRONZINI
AND MARTIN H. GREENBERG

DOUBLEDAY & COMPANY, INC.

GARDEN CITY, NEW YORK

1986

All of the characters in this book
are fictitious, and any resemblance
to actual persons, living or dead,
is purely coincidental.

Acknowledgments

"Raiders Die Hard" by John M. Cunningham. Copyright © 1952 by Popular Publications, Inc. First published in *Dime Western.* Reprinted by permission of the author and Knox Burger Associates.

"Mission with No Record" by James Warner Bellah. Copyright © 1947 by The Curtis Publishing Company. First published in *The Saturday Evening Post.* Reprinted by permission of Scott Meredith Literary Agency, Inc., 845 Third Avenue, New York, New York 10022.

"The Hanging Tree" by Dorothy M. Johnson. Copyright © 1957 by Dorothy M. Johnson; copyright © renewed 1985 by Raymond J. Fox, Executor of the Estate of Dorothy M. Johnson. Reprinted by permission of McIntosh and Otis, Inc.

Library of Congress Cataloging-in-Publication Data
Main entry under title:
The Third reel west.
Contents: The luck of Roaring Camp/Bret Harte—
The parson of Panamint/Peter B. Kyne—
The caballero's way/O. Henry—[etc.]
1. Western stories.   2. Western stories—Film adaptations.
3. Short stories, American.   I. Pronzini, Bill.
II. Greenberg, Martin Harry.
PS648.W4T45   1986   813'.0874'08   85–31111
ISBN 0-385-23406-6

First Edition

Contents

Publisher 6/86

Introduction

Like the two volumes which preceded it, *The Reel West* (Doubleday, 1984) and *The Second Reel West* (Doubleday, 1985), *The Third Reel West* is an anthology of outstanding Western short stories which were the bases for noteworthy films. In our introductions to the first two volumes we made a point which is also applicable here: some of the tales in these pages have not been faithfully transferred to the screen, while others contributed only the basic idea to the movies they became. None is exactly like its Hollywood adaptation; some are barely recognizable as source material, after having gone through the multifarious hands of producers, directors, actors, and (especially) screenwriters. A comparison of the two versions of each entry can be educational, in that it offers an insight into the workings of the "Hollywood mind."

To begin with, we'll look at each of the films in chronological order:

The Cisco Kid (1931) is based on "The Caballero's Way" by the noted short story writer O. Henry (William Sydney Porter), a story which introduced the Cisco Kid, one of the most enduring of Western characters. Some two dozen feature films, from the silent French production of *The Caballero's Way* in 1914 to *The Girl from San Lorenzo* in 1950, featured this romantic, dashing figure. (At least he became a romantic, dashing figure in his cinematic incarnations; ironically, the character as originally conceived by O. Henry is anything but a "Robin Hood of the Old West.") In addition, the Kid appeared on radio in 1943, with Jackson Beck in the lead role, and of course on television; 156 episodes of "The Cisco Kid" were aired between 1951 and 1955, and are still in syndication. Unfortunately, the television version contains quite stereotypical Hispanics and has been attacked by representatives of this group. Duncan Renaldo starred as TV's Cisco, and Leo Carrillo as his good-natured sidekick, Pancho. The 1931 film version featured Warner Baxter in a reprise of the role that won him an Oscar in *In Old Arizona* (1929), the first all-sound Western talkie. Edmund Lowe also repeated his role as the Texas Ranger from the earlier film, while Nora Lane and Conchita Montenegro provided the love interests. Also appearing was Chris-Pin Martin, a fine actor who would find steady employment in a long string of Hollywood Westerns. Baxter played Cisco once more, in *The Return of the Cisco Kid* (1939).

The Luck of Roaring Camp (1937) is based on the famous Bret Harte story of the same title. This production was one of hundreds turned out by Monogram Pictures, perhaps the leading institution on Hollywood's "Poverty Row," and suffers from the tiny budget within which director Irving Willat had to work. Nevertheless, the film effectively captures the sentimentality of the story and has some good moments. Monogram regulars Joan Woodbury and Charles King starred.

Peter B. Kyne's *Saturday Evening Post* novelette provided the plot for *The Parson of Panamint* (1941), an entertaining, low-key film about a Western preacher (played by Philip Terry) who tries to reform a rugged mining town down on its luck. Directed by Harry Sherman, it also features Charles Ruggles, Ellen Drew, and that too-little-known product of the Yiddish theater, Joseph Schildkraut.

The final installment of John Ford's acclaimed "cavalry trilogy," *Rio Grande* (1950), was based on James Warner Bellah's story "Mission with No Record" and has an impressive cast that includes John Wayne, Maureen O'Hara, Victor McLaglen, Ben Johnson, J. Carrol Naish, Chill Wills, and Ken Curtis. As memorable as script (written by James K. McGuinness), acting, and direction is the cinematography, which features some superb vistas of Monument Valley. As are the other two films in the trilogy, *Fort Apache* (1948) and *She Wore a Yellow Ribbon* (1949), *Rio Grande* is concerned with personal heroism and unabashed patriotism, as a common enemy (the Apaches) unites soldiers from the North and South who only a few years before had been fighting each other in the Civil War.

John M. Cunningham's *Dime Western* pulp novelette "Raiders Die Hard" served as the basis for 1958's excellent *Day of the Bad Man*, directed by Harry Keller. The film stars Fred MacMurray as a circuit judge who refuses to give in to threats made by the four brothers of a convicted murderer, and is packed with the same kind of tension that makes *High Noon* (also based on a Cunningham short story) such a classic. Joan Weldon, John Ericson, Robert Middleton, Edgar Buchanan, and Lee Van Cleef had supporting roles.

The Hanging Tree (1959), adapted from Dorothy M. Johnson's poignant novella of the same title, features another outstanding performance by Gary Cooper. In his next-to-last Western film, Cooper portrays a doctor trying to forget his past in a mountain mining camp, until the blinded survivor of an Indian raid (played by Maria Schell) gives him a new lease on life. The supporting cast is uniformly excellent. George C. Scott (in a memorable role as a mad preacher) and Ben Piazza made their screen debuts; and Karl Malden (who doubled as emergency director when illness struck Delmer Daves) gives his usual flawless performance.

These, then, are the films; now for the stories that inspired them— stories that, like those in *The Reel West* and *The Second Reel West,* are among the most entertaining in the Western genre. Good reading.

—Bill Pronzini and
Martin H. Greenberg,
October 1985

The Third Reel West

The Luck of Roaring Camp

BY BRET HARTE

(The Luck of Roaring Camp)

Like his friend (and later rival) Mark Twain, Bret Harte (1836–1902) was a California resident during the years following the 1849 Gold Rush and wrote hundreds of stories and sketches about that lusty period in American history. The Writings of Bret Harte *were published in twenty volumes —eighteen of fiction, two of poetry—between 1896 and 1904, and comprise the most complete and colorful body of imaginative work about the Gold Rush era. Numerous films were made from Harte's short fiction, most of them silents. In addition to* The Luck of Roaring Camp, *other talkies of note are* Tennessee's Partner *(1955), with John Payne and Ronald Reagan, from the story of the same title (see* The Reel West); *and two versions of* The Outcasts of Poker Flat, *also from the story of the same title (included in* The Second Reel West), *the first version made in 1937 with Preston Foster and Van Heflin, the second in 1952 with Dale Robertson and Cameron Mitchell.*

There was commotion in Roaring Camp. It could not have been a fight, for in 1850 that was not novel enough to have called together the entire settlement. The ditches and claims were not only deserted, but "Tuttle's grocery" had contributed its gamblers, who, it will be remembered, calmly continued their game the day that French Pete and Kanaka Joe shot each other to death over the bar in the front room. The whole camp was collected before a rude cabin on the outer edge of the clearing. Conversation was carried on in a low tone, but the name of a woman was frequently repeated. It was a name familiar enough in the camp—"Cherokee Sal."

Perhaps the less said of her the better. She was a coarse and, it is to be feared, a very sinful woman. But at that time she was the only woman in Roaring Camp, and was just then lying in sore extremity, when she most needed the ministration of her own sex. Dissolute, abandoned, and irreclaimable, she was yet suffering a martyrdom hard enough to bear even when veiled by sympathizing womanhood, but now terrible in her loneliness. The primal curse had come to her in that original isolation which must have made the punishment of the first transgression so dreadful. It was, perhaps, part of the expiation of her sin that, at a moment when she most lacked her sex's intuitive tenderness and care, she met only the half-contemptuous faces of her masculine associates. Yet a few of the spectators were, I think, touched by her sufferings. Sandy Tipton thought it was "rough on Sal," and in the contemplation of her condition, for a moment rose superior to the fact that he had an ace and two bowers in his sleeve.

It will be seen also that the situation was novel. Deaths were by no means uncommon in Roaring Camp, but a birth was a new thing. People had been dismissed the camp effectively, finally, and with no possibility of return; but this was the first time that anybody had been introduced *ab initio*. Hence the excitement.

"You go in there, Stumpy," said a prominent citizen known as "Kentuck," addressing one of the loungers. "Go in there, and see what you kin do. You've had experience in them things."

Perhaps there was a fitness in the selection. Stumpy, in other climes, had been the putative head of two families; in fact, it was owing to some legal informality in these proceedings that Roaring Camp—a city of refuge—was indebted to his company. The crowd approved the choice, and Stumpy was wise enough to bow to the majority. The door closed on the extempore surgeon and midwife, and Roaring Camp sat down outside, smoked its pipe, and awaited the issue.

The assemblage numbered about a hundred men. One or two of these were actual fugitives from justice, some were criminal, and all were reckless. Physically they exhibited no indication of their past lives and character. The greatest scamp had a Raphael face, with a profusion of blond hair; Oakhurst, a gambler, had the melancholy air and intellectual abstraction of a Hamlet; the coolest and most courageous man was scarcely over five feet in height, with a soft voice and an embarrassed, timid manner. The term "roughs" applied to them was a distinction rather than a definition. Perhaps in the minor details of fingers, toes, ears, etc., the camp may have been deficient, but these slight omissions did not detract from their aggregate force. The strongest man had but three fingers on his right hand; the best shot had but one eye.

Such was the physical aspect of the men that were dispersed around the cabin. The camp lay in a triangular valley between two hills and a river.

The only outlet was a steep trail over the summit of a hill that faced the cabin, now illuminated by the rising moon. The suffering woman might have seen it from the rude bunk whereon she lay—seen it winding like a silver thread until it was lost in the stars above.

A fire of withered pine boughs added sociability to the gathering. By degrees the natural levity of Roaring Camp returned. Bets were freely offered and taken regarding the result. Three to five that "Sal would get through with it"; even that the child would survive; side bets as to the sex and complexion of the coming stranger. In the midst of an excited discussion an exclamation came from those nearest the door, and the camp stopped to listen. Above the swaying and moaning of the pines, the swift rush of the river, and the crackling of the fire rose a sharp, querulous cry— a cry unlike anything heard before in the camp. The pines stopped moaning, the river ceased to rush, and the fire to crackle. It seemed as if Nature had stopped to listen too.

The camp rose to its feet as one man! It was proposed to explode a barrel of gunpowder; but in consideration of the situation of the mother, better counsels prevailed, and only a few revolvers were discharged; for whether owing to the rude surgery of the camp, or some other reason, Cherokee Sal was sinking fast. Within an hour she had climbed, as it were, that rugged road that led to the stars, and so passed out of Roaring Camp, its sin and shame, forever. I do not think that the announcement disturbed them much, except in speculation as to the fate of the child. "Can he live now?" was asked of Stumpy. The answer was doubtful. The only other being of Cherokee Sal's sex and maternal condition in the settlement was an ass. There was some conjecture as to fitness, but the experiment was tried. It was less problematical than the ancient treatment of Romulus and Remus, and apparently as successful.

When these details were completed, which exhausted another hour, the door was opened, and the anxious crowd of men, who had already formed themselves into a queue, entered in single file. Beside the low bunk or shelf, on which the figure of the mother was starkly outlined below the blankets, stood a pine table. On this a candlebox was placed, and within it, swathed in staring red flannel, lay the last arrival at Roaring Camp. Beside the candlebox was placed a hat. Its use was soon indicated. "Gentlemen," said Stumpy, with a singular mixture of authority and *ex officio* complacency—"gentlemen will please pass in at the front door, round the table, and out at the back door. Them as wishes to contribute anything toward the orphan will find a hat handy." The first man entered with his hat on; he uncovered, however, as he looked about him, and so unconsciously set an example to the next. In such communities good and bad actions are catching. As the procession filed in comments were audible—criticisms addressed perhaps rather to Stumpy in the character of showman: "Is that him?" "Mighty small specimen;" "Hasn't more'n got the color;" "Ain't bigger nor a derringer." The contributions were as characteristic: A silver tobacco box; a doubloon; a navy revolver, silver mounted; a gold specimen; a very beautifully embroidered lady's handkerchief (from Oakhurst the gambler); a diamond breastpin; a diamond ring (suggested by the pin, with the remark from the giver that he "saw that pin and went two diamonds better"); a slung shot; a Bible (contributor not detected); a golden spur; a silver teaspoon (the initials, I regret to say, were not the giver's); a pair of surgeon's shears; a lancet; a Bank of England note for £5; and about $200 in loose gold and silver coin. During these proceedings Stumpy maintained a silence as impassive as the dead on his left, a gravity as inscrutable as that of the newly born on his right. Only one incident occurred to break the monotony of the curious procession. As Kentuck bent over the candlebox half curiously, the child turned, and, in a spasm of pain, caught at his groping finger and held it fast for a moment. Kentuck looked foolish and embarrassed. Something like a blush tried to assert itself in his weather-beaten cheek. "The d—d little cuss!" he said, as he extricated his finger, with perhaps more tenderness and care than he might have been deemed capable of showing. He held that finger a little apart from its fellows as he went out, and examined it curiously. The examination provoked the same original remark in regard to the child. In fact, he seemed to enjoy repeating it. "He rastled with my finger," he remarked to Tipton, holding up the member, "the d—d little cuss!"

It was four o'clock before the camp sought repose. A light burnt in the cabin where the watchers sat, for Stumpy did not go to bed that night. Nor did Kentuck. He drank quite freely, and related with great gusto his experience, invariably ending with his characteristic condemnation of the newcomer. It seemed to relieve him of any unjust implication of sentiment, and Kentuck had the weaknesses of the nobler sex. When everybody else had gone to bed, he walked down to the river and whistled reflectingly. Then he walked up the gulch past the cabin, still whistling with demonstrative unconcern. At a large redwood tree he paused and retraced his steps, and again passed the cabin. Halfway down to the river's bank he again paused, and then returned and knocked at the door. It was opened by Stumpy. "How goes it?" said Kentuck, looking past Stumpy toward the candlebox. "All serene!" replied Stumpy. "Anything up?" "Nothing." There was a pause—an embarrassing one—Stumpy still holding the door. Then Kentuck had recourse to his finger, which he held up to Stumpy. "Rastled with it—the d—d little cuss," he said, and retired.

The next day Cherokee Sal had such rude sepulture as Roaring Camp afforded. After her body had been committed to the hillside, there was a formal meeting of the camp to discuss what should be done with her infant. A resolution to adopt it was unanimous and enthusiastic. But an animated discussion in regard to the manner and feasibility of providing for its wants at once sprang up. It was remarkable that the argument partook of none of those fierce personalities with which discussions were usually conducted at Roaring Camp. Tipton proposed that they should send the child to Red Dog—a distance of forty miles—where female attention could be procured. But the unlucky suggestion met with fierce and unanimous opposition. It was evident that no plan which entailed parting from their new acquisition would for a moment be entertained. "Besides," said Tom Ryder, "them fellows at Red Dog would swap it, and ring in somebody else on us." A disbelief in the honesty of other camps prevailed at Roaring Camp, as in other places.

The introduction of a female nurse in the camp also met with objection. It was argued that no decent woman could be prevailed to accept Roaring Camp as her home, and the speaker urged that "they didn't want any more of the other kind." This unkind allusion to the defunct mother, harsh as it may seem, was the first spasm of propriety—the first symptom of the camp's regeneration. Stumpy advanced nothing. Perhaps he felt a certain delicacy in interfering with the selection of a possible successor in office. But when questioned, he averred stoutly that he and "Jinny"—the mammal before alluded to—could manage to rear the child. There was something original, independent, and heroic about the plan that pleased the camp. Stumpy was retained. Certain articles were sent for to Sacramento. "Mind," said the treasurer, as he pressed a bag of gold dust into the expressman's hand, "the best that can be got—lace, you know, and filigree work and frills—d—n the cost!"

Strange to say, the child thrived. Perhaps the invigorating climate of the mountain camp was compensation for material deficiencies. Nature took the foundling to her broader breast. In that rare atmosphere of the Sierra foothills—that air pungent with balsamic odor, that ethereal cordial at once bracing and exhilarating—he may have found food and nourishment, or a subtle chemistry that transmuted ass's milk to lime and phosphorus. Stumpy inclined to the belief that it was the latter and good nursing. "Me and that ass," he would say, "has been father and mother to him! Don't you," he would add, apostrophizing the helpless bundle before him, "never go back on us."

By the time he was a month old the necessity of giving him a name became apparent. He had generally been known as "The Kid," "Stumpy's Boy," "The Coyote" (an allusion to his vocal powers), and even by Kentuck's endearing diminutive of "The d—d little cuss." But these were felt to be vague and unsatisfactory, and were at last dismissed under another influence. Gamblers and adventurers are generally superstitious, and Oakhurst one day declared that the baby had brought "the luck" to Roaring Camp. It was certain that of late they had been successful. "Luck" was the name agreed upon, with the prefix of Tommy for greater convenience. No allusion was made to the mother, and the father was unknown. "It's better," said the philosophical Oakhurst, "to take a fresh deal all round. Call him Luck, and start him fair." A day was accordingly set apart for the christening. What was meant by this ceremony the reader may imagine who has already gathered some idea of the reckless irreverence of Roaring Camp. The master of ceremonies was one "Boston," a noted wag, and the occasion seemed to promise the greatest facetiousness. This ingenious satirist had spent two days in preparing a burlesque of the Church service, with pointed local allusions. The choir was properly trained, and Sandy Tipton was to stand godfather. But after the procession had marched to the grove with music and banners, and the child had been deposited before a mock altar, Stumpy stepped before the expectant crowd. "It ain't my style to spoil fun, boys," said the little man, stoutly eying the faces around him, "but it strikes me that this thing ain't exactly on the squar. It's playing it pretty low down on this yer baby to ring in fun on him that he ain't goin' to understand. And ef there's goin' to be any godfathers round, I'd like to see who's got any better rights than me." A silence followed Stumpy's speech. To the credit of all humorists be it said that the first man to acknowledge its justice was the satirist thus stopped of his fun. "But," said Stumpy, quickly following up his advantage, "we're here for a christening, and we'll have it. I proclaim you Thomas Luck, according to the laws of the United States and the State of California, so help me God." It was the first time that the name of the Deity had been otherwise uttered than profanely in the camp. The form of christening was perhaps even more ludicrous than the satirist had conceived; but strangely enough, nobody saw it and nobody laughed. "Tommy" was christened as seriously as he would have been under a Christian roof, and cried and was comforted in as orthodox fashion.

And so the work of regeneration began in Roaring Camp. Almost imperceptibly a change came over the settlement. The cabin assigned to "Tommy Luck"—or "The Luck," as he was more frequently called—first showed signs of improvement. It was kept scrupulously clean and white-washed. Then it was boarded, clothed, and papered. The rosewood cradle, packed eighty miles by mule, had, in Stumpy's way of putting it, "sorter killed the rest of the furniture." So the rehabilitation of the camp became a necessity. The men who were in the habit of lounging in at Stumpy's to see "how 'The Luck' got on" seemed to appreciate the change, and in self-defense the rival establishment of "Tuttle's grocery" bestirred itself and imported a carpet and mirrors. The reflections of the latter on the appearance of Roaring Camp tended to produce stricter habits of personal clean-liness. Again Stumpy imposed a kind of quarantine upon those who aspired to the honor and privilege of holding The Luck. It was a cruel mortification to Kentuck—who, in the carelessness of a large nature and the habits of frontier life, had begun to regard all garments as a second cuticle, which, like a snake's, only sloughed off through decay—to be debarred this privilege from certain prudential reasons. Yet such was the subtle influence of innovation that he thereafter appeared regularly every afternoon in a clean shirt and face still shining from his ablutions. Nor were moral and social sanitary laws neglected. "Tommy," who was supposed to spend his whole existence in a persistent attempt to repose, must not be disturbed by noise. The shouting and yelling, which had gained the camp its infelicitous title, were not permitted within hearing distance of Stumpy's. The men conversed in whispers or smoked with Indian gravity. Profanity was tacitly given up in these sacred precincts, and throughout the camp a popular form of expletive, known as "D—n the luck!" and "Curse the luck!" was abandoned, as having a new personal bearing. Vocal music was not interdicted, being supposed to have a soothing, tran-quilizing quality; and one song, sung by "Man-o'-War Jack," an English sailor from her Majesty's Australian colonies, was quite popular as a lul-laby. It was a lugubrious recital of the exploits of "the Arethusa, Seventy-four," in a muffled minor, ending with a prolonged dying fall at the burden of each verse, "On b-oo-o-ard of the Arethusa." It was a fine sight to see Jack holding The Luck, rocking from side to side as if with the motion of a ship, and crooning forth this naval ditty. Either through the peculiar rocking of Jack or the length of his song—it contained ninety stanzas, and was continued with conscientious deliberation to the bitter end—the lullaby generally had the desired effect. At such times the men would lie at full length under the trees in the soft summer twilight, smok-ing their pipes and drinking in the melodious utterances. An indistinct idea that this was pastoral happiness pervaded the camp. "This 'ere kind o' think," said the Cockney Simmons, meditatively reclining on his elbow, "is 'evingly." It reminded him of Greenwich.

On the long summer days The Luck was usually carried to the gulch from whence the golden store of Roaring Camp was taken. There, on a blanket spread over pine boughs, he would lie while the men were working in the ditches below. Latterly there was a rude attempt to decorate this bower with flowers and sweet-smelling shrubs, and generally some one would bring him a cluster of wild honeysuckles, azaleas, or the painted blossoms of Las Mariposas. The men had suddenly awakened to the fact that there were beauty and significance in these trifles, which they had so long trodden carelessly beneath their feet. A flake of glittering mica, a fragment of variegated quartz, a bright pebble from the bed of the creek, became beautiful to eyes thus cleared and strengthened, and were invariably put aside for The Luck. It was wonderful how many treasures the woods and hillsides yielded that "would do for Tommy." Surrounded by playthings such as never child out of fairyland had before, it is to be hoped that Tommy was content. He appeared to be serenely happy, albeit there was an infantine gravity about him, a contemplative light in his round gray eyes, that sometimes worried Stumpy. He was always tractable and quiet, and it is recorded that once, having crept beyond his "corral"—a hedge of tessellated pine boughs, which surrounded his bed—he dropped over the bank on his head in the soft earth, and remained with his mottled legs in the air in that position for at least five minutes with unflinching gravity. He was extricated without a murmur. I hesitate to record the many other instances of his sagacity, which rest, unfortunately, upon the statements of prejudiced friends. Some of them were not without a tinge of superstition. "I crep' up the bank just now," said Kentuck one day, in a breathless state of excitement, "and dern my skin if he wasn't a-talking to a jay bird as was a-sittin' on his lap. There they was, just as free and sociable as anything you please, a-jawin' at each other just like two cherrybums." Howbeit, whether creeping over the pine boughs or lying lazily on his back blinking at the leaves above him, to him the birds sang, the squirrels chattered, and the flowers bloomed. Nature was his nurse and playfellow. For him she would let slip between the leaves golden shafts of sunlight that fell just within his grasp; she would send wandering breezes to visit him with the balm of bay and resinous gum; to him the tall redwoods nodded familiarly and sleepily, the bumblebees buzzed, and the rooks cawed a slumbrous accompaniment.

Such was the golden summer of Roaring Camp. They were "flush times," and the luck was with them. The claims had yielded enormously. The camp was jealous of its privileges and looked suspiciously on strangers. No encouragement was given to immigration, and, to make their seclusion more perfect, the land on either side of the mountain wall that surrounded the camp they duly preempted. This, and a reputation for singular proficiency with the revolver, kept the reserve of Roaring Camp inviolate. The expressman—their only connecting link with the surrounding world—sometimes told wonderful stories of the camp. He would say, "They've a street up there in 'Roaring' that would lay over any street in Red Dog. They've got vines and flowers round their houses, and they wash themselves twice a day. But they're mighty rough on strangers, and they worship an Ingin baby."

With the prosperity of the camp came a desire for further improvement. It was proposed to build a hotel in the following spring, and to invite one or two decent families to reside there for the sake of The Luck, who might perhaps profit by female companionship. The sacrifice that this concession to the sex cost these men, who were fiercely skeptical in regard to its general virtue and usefulness, can only be accounted for by their affection for Tommy. A few still held out. But the resolve could not be carried into effect for three months, and the minority meekly yielded in the hope that something might turn up to prevent it. And it did.

The winter of 1851 will long be remembered in the foothills. The snow lay deep on the Sierras, and every mountain creek became a river, and every river a lake. Each gorge and gulch was transformed into a tumultuous watercourse that descended the hillsides, tearing down giant trees and scattering its drift and debris along the plain. Red Dog had been twice under water, and Roaring Camp had been forewarned. "Water put the gold into them gulches," said Stumpy. "It's been here once and will be here again!" And that night the North Fork suddenly leaped over its banks and swept up the triangular valley of Roaring Camp.

In the confusion of rushing water, crashing trees, and crackling timber, and the darkness which seemed to flow with the water and blot out the fair valley, but little could be done to collect the scattered camp. When the morning broke, the cabin of Stumpy, nearest the riverbank, was gone. Higher up the gulch they found the body of its unlucky owner; but the pride, the hope, the joy, The Luck, of Roaring Camp had disappeared. They were returning with sad hearts when a shout from the bank recalled them.

It was a relief-boat from down the river. They had picked up, they said, a man and an infant, nearly exhausted, about two miles below. Did anybody know them, and did they belong here?

It needed but a glance to show them Kentuck lying there, cruelly crushed and bruised, but still holding The Luck of Roaring Camp in his arms. As they bent over the strangely assorted pair, they saw that the child was cold and pulseless. "He is dead," said one. Kentuck opened his eyes. "Dead?" he repeated feebly. "Yes, my man, and you are dying too." A smile lit the eyes of the expiring Kentuck. "Dying!" he repeated; "he's a-taking me with him. Tell the boys I've got The Luck with me now;" and the strong man, clinging to the frail babe as a drowning man is said to cling to a straw, drifted away into the shadowy river that flows forever to the unknown sea.

The Parson of Panamint

BY PETER B. KYNE

(The Parson of Panamint)

Peter B. Kyne (1880–1957) was a widely read and much loved author during the early years of this century. Particularly popular was his series chronicling the amusing adventures of a Pacific Coast entrepreneur named Cappy Ricks and his son-in-law, Matt Peasley. Kyne also wrote four Western novels, and numerous Western short stories (the best of which can be found in his 1929 collection, The Parson of Panamint and Other Stories). *One of the novels,* Three Godfathers, *was filmed no less than six times, most notably in 1948 as* The Three Godfathers, *with John Ford directing. Dozens of silent films were produced from Kyne's works, and several other sound films as well—all of them of negligible interest.*

I had been prospecting with Chuckwalla Bill in the Coso Range, working eastward out of Darwin into the desolate region stretching away toward Death Valley. Along in the late afternoon we passed through a rocky defile and emerged into a sage flat about a mile square hemmed in by naked red buttes; and shortly thereafter I commenced to make frequent discoveries in the stunted sage of ancient, rust-corroded tin cans. These indicating that we were approaching a camp, I mentioned my suspicions to Chuckwalla Bill.

"Yes," he replied dully; "we're gettin' right close to Panamint."

We pressed slowly onward, herding the burros before us, and at sunset we came on the camp. Chuckwalla Bill saw it first.

"There's Panamint," he said, pointing; and added: "Philip's church is gone at last."

I gazed ahead into the violet shadows trooping up the valley and beheld a huge heap of rusty tin cans of assorted sizes, similar to those we had passed earlier in the day. They were scattered over nearly an acre of ground and piled to a depth of several feet; wherefore, in the absence of other sign of human habitation, past or present, I was not long in fixing the exact geographical locus of Panamint. It lay in the heart of old Chuckwalla Bill, as his next remark fully convinced me.

"I was mayor o' that city oncet," he said wistfully, and recited an extemporaneous paraphrase of an old poem:

> "Her picks is rust;
> Her bones is dust
> It's thirty years since she went bust."

Son, let's crack along over to the foot o' Amethyst Avenoo an' bed down for the night at Jake Russell's well."

After supper he told me this tale of the Parson of Panamint.

Yes, sir [began Chuckwalla Bill] I make the first strike in these parts, an' when I pack back to Darwin for more grub an' dynamite, an' show my samples, I start a stampede. In six months we have a city three thousand strong, not countin' Injuns an' Greasers, of which we have our share in them days. Panamint's a silver camp, an' all this I'm goin' to tell you is pulled off before silver gets demonetized an' silver mines so far from everywhere as Panamint can't be worked no more at a profit, which is why Panamint goes bust. An' when a minin' camp goes bust oncet, she's got a black eye forever an' don't revive nohow. Besides, we don't have much water in Panamint; an' that's a drawback. Teamin' water in from Darwin runs up the cost o' livin' too high, with silver down to sixty-seven.

Son, my tomato cans is the first on that dump—an' the last. I stake out the Panamint Lily, an' a dozen good claims besides, before ever I tip off the news o' my strike; an' then I sell the Lily for five hundred thousand cash an' lease my other claims on a good royalty. I cal'late mebbe I'm worth at the time a coupler million dollars; so nachelly I can't see my way clear to labor none, an' I look round for a hobby.

I find her in Panamint.

Son, Panamint's my sweetheart. I'm raisin' thirty years at the time, full o' blue blood an' conceit, like a barber's cat; an' folks takes to callin' me the Father o' Panamint. Nachelly, me bein' responsible for the camp, as the feller says, I'm prouder'n a roadrunner of it.

I get to dreamin' big dreams o' the future o' Panamint, an' I sink a deal o' money in local real estate, start a bank, import a printin' press an' an editor, an' a rig to drill for water; an', in general, I get behind Panamint with my personality an' my bank roll, an' boost the municipality.

I reckon we're about eight months old, an' growin' like a stall-fed calf, when Hank Bartlett—Hank's a scholar an' a gentleman, an' I stake him to a daily paper called the Panamint Nugget, an' subsidize him till he's on a payin' basis—writes an editorial advocatin' the incorporation o' the camp as a regular city.

The idee's a hummer an' I get back of it right off; so we incorporate Panamint an' I run for mayor agin a party by the name o' Jedge Tarbox.

The jedge 'lows as how his record in the Civil War's bound to help him; but I'm the daddy o' Panamint, an' I'm swept into office—me an' my ticket—by such a majority the jedge comes out with a signed article in the Nugget apologizin' for livin', an' moves to make it unanimous. I'm so proud o' that ol' warrior I give the city-attorney-elect a thousand dollars to resign his office so's I can app'int Jedge Tarbox in his place.

As I remarks previous, I'm all wrapped up in Panamint. I'm plannin' to make her the biggest silver camp in the West an' advancin' her interests every way I know how, so, right after I'm sworn in as mayor, me an' Hank Bartlett puts our heads together an' holds a potlatch.

As a result Hank writes an editorial callin' for a mass meetin' to advocate the three things the camp's got to have if she's goin' to press for'd to her destiny. Them three things is a town hall, a schoolhouse an' a church; for, though Panamint's a camp with the hair on her—an' I wouldn't give a damn to be mayor o' no other kind—still, there's plenty o' women an' children, an' good, solid citizens with us already, an' more willin' to come if we give 'em the things they're used to in more cultivated sections that lies closer to water an' railroads.

Well, son, we hold that mass meetin', an' Hank Bartlett makes a speech that shore gets the money. Me, I ain't never what the feller calls silver-tongued, but I make a brief talk, nevertheless, to sorter back up Hank's play an' give it official sanction. Then I call for subscriptions to the buildin' fund, an' as mayor I start the ball rollin' with ten thousand dollars an' pledge the camp treasury for five more if the citizens at large'll make up the rest. We're askin' for fifty thousand dollars until Panamint's on a self-supportin' basis; an' in half an hour I have it and the committees are app'inted.

It's sixty days before we get the lumber freighted in from Mojave, an' the church an' the schoolhouse up. Meantime Hank Bartlett, whose hand-writin' is somethin' to admire, has wrote to the state superintendent o' schools askin' him to send us a bang-up schoolmarm, which the super done; an' as I remember she was right satisfactory. Also, the Committee on Ree-ligion—which I'm the committee—has pulled out for San Francisco to round up a preacher, aimin' to come back with him about the time the parsonage is up.

Now this question of a preacher's been worryin' me no little. We got a coupler Jews in commercial lines, an' some Irish Catholics; but, by an' large, the bulk o' the population o' Panamint is Protestant. We got Methodists an' Baptists an' Congregationalists an' Mormons an' Unitarians an' Episcopals, an' what-all; but I figure it out as how all these here sects nachelly comes under the same general head, an' one good, bang-up parson that don't stir up no secular strife is shore bound to please all hands.

Pers'nally I don't have no more ree-ligious convictions than a tarantula, but, all the same, I don't lose sight o' the fact that ree-ligion is a heap o' comfort to a lot o' people; so nachelly I'm careful in makin' my selection. I'm the butt end of a month sortin' over parsons an' conferrin' with bishops, lookin' for a big, broad-gage young feller that don't take his ree-ligion too hard; for I realize that a parson with the ingrowin' brand o' faith ain't goin' to be popular in Panamint. As I say, she's a camp with the hair on her, but her heart's right an' she means well; an' all a feller has to do is overlook a few things that are peculiar to boom camps an' can't be helped nohow.

Son, that time I put in lookin' for my ideal of a preacher is about the hardest three weeks I'm ever through. My previous experience with parsons an' bishops is limited; an', havin' allers been used to a free range an' free speech, I suppose I don't make a hit with a lot of them. They're all a-wonderin' what Panamint looks like if I'm her mayor, I guess; an' none of 'em is inclined to take a chance, even if I let 'em, which I do not, because I don't see none that measures up to my standards. I'm plumb discouraged when Fate, as the feller says, bumps me up agin the Reverend Philip Pharo. We meet this way:

There's a strike on in the mee-tropolis while I'm there preacher-prospectin'. I'm leavin' the Occidental Hotel for a little *pasear* up Montgomery Street when I'm aware o' some excitement. A feller comes chargin' down the street to beat four of a kind, with mebbe a dozen men a-chasin' him an' yellin': "Scab! Scab! Kill the scab!"

Now, son, I'm not interested a little bit in this round-up. In Panamint it's the custom to let every man roll his own hoop; an', as this fugitive is makin' fast headway, I don't feel called on to interfere, particularly as it looks to me like there's goin' to be a heap o' yellin' an' no killin'. In consequence I'm a mite surprised when a half a brick reaches the runner in the back o' the head an' he falls almost in front o' me.

"That mob'll kick him to death," says a voice alongside o' me; an' a

young feller jumps past me, grabs the victim by the collar an' drags him
into a doorway, where they can't get at him. Then he faces the mob with
his fists an' drops the first two men that closes in on him.

Son, I'm a fightin' tarantula in them days. There ain't nothin' I won't
tackle, once the play is up to me fair; an' it gravels me to see a dozen men
pickin' on one. Also it pleases me to see the businesslike way this interferin' stranger faces the music, a-knowin' they're goin' to tromp him to
death an' make a rag baby out o' him in half a minute; so while they're
swarmin' over him I'm gettin' out my artillery an' fixin' to help the young
feller out a little.

Before they can get him down I'm wadin' into the riot, tampin' sociable
left an' right with my weepon; an' in half a minute me an' this young
stranger ee-merges from the conflict, bloody but victorious, an' in the
hands of a dozen policemen.

They take my gun away from me, which I'm too law-abidin' to object,
an' then we're took to a hospital an' patched up, though there ain't
nothin' serious wrong with either of us. We got forty fights left in us yet.
From the hospital we're taken to the police station, where the young
feller's booked for incitin' a riot, with his bail fixed at five hundred dollars;
an' me—son, I'm charged with assault with a deadly weepon. The ar-
restin' officer says as how I'm a gun-fighter an' a dangerous character, an'
they make my bail a thousand dollars.

I can see my feller criminal is staggered at this state of affairs, but it's
plumb amusin' to me. I have a money belt under my shirt next my skin,
which I hauls her out an' counts out fifteen hundred dollars on the
counter.

"Gimme a receipt," I says. "This young friend o' mine is John J. Jones,
an' I'm Chuckwalla Bill Redfield, mayor o' Panamint, which Panamint's
the biggest-feelin' camp on earth." I'm that patriotic nothin' can keep me
from advertisin' Panamint.

So the officer takes us to another feller at a desk, an' he rakes in my
fifteen hundred, gives me separate receipts, an' tells us to come back for
trial in the mornin'.

When we're safe outside the police station the young feller thanks me
kindly. He says if I'm not there with his bail money he'd shore have been
disgraced.

"Which you're a fightin' bobcat, young feller," I says, "an' I'm proud to
have been arrested with you." Then I interduced myself; an' I learn his
name is Philip Pharo.

"Mr. Redfield, I had no call to drag you into this mess," he says, "only I can't bear to see murder done."

"Same here," I says, "only call me Chuckwalla or Bill. I been mighty lonesome in this here city an' if you call me by my Christian name I'll feel more to home. Down in Panamint we got a vacancy for a preacher, an' I'm here to round one up if I can ever find one to fit the job."

"Why, Chuckwalla," he says, "I'm a minister o' the Gospel."

"The hell you are!" I says. "You don't fight like one."

"I'm brand-new," he says grinnin'. "I'm only ordained yesterday, an' I'm on my way to a tailor's to be measured for a parson's suit when I feel myself called on to save the life o' that unfortunate scab. Now, if I'm fined or jailed for incitin' a riot I can't get that suit, an' mebbe the bishop'll call a conference an' heave me out o' the church."

"Philip," I says, "if the bishop does that I'll shore make him hard to catch. However, don't you worry, because you ain't goin' to have to stand trial. We'll just nachelly jump our bail."

The young feller give a laugh that would have warmed the heart of a banker.

"Why, I won't hear to it, nohow," he says. "You'll lose fifteen hundred dollars."

"It won't be the first fifteen hundred I've lost," I says. "I ain't worryin' about that. I'm richer'n a fool, an' can afford it. What I ain't bankin' on is havin' a black mark unjustly chalked up agin the only red-blooded parson I've seen in three weeks. To hell with the money!"

"Chuckwalla," he says, "you're immense!"

"Let's talk about you, Philip," I says. To save my soul I can't call him parson. He's too much like a friend. "Be you lookin' for a job preachin' the Gospel?"

"I shore am," he says. "Do you reckon I could fill that vacancy you mention?"

"Well," I says, "I'm the mayor o' Panamint, daddy o' the camp an' the Committee on Ree-ligion; an' what I say goes or I'll know the reason why. I've looked over a lot o' parsons, but they don't grade high enough for Panamint; an' though you look mighty good to me, still there's a chance that Panamint don't grade high enough for you. She's a minin' camp that ain't had the edges knocked off her yet, an' it's only fair I should warn you before talkin' terms."

"Chuckwalla," he says, layin' his hand on my arm like he'd knowed me all his life, "I'm out to preach the Gospel, an' I don't care a hoot in a hollow where I preach it. That's me!"

Son, I'm overcome.

"Philip," I says, "suppose me an' you go somewhere while we talk this thing over."

"All right," he says; an' we went over to the Palace Hotel restauraw an' sat down to discuss the matter.

The Reverend Pharo he has a glass o' buttermilk an' I have some red liquor, to which he don't offer no objections an' tell me a lot o' things about red liquor that I know already a durned sight better'n him. I chalk a white mark up to him for that, an' then I put him through his examination.

"Philip," I says, "do you believe in hell?"

"Well, Chuckwalla, my friend," he says, "the constitution an' by-laws o' my church recognizes it, but there ain't no orthodox hell; an' the first time I get up in a pulpit I'm going to say so."

"On what grounds do you base them views?"

"On common sense. Our Lord can't take enjoyment in fryin' people. It's agin all the compassion He showed to human bein's while He was here on earth."

"How many roads is there to heaven?" I says.

"So blamed many, Chuckwalla, it's no wonder a lot of us get lost in transit. The Bible says: 'In my Father's house there is many mansions.' An' I guess there's enough spare rooms for all of us, Jew an' Gentile, if we play the game o' life square with ourselves."

"Philip," I says, "the job's your'n if you'll take it; an' if you don't take it I'm goin' to set right here an' get drunk an' drown my sorrer."

"I'll take it," he says, "providin' the bishop is willin'. I suppose my congregation'll approve your choice o' parson?"

"I dunno," I says; "an' what's more, I don't give a goddam. I know what's good for Panamint, an' if they reject you I'll build another church at my own expense an' run 'em out o' business. All I know is you're my parson, providin' you ain't a Baptist."

"No, Chuckwalla," he says, "I ain't. You got a grudge agin the Baptists?"

"I shore ain't no bigot," I says; "but we got to haul our water in bar'ls twelve mile to camp." He laughed himself into a fit at that.

"Chuckwalla," he says, "I repeat it—you're immense! I love you like a brother."

Then we talked salary, an' I offered him five hundred, which he says, as shy as a sheep-killin' dog, five hundred ain't quite enough, an' the very least he can get along on is seven hundred. I'm embarrassed a heap to think mebbe I've showed Panamint in the light o' bein' cheap an' small in money matters, an' I tell him, in order to be safe, I'll guarantee him a thousand; the congregation can fix the regular rate, an' I'll make up the dee-ficit personally.

Thinkin' to ease his mind on the financial question I draw a check on the Panamint Bank & Trust Company for a thousand and give to him. "There, Philip," I says, "is your first month's salary in advance."

"Month!" he yells. "You frontier comedian, I'm talkin' about years!" An' he laughs so long an' hearty the head waiter comes over an' tells us we'll have to be quiet or git out. "Why, bless your heart, Chuckwalla," Philip continues, "a hundred a month is princely as preacher's salaries goes in the country!"

"Then," I says "the good Lord help them in the city, for nine-tenths o' the preachers I see are that grave an' solemn I got a notion they're worried over money matters; but you're different. I got a notion mebbe sometime I'll come to church an' listen to you preach."

"Well, Chuckwalla," he says, "don't do nothin' that hurts you, unless it happens to be the right thing to do. An' now," he says, "I'll go an' explain my damaged appearance to the bishop an' talk it all over with him." Which he done; an' in two hours he's back an' I have his final acceptance.

We start right out shoppin'. First I buy me a new gun, because I don't feel dressed up since the police take my other gun away from me; an' then we buy a big, bang-up organ for the church. That's my gift an' it costs me close to two thousand. Also, I buys the hymn books, etcetry; an' I make Philip pick out the fixin's an' furnishin's for his parsonage himself. I aim to make him comfortable, an' I have a heap o' difficulty convincin' him he's headed for Panamint, where the best ain't none too good; an' most likely, at that, it's regarded with suspicion!

While we're shoppin' I learn a heap about Philip. He's got no kin; an', as near as I can make out, his pa leaves him just about enough to educate him an' clothe him till he's twenty-one. He's been through a big Eastern college an' has a string o' letters after his name like the tail of a comet. He's probably the most wholesome, handsomest young feller I ever meet, an' when it comes to sand he's got more o' that commodity in his craw than a grizzly bear. He's as good-natured as a baby an' laughin' all the time he's with me. Durned if I see what he finds to laugh at, unless it's mebbe because I treat him like he's a pin-feather boy. I'm five year older'n him in p'int o' years; but in p'int of experience with life I'm dyin' of old age compared with Philip.

Well, when everything is bought an' the shippin' instructions given, me an' Philip lights out for San José, so the police won't ketch us on a bench warrant for jumpin' our bail next day. In San José we patronize an expensive tailor, an' when our clothes are ready we head for Panamint.

We don't make no noise comin' into town, for I'm dead set agin this Wild West hip!-hip!-hurrah! business every time some sucker wins a big pot. We put up at the hotel while waitin' for the furnishin's for the parsonage an' the organ to be freighted in, an' I take Philip around an' interduce him to everybody in Panamint. He's received with favor an' I'm complimented a heap on my jedgment.

It's mebbe two weeks before the freight gets in, but during that time Philip organizes his congregation with a membership roll, an' the congregation gets together an' elects a governin' board, called the elders. As near as I recollect there's a dozen o' these elders. I don't favor the notion nohow, bein' dead set agin anybody bossin' Philip; but as I ain't a member o' the church an' don't intend to be, an' as it's Philip's game, I figger he knows what he's up to, an' that there ain't no call for me to horn in on the play. If I'd knowed as much about elders as I do now I'd have named a slate an' put Philip up to an opposition ticket.

The elders is all composed o' the solid citizens o' the town. The presidin' elder is an old silvertip by the name o' Absalom Randall. Absalom's been clerkin' in a country bank in Kansas about twenty year, an' when I organized the Panamint Bank & Trust Company one o' the directors recommends him for the job o' vice-president an' manager, particular since Absalom's got five thousand dollars he's willin' to invest in the stock.

I'm for him on account of his bankin' experience, which is why he gets the job. I'm president myself, but I don't take no interest in the bank's affairs. I leave that to hirelin's, as I'm never inside the bank except to draw checks agin my own account; which, lookin' back at it all now, 'pears to me I all but lived in front o' the payin' teller's winder.

The super o' the Panamint Lily, an' the druggist, an' some leadin' merchants an' family men makes up the rest o' the list; but Absalom Randall, he sticks out in my memory most. He shore was a ornery old sidewinder.

Well, son, I don't make no mistake in pickin' the Reverend Philip Pharo. The first Sunday the house is packed, an' Philip's sermon is a snorter. Also, he takes occasion to pass out a few complimentary remarks about me, which if I'm in church when he makes 'em I'd have been embarrassed.

The Almighty's just cut Philip out for a minin'-camp parson, an' filled him up with love for his feller man. It ain't no time before that boy is workin' himself sick doin' things for the unfortunates that romps into every minin' camp, where they promptly find themselves unfit and bog down, sick an' busted.

We've built him a nice little five-room parsonage up on Amethyst Avenoo—son, we're settin' in his back yard right now—but he never gets to enjoy it none. Right off he digs up a busted Cousin Jack miner that's been leaded, an' a tin-horn gambler dyin' o' consumption, an' houses 'em at the parsonage, after which he installs a drunken old bandit answerin' to the name o' Crabapple Thompson, an' nominates Crabapple chief cook an' head nurse

"Philip," I says, when I spot Crabapple Thompson on the premises, an' me knowin' his capacity for red liquor, "fire this here attendant o' your'n an' I'll round you up a responsible party."

"No, Chuckwalla," he says; "Crabapple needs me worse'n I need him. If he's round where I can keep my eye on him he'll stay in line. Besides, I like the old sinner. There's a heap o' character in Crabapple when you catch him sober."

Well, I seen there wasn't no use arguin' with him, particular after he says:

"Chuckwalla, did you ever notice how prone a lot o' preachers is to surround themselves with respectable people an' visit round among the congregation, an' make themselves agreeable to agreeable people?"

"No," I says; "I ain't had no experience that way. You're the first parson I ever see on the job—that is, at close range."

"Well," he says, "it's a fact. A lot o' my worthy brethren seem to have an idee that fellers like Crabapple Thompson an' that there consumptive gambler is the legitimate prey o' so-called settlement workers an' public institootions. I don't subscribe to them theories. I'm a-tryin' to foller in His steps. He went round healin' the sick an' bein' kind to sinners, an' mixin' up with the lowly o' the earth, regardless. Chuckwalla, good people don't need my services; an' so long as I'm the parson o' Panamint I don't aim to spend my time drinkin' tea with the ladies of the congregation, or walkin' round hand-shakin' myself into popularity. I ain't been here long, but I can see already I got a real he-job in this camp an' I'm not goin' to be no kid-glove preacher. Sinners is too thick here for me to waste my time in social frivolity."

I've hardly left him before a faro dealer in the Pick an' Drill, feelin' jealous o' his light-o'-love, shoots the lady up somethin' scandalous. It's four days before I learn Philip has the unfortunate up at the parsonage. Me, I've got that many things to think of, I've forgot to rig up a hospital;

an' as nobody seems anxious to care for this here gal, Buckskin Liz, why, the parson has her toted up to the parsonage. He gives up his own bed to the critter, while he takes a blanket an' goes over to the church nights, aimin' to roost in the organ loft. As soon as I find this out I have Buckskin Liz moved out to Darwin, to the Miners' Hospital.

Now, of course, like all lovable, good-natured boys, Philip ain't in camp a week till there's forty corn-fed girls out to rope him. They're pesterin' the boy to such an extent that it takes him two hours to get to the post office an' back. While he's got Buckskin Liz on his hands he asks one after the other o' these young women to come up an' nurse Liz. He says as how a little charity an' gentleness at this time mebbe reclaims Liz from a life o' shame. Finally he gets one out o' the lot who 'lows mebbe she'll take a chance; but she ain't on the job more'n an hour when Liz calls the parson in.

"Reverend," she says, "if you don't fire this here volunteer nurse I'm a-goin' to leave. I'm what I am, an' I know it; but it shore does gravel me to be told about it."

So Philip, he thanks the lady kindly an' says he's much obliged, but perhaps he's asked her to do somethin' he oughtn't to; an' he guesses he'll manage somehow. He don't have to give her more'n half an' openin' before she's gone.

Women don't take to Buckskin Liz worth a whoop, an' Philip he has to fall back on Crabapple Thompson, which the sot ain't half bad, accordin' to Liz. She says he understands her; an' first thing her an' Crabapple gets to arguin' religion, an' Liz, she warns the Crabapple if he ever gets drunk round the parson, an' she gets well an' finds it out, she'll shore make him hard to catch.

No, Philip's too busy to go feedin' round to a new house every night, an' he ain't the kind of a man to go peddlin' out small talk an' compliments to a lot o' women just because they stand ready to fall in love with him. Philip, he's a regular man, an' there ain't no female in Panamint that grades high enough for him; an' there ain't no bunch o' females that's goin' to make a mollycoddle outer him, either.

"Chuckwalla," he says—he comes to me for comfort when he can't stand it no longer—"it's an awful strain on a parson to be rubbin' up agin folks that wears their best side outside when they meet up with the minister. Me, I like my souls turned inside out—an' mostly I like 'em when they're naked an' I can see all the sin."

Well, son, this Buckskin Liz ee-pisode creates some little talk an' a diversity of opinion. It sorter jolts all hands in the congregation, an' some of the good people makes so bold as to remonstrate with Philip. In particular the chief elder, Absalom Randall, he talks to Philip like a son, an' says he must be careful an' not cause no talk.

"Absalom Randall," says Philip, "let me an' you have a show-down right here an' now. I'm a plain minister o' the Gospel an' not a divinity. I object seriously to this idea of a congregation electin' to think their pastor's so blamed pure he mustn't let himself go near sin an' sordidness in male or female. I'm a-tryin' to do this job accordin' to my Master's example. Elder, did you ever hear of a woman named Mary Magdalene?"

"Yes, yes!" says this hoary-headed old hypocrite. "I understand, parson; but you're young and I'm only warnin' you about people that may not understand."

"Your wife an' daughter, I take it, is included in that category," says Philip. "I recall I asked both of 'em to step up to the parsonage an' help me manage Buckskin Liz; but they don't oblige me."

"That's work for a trained nuss, my dear Mr. Pharo," says ol' Silvertip —I allers call him that, because he's a heap like a b'ar in many ways; an', havin' pulled himself out of a mean hole which Philip plunges him into, he takes up his hat an' goes back to the bank.

That night me an' Philip is settin' on the front porch o' the parsonage and he tells me about it. I don't say nothin'; but when Silvertip comes prancin' down to the bank next mornin' I'm settin' in at his desk—an' Silvertip's fired!

"Silvertip," I says, "hereafter you'll leave the Reverend Mr. Pharo to run his game without interference. Now you trot along to the cashier an' he'll give you back the five thousand you invested, at bankin' interest to date; an' don't you come in here no more. If you do I'll skelp you!"

What does this old Silvertip do? Son, I'm ashamed to tell you. He runs blubberin' to Philip an' begs him to use his influence with me to get him back his job; an' o' course, when Philip comes over an' tells me I don't know how to run a bank an' to get away from that desk an' let Silvertip do his work, I ain't got no option but to oblige him. Anyway, I've put Silvertip in his place, an' I'm figgerin' he'll leave Philip alone hereafter.

Now there's lately come to town a person callin' himself Bud Deming. I know Bud well. He's a gambler, but he's tee-totally on the square; so when he applies for a license to open up a combination gamblin' hall, dance-hall, saloon an' restauraw, nachelly he gets it. I'm for encouragin' legitimate commercial enterprises every time, an' the only mistake I make in Bud Deming's case is failin' to look over the plans o' Bud's deadfall. I'll explain later.

Well, when Bud's place o' business is ready he plans to give a banquet to the leadin' citizens an' the future patrons o' his house as a sort o' grand openin'. Me bein' the mayor an' the daddy o' the camp, nachelly he invites me, an' still further honors me by insistin' that I'm to be the toastmaster. I'm agreeable; then me an' Bud arranges the program o' speakers an' toasts, an' Bud has a bright idee.

"How'd it do," he says, "to invite the parson? Think he'd come?"

"Try him an' see, Bud," I says. "All I know is you won't offend him by askin'."

So Hank Bartlett gets out the printed invitations an' the programs over on the Nugget Press, an' Bud mails one to Philip. Right off Philip writes Bud a letter, acceptin' with thanks, an' says he'll shore be there when the dinner bell rings. A invite like that might have riled some parsons; but Bud's meanin' well, an' Philip knows he is, an' he's never missin' any opportunities for gettin' acquainted with Bud's kind o' people. So he accepts just like you or me.

Son, that banquet shore was a hummer! I make Bud the address o' welcome an' interduce the speakers. Philip says grace before an' after meals an' responds to the toast: Panamint; Her Dull Past an' Brilliant Future. An' if he don't make a hit I'm a Chinaman! Sunflower Sadie, which Sadie's Bud's light-o'-love, as the feller says, declares he's a wonder; an' after the banquet she comes up an' shakes hands with him an' tells him so.

Is Philip embarrassed when Sunflower Sadie shakes his flipper? Not a bit. Does he give her a ree-ligious talk an' tell her to abandon the sinful life she's leadin'? No, sir! This parson of ours is a gentleman an' don't get familiar on brief acquaintance. A-lookin' back on them days now I think I figger out Philip's system, which was to be so good an' kind an' gentle an' human an' natural an' noble that everybody's just got to love him; an' then he has things all his own way, an' you're ready to bust a laig runnin' to church to holler "Halleluiah!" Me, I love that boy like he's my own son, for he grades high. He's the biggest man that ever come to Panamint. Somehow he manages to pull all the burs off'n religion an' make it as smooth as long sweetenin'.

Hank Bartlett runs an account o' the banquet in the Nugget, an' I'm down at the post office when old Silvertip gets his paper an' reads about the banquet. He just goes staggerin' back to the bank, lookin' like he's goin' to have some sort of a fit. I'm looking for breakers, as the feller says, an' I ain't disapp'inted. Pretty soon the druggist comes pussy-footin' it into the bank an' him an' Silvertip goes into executive session. As he's leavin' I'm lingerin' by the door an' I hear him say:

"It's an outrage! I'm goin' to see the other elders an' call a meetin', Randall, if you don't."

I steps out an' takes the druggist by the arm.

"Neighbor," I says, "if you call that meetin' this here bank'll call your note. We got a majority o' you elders represented in our Bills Receivable account, an' I guess, as the feller says, Chuckwalla Bill Redfield's got the situation well in hand."

They didn't call no meetin'.

However, a-gettin' back to this here Bud Deming: He's caterin' to the select trade o' the camp, an' if there's one thing he prides himself on it's the grub in his restauraw. He don't spare no expense; an', as Philip sees right off the night o' the banquet Bud's fodder is the real quill, the follerin' evenin' he drops into the restauraw for his supper.

As a cook, Crabapple Thompson don't grade higher'n flapjacks an' *frijoles;* an' it's plain wearin' on Philip to dine out with the members o' his flock, who treat him like he's a superior person. Bud has some good soup an' a light dessert that's something to admire; an' when he's finished his grub Philip calls the waiter an' 'lows he'll buy some for his patients up at the parsonage if the cook'll load up a basket for him to carry it in; which the cook done the same an' Philip's goin' out with the basket—when Bud spots him.

Now, after ascertainin' what he's got in the basket, Bud Deming, which he has a heart as big as all outdoors, says to Philip:

"Parson, I ain't no church-goin' man, but when it comes to feedin' the hungry an' slippin' a dollar to a down-an'-outer, that's my religion. As a business man I'm willin' to let you pay for your own scoffin's, but this grub you're totin' home for them sick fellers you got on your hands, that's on the house; an' it'll continue to be on the house—three times a day, twenty-one times a week—while I'm runnin' this restauraw. You come yourself or send Crabapple, an' the cook'll have instructions to have it ready an' waitin' for you."

"Bud," says the parson, "you're a no-good ol' skunk, but you're shore a-layin' up treasures in heaven for yourself!" An' then him an' Bud laughs an' has their little joke an' walks arm an' arm together to the door.

Speakin' o' this door, it's the sole entrance to Bud's hall o' sin. As you come in there's the long bar on the left; in the center there's a space for dancin', an' the gamblin' layouts is along the right wall; while in the rear there's a glass door leadin' into the restauraw.

This glass door is the only way in, an' likewise it's the only way out; in consequence of which, when Philip takes to patronizin' Bud's restauraw he has to pass through the departments out in front.

Philip ain't been feedin' at the restauraw three weeks before he's on speakin' terms with every barkeeper, gambler, swamper an' dance-hall girl in the place. He don't stop to talk with them at all when he comes in, but as he walks through he has a nod an' a smile for all hands. It's "Howdy, Bill, you ol' pelican!" or "Good evenin', Tessie!" an' he's back in the restauraw. Same thing when he comes out.

An' to show you the effect o' this simple treatment on them denizens o' Bud's place, every man an' woman, from time to time, takes occasion to apologize to Philip for the architect that draws Bud's plans! Why, that parson has more friends among them people than me—an' I have money to give away. What's more, I'm a-givin' it too!

Well, as I say, things goes along this way mebbe a month, when Chappie Ellerton comes to town. Speakin' o' Chappie reminds me o' that sayin' from the Scriptures: "Consider the lilies of the field; they toil not, neither do they spin; yet Solomon in all his glory was not arrayed as one o' these."

In face an' figger Chappie's a heap like Philip. Hank Bartlett allers 'lows as how he's a poet gone wrong. He's allers lookin' like he'd stepped out of a ban'box; an' I suppose if somebody'd killed him the night him an' Philip meet up, he'd dress mebbe two thousand dollars on the hoof in jewelry an' glad raiment.

Son, if Solomon ever put on half the dog Chappie Ellerton does the ol' gentleman sure was a sport! Chappie's shore a lily o' the field in p'int o' looks an' labor; but when it comes to spinnin', right there him an' the lily forks trails. Chappie's a spinner from 'way back, him controllin' the destinies of a little ivory ball in a circle o' numbers an' colors, the same bein' known to science as a roulette wheel.

It's Chappie's first night on shift in Bud Deming's place, along in the shank o' the evenin', when there ain't nothin' much doin'. He's standin' back o' the wheel waitin' for the play to start; an' him an' the night both bein' young, he's singin' a little song of his own devisin':

> "Roun' she goes an' roun' she goes;
> An' where she stops nobody knows
> But the Lord!—an' He won't tell!"

Philip's just comin' out o' the restauraw an' is stoppin' a brief second at the end o' the bar to thank Bud for his daily contribution to the sick an' destitoot; so nachelly he hears Chappie croonin' his little ditty over an' over again! There ain't a soul at the wheel but Chappie, but he's spinnin' the ball just the same—for practice, I guess; an' singin' because he knows from experience that advertisin' pays.

Well, son, the preacher, hearin' the song, turns around for a look at the blasphemer; Chappie, who's sensitive to a degree, feels somebody sizin' him up; so he glances round an' spots the preacher. Then them two looks at each other.

Now, the Reverend Pharo's a new one on Chappie. He don't figger none on meetin' a preacher in a gamblin' hall; consequently the sight completely busts Chappie's ideals wide open, an' he grins at the parson.

On his part the parson 'lows as how Chappie's a new one on him. He's such a kid to be herdin' a roulette wheel, an' his smile's plumb irresistible; so the preacher smiles back an' crosses over to him. It's the first time on record he ever lingers in the gamblin' hall.

"Friend," he says, "ain't it possible for you to ply your vocation without draggin' the name o' the Lord into it? I should jedge, from a casual inspection o' your head, that you got imagination enough to invent some other madrigal not contrary to the Second Commandment."

"If I'd known there was a preacher driftin' round loose in this here haunt o' the particular an' the unparticular, the quick an' the quicker, the secular an' the insectivorous, I'd 'a' done it without askin'," says Chappie. He spins the ball again an' sings:

> "Roun' she goes an' roun' she goes;
> An' where she stops nobody knows.
> An' nobody gives a turiloo, turille-addy!"

"Now that's just as good," says the sky pilot, laughin'.

"Try your luck!" says Chappie. He's a mite fresh, is Chappie, an' inclined to have a little fun with any preacher he ketches in a gamblin' house.

"My jovial friend," says Philip, "I never gamble. I've never been this close to a roulette wheel before."

"This ain't gamblin'," says Chappie; "it's just a mortal cinch in favor o' the house. D'ye suppose Bud'd be reskin' his bank roll if it wasn't? The odds is thirty-eight to thirty-five agin you."

"Then why should I try my luck?" says Philip.

"To be a good feller," says Chappie. "You bein' a parson an' hornin' into my game thataway, I got a notion you've jinxed the wheel; an' presently some mucker comes along an' busts the bank. You ought to lug that jinx away with you when you leave."

"How?"

"By pikin' a dollar to take away the curse."

"You young rascal!" says Philip laughin'. "You're darin' me to gamble just because I'm a preacher, an' I got a good notion to take you up. Remember what the Scriptures say: 'Them that lives by the sword shall perish by the sword.'"

"Meanin' what, dominie?"

"Meanin', in your own classical language, that I might bust the bank."

"No danger," says Chappie. "I'm game. Come on, parson! Be a sport!"

"All right," says Philip, "I'll gamble with you—on one condition."

"It's accepted. What does she look like?"

"Since a preacher in a gamblin' house playin' a roulette wheel for money is an unusual sight," says Philip, "a gambler in church ought to prove an equally interestin' attraction. It ain't fair for me to furnish the whole show; so if I play your game you'll have to play mine. That's fair, ain't it?"

"I should tell a man!" says Chappie, laughin' to see the trap Philip's sprung on him. "Parson, you've shore got me in the nine-hole that time."

"That bein' thoroughly understood I'll expect to see you in church next Sunday. I shall now tempt the tongue o' scandal," says Philip. "Also, by reason o' you remarkin' that I got you in the nine-hole, whatever that may be, I shall take you at your word an' play the nine." An' he lays his dollar on the Curse o' Scotland.

"Yes," says Chappie, "I've seen fellers play them hunches before." An' he spins the ball an' sings, plumb forgetful o' present company:

> "Roun' she goes an' roun' she goes;
> An' where she stops nobody knows
> But the Lord!—an' He won't tell!"

"There you go again, bustin' the Second Commandment!" says Philip —an' the ball drops into the pocket.

"Nine, red, odd, low, third column, an' first twelve," says Chappie in his professional tones. "How'll you have it, parson?"

Now the fact o' the matter is, Philip don't have no more idee o' roulette than that Champagne Charley jackass o' mine has of astronomy. He don't even know he's won an' that Chappie's askin' him whether he'll take chips or silver, for he ain't thinkin' of gamblin' at all; but what a shame it is that a nice-appearin' young feller like this ain't doin' some good in life.

So Chappie, figgerin' the parson won't bet any more an' hence won't need chips, shoves over a stack o' thirty-five dollars. It's only then that

Philip sees he's won, an' the shock of it scares him stiff. He don't figger that anything like this is goin' to happen; an', what's more, he don't want it to happen, because he only intends to play a dollar an' quit after he's got the strangle hold on Chappie an' rounded him up for the church! He stands there kinder stupid, thinkin' it over.

"Oh," says Chappie, "I guess I got you sized up all wrong after all. Goin' to let her ride, eh? Well, you are a sporty parson, ain't you? However, I'm sorry to say the house won't let you pyramid your bets." An' he points over his shoulder with his thumb to the sign on the wall above him: Ten-Dollar Limit!

Then he reaches over, pinches the parson's stack down to ten dollars an' spins the ball again.

> "Roun' she goes an' roun' she goes;
> An' where she stops nobody knows
> But the Lord!—an' He won't tell!"

"Didn't I warn you agin that third line?" says Philip, an' the ball drops home.

"Nine! The Curse o' Scotland repeats," says Chappie, reachin' casual for the tray containin' the gold an' currency; an' then Philip wakes up to what's happenin'.

Nevertheless, he don't like it one little bit, for he ain't a gambler an' winnin' don't excite him like it does most people. He's just a human preacher sparrin' with Satan for a soul, an' the thought o' winnin' a lot of unclean money is plain repugnant to him. Not for all the wealth o' Panamint will he touch a cent o' the wages o' sin. Still, he's a human bein'—an' as curious as a pet coon. He's just nachelly got to see how rich he is if he ain't got a conscience; so he starts countin' the money without drawin' down his ten-dollar bet, which is still ridin'.

Chappie, not bein' familiar with sportin' parsons, gives Philip a look of admiration an' sorrer combined; an', takin' it for granted the parson's game for another little whirl on the nine, he spins his ball an' sings his little song again. She repeats! Chappie shoves three hundred an' fifty dollars across to Philip.

"Parson," he says, "you're a lucky man; but as there's only luck in odd numbers, as a rule, an' you've won three times hand runnin' on the nine, your luck's due to change. It's time to shift your bet. Durned if I don't believe you've jinxed my wheel so bad you could win on the hoodoo number!"

"What's that?"

"Thirteen."

Philip looks at Chappie, an' he's tempted. He's only foolin', but he sees that Chappie is dead serious. Consequently, because it's only innercent pastime to Philip, like a boy playin' marbles, he shoves his bet over on to the thirteen. You see his play, don't you, son? He wants to lose it on the hoodoo number an' retire gracefully when his winnin's is all back in Chappie's tray.

The ball drops into the thirteen pocket! Chappie gets out his white handkerchief an' wipes his corrugated brow, as the feller says, meantime eyein' the parson suspicious-like. On his part, Philip, enjoyin' the knowledge that he's got Chappie fannin' the air, grins back at him—an' Bud Deming, seein' the dinero in front o' the reverend, strolls over to poke some fun at the foreman o' his roulette wheel.

"Hello, Chappie!" he says. "The parson got you goin' south?"

"No," says Chappie; "but, all the same, he's luckier'n a fool. If I hadn't held him to the limit first off I'd be raidin' one o' the other games for more cash right now."

"What?" says Bud, aimin' to be agreeable an' pleasant. "Is the ten-dollar limit annoyin' our clerical friend?"

"He wants to pyramid his bets, startin' right in," complains Chappie. "Plays a dollar on the nine, ketches it, an' lets her ride. I had to pinch him down."

"That so?" says Bud. "Well, the roof is off! Anything the parson wants in this house goes while I'm the proprietor."

"Spread my bets for me, Bud," says Philip. Gawd bless him, he's a lamb!

"He'll win wherever you spread 'em," Chappie warns Bud.

"We'll see," says Bud.

An' he places a hundred on the double-O, a hundred on the green an' a hundred on the even; whereupon Chappie spins the ball an' she drops into the green double-O, winnin' all three bets. The green an' the even pays double, an' the double-O pays thirty-five to one.

"That's what you get for interferin', boss," says Chappie carelesslike.

He reaches into the dinero an' shoves hundred-dollar bills acrost to the parson until the place begins to look like a patch of alfalfa. An' still the bets goes ridin' as they lay.

Again Chappie spins the ball; again from force o' habit he sings:

> "Roun' she goes an' roun' she goes;
> An' where she stops nobody knows—"

An' then he waits, holdin' the tune while the ball circles slower an' slower. In a second she's due to run off the right o' way an' go slippin' an' bumpin' among the pegs an' pockets before settlin'.

"Finish your little song, ol'-timer," says the parson.

The ball commences to bump, with the double-O so clost to hand it's even money the ball drops into it, when Chappie sings the last line:

"An' nobody gives a turiloo, turilee-addy!"

The ball drops into the double-O, hesitates—an' pops out into the next pocket, when, accordin' to all the laws o' averages she should have stayed in the double-O! Chappie gives a sort o' suckin' sob an' rakes in the three hundred dollars.

Now all this is just the most wonderful luck in the world, an' Chappie an' Bud ain't never seen or heard o' nothin' like it; but the parson, being free from superstition an' previous experience, don't see nothing so very wonderful in it, because he knows the Lord ain't on the side o' no gambler, an' if he stays with the game long enough he's bound to lose all he's got. However, he's smart enough to see he's built a fire under Chappie; so he says:

"Now that's a heap better, Chappie. Don't that last turn prove to you there ain't no luck in usin' the name o' the Lord in vain?"

"It shore does look that way," says Chappie; "but I happen to know the Lord ain't got nothin' to do with it. There ain't nothing on earth can control that little ball 'ceptin' the law of averages, an' your luck's been runnin' beyond the wildest dreams o' average."

Havin' won a bet at last Chappie's feelin' cheerful again.

Now the parson knows he ain't goin' to take the money, even if he wins it; so consequently he figgers this is all innercent fun an' no harm to nobody. He sees Chappie an' Bud are takin' him dead serious, an' he's so almighty human he can't help having a little fun with them by a-testin' o' their nerves. Besides, he's plumb anxious to get rid o' the wealth he's accumulated an' remove himself from the occasions o' sin. He figgers he's been lingerin' there too long already, as it is; an', since his luck's had one setback, he 'lows as how the tide has turned, an' if he crowds his hand he'll go bust in five minutes.

"My friends," he says, "I'm only a parson, I know, an' gamblin' ain't my long suit; but, nevertheless, when I'm out for a little mild mental relaxation I likes to bet 'em as high as a hound's back, an' this suspense is aggervatin' to me. I'll bet every dollar before me on number thirteen an' let the tail go with the hide; an' if you're a dead game sport, Bud, you won't take a dare like that from a preacher."

"Boss," says Chappie, "you goin' to let this sportin' parson back you down?"

Now Bud; he knows just as well as Chappie that it ain't in nature to beat a roulette wheel if a man stays with it. Also, the parson's playin' the hoodoo number an' the chances is thirty-five to one against him, not countin' the hoodoo; an' as Bud's as superstitious as any gambler, an' as game as the best, he takes the parson up.

"I'll go you parson," he says; "only I warn you in advance if you win you got upward o' one hundred an' fifty thousand dollars comin' to you, an' I ain't got that much money."

"Bet the house, lock, stock an' barrel," says the parson, "an' we'll call it square at that!"

"Fair enough," says Bud. "Spin the ball, Chappie, an' be right sure you don't take the name o' the Lord in vain. I ain't lookin' to bust the hoodoo on that number."

Now for the first time the Reverend Philip Pharo gets wise to the fact that Chappie an' Bud's as superstitious as two Chinamen, an' this knowledge amuses him a heap.

Consequently, for purposes o' plain human enjoyment, he thinks he'll enter into the sperrit o' the evenin' an' make out as how he's somethin' of a conjurer with a roulette wheel.

" 'Twon't do you no good whatever, Bud," he says. "I'm goin' to jinx the wheel." An' he runs his finger clear round it an chants a line, which he tells me afterward he swipes from a play: " 'Roun' her form I draw the awful circle of our solemn church!' "

Then he spills somethin' in a furrin language—it's Greek, which Philip's learned in college; but Chappie an' Bud don't know it, an' both are some apprehensive as Chappie spins the ball an' sings his song.

Son, there ain't nothing like that parson's luck ever seen. The ball pops straight into the thirteen pocket first thing—an' stays there! The Reverend Philip Pharo's busted the bank! Bud Deming's a pauper, an' Chappie Ellerton's workin' for the preacher, who's the sole proprietor of a gamblin' hall!

Chappie Ellerton's as white as a miller an' Bud Deming's face is as yaller as an old cheese. But he's game, is Bud—none more so. He just steps back an' bows to the parson with all respect.

"Parson," he says, "the shack is yours. All hands was paid off at six o'clock tonight an' the title's clear. I don't suppose there's nothin' for me

to do round here 'cept to state that it shore was poor jedgment on my part
havin' only one entrance to my place o' business."

Well, son, Philip just stands there, with his mouth wide open like a kid
seein' things at night. Chappie Ellerton is absolutely overcome an' stands
starin' at Philip, with *his* mouth open; an' Bud's the only cool man at the
table, for he's been busted many a time an' oft, as the poet says, an' the
prospect don't worry him none, providin' he can find a job right away. It
occurs to Bud that the quickest way to do this is to ask Philip for it—
which he done an' that brings the Reverend Philip Pharo out of his
trance.

"Why, Bud, you blessed ol' sinner," he says, "whatall d'ye suppose I
am?"

"You might be just smeared with luck from heels to hair, but I doubt
it," says Bud. "However, that ain't neither here nor there. This here place
is a payin' property; an', since it ain't the kind of a place that can be run
by a preacher or ex-preacher, it stands to reason you got to have a manager
for it. Though I ain't fixin' to throw bouquets at myself, I been runnin'
this house with tolerable success up till now, an' I'll leave it to Chuckwalla
here if I ain't square."

I've just dropped in an' I'm not conversant with the lay o' the land; so I
don't ask no questions, but proceed to give Bud a reputation.

Now Philip wants to assure Bud he don't want the place nohow an'
wouldn't tech it for a million dollars, because the whole thing starts with a
little innercent joke between him an' Chappie Ellerton; but, knowin' the
kind of a gambler Bud is, the boy figgers he'll mebbe hurt his feelin's by
pressin' his property back on to him in the presence o' third parties.

While he's figgerin' a graceful way out Chappie Ellerton still further
complicates matters by quotin' a little Scripture:

" 'Them that lives by the sword shall perish by the sword.' An' truer
words than them was never spoke. Bud, this here sportin' parson warns me
startin' out exactly how this fiesta's goin' to end! The age o' miracles ain't
past yet, an' I don't have to have the parson's church fall on me before I
take the hint. Me, I'm through gamblin' forever! Parson, be a good feller
an' give me a job slingin' hash in the restauraw till I can get a road stake
together." An' that's the first intimation Panamint ever has that Chappie's jewelry ain't what it's cracked up to be.

Now, son, mark the fix that remark puts Philip in—from Philip's p'int
o' view. Startin' out, he's made up his mind there's somethin' awful good
in Chappie Ellerton an' he's goin' to bring it out. Bein' a parson, nobody
knows better'n Philip that the Almighty moves in devious ways His won-

ders to perform; an' here He is proclaimin' in plain English that this brand, Chappie Ellerton, is ready to be hauled out o' the fire! To Chappie the fact that Philip busts the bank ain't nothin' unusual, but the way the play comes up it is! He's regardin' it as a good, broad hint from the Almighty to quit gamblin'—an' he's quit. Mebbe he's superstitious. Well, all right, but if his superstition makes a good man out o' him, then Philip's ready to praise Gawd for installin' the superstition into this gambler. He's got Chappie fannin' for fair, an' it occurs to him if he catches Chappie on the rebound, as the feller says, he's got him.

On the other hand, if he lets on that his winnin' Bud's gamblin' house is just plain luck, an' he ain't invoked the aid o' the Lord nohow, he disillusions Chappie; an' mebbe the young feller goes to gamblin' again. Also, this newly acquired property o' his is the haunt o' sinners o' both sexes; an', with him bein' boss as well as pastor, he gets closer than ever to them. An' he's smart enough to know you got to get awful close to a sinner to get his confidence in anything ree-ligious.

It does appear to Philip that he ain't got nothin' to gain by declinin' his winnin's, an' he's got a whole lot to lose. On the other hand, since he never means to possess this deadfall, Bud ain't got nothin' to lose—only he don't know it! Then, again, Philip's tempted to think the Lord has delivered Bud Deming's place into his hands in order that he may close it up! However, Philip's broad-minded. He don't aim to cram his ree-ligion down nobody's throat agin their will. So right off he resolves to play a waitin' game.

"All right, Bud," he says; "you're my manager, an' you name your own salary. Chappie, Bud'll fix you up with that job in the restauraw. An' now, if you'll excuse me, gentlemen, I'll just mosey along back to the parsonage. This grub I've got in this basket'll be gettin' cold; an', moreover, I greatly fear Crabapple Thompson has a bottle hid out, an' if I ain't there to steady the ol' rascal he'll get drunk on my hands. Thank you for a pleasant five minutes' entertainment." An', smilin' cordial to all hands, the Reverend Philip Pharo dusts out o' that gambling house like the devil's at his tail a-wallopin' him at every jump.

I get the story o' what's happened from Bud an' Chappie; an', on account o' being able to guess Philip's attitood toward gamblin' an' knowin' him better'n them, I see it ain't goin' to do the parson no good to have the news leak out. Also, I know Philip just nachelly don't intend to consider himself the owner o' Bud's place, for I can see by the light in his eye he's bustin' with laughter 'way back inside; so I warns Bud an' Chappie to go slow an' not spread the news yet awhile. An' as both gents is smart enough to see they're going to be deviled out o' camp on account o' workin' for a preacher, they're right glad to keep their business to themselves.

Somethin' tells me Philip wants to see me and talk things over, for whenever he's in doubt or trouble the boy allers comes a-runnin' to his ol' Bill-pardner; so I takes a little *pasear* up to the parsonage. I find Philip on his knees in his front room, prayin' Gawd to forgive him. Also, he don't neglect to thank the Lord for plantin' the seed o' redemption in Chappie Ellerton's heart, an' prays that Chappie'll be given the strength to hold to his high resolve; an', as a grand wind-up, he asks the Almighty to direct him in the predicament he's in. I can hear him prayin' out loud as I come in.

"Well, Philip," I says, "pendin' a tip from On High, take a little advice from Chuckwalla Bill. You stay away from that gamblin' hall hereafter, unless you're aimin' to cause fits among your flock."

"I got justification for my course right here," he says, an' lays his hand on his Bible.

"I know it," I says—which I don't; but I'm willin' to take that boy's word for anything. "But you stay away, an' have your grub sent up by Crabapple Thompson hereafter. Meantime we'll let Chappie an' Bud suffer under your little joke until you've had a chance to get Chappie into church oncet. Then I'll quietly slip the word to Bud just how you regard this here transaction, an' I'll make him understand it's all right."

"Will you do that, Chuckwalla?" he says, greatly relieved; an' I promised.

Well, Crabapple Thompson's drunk that night, an' he stays loaded three days; which nachelly throws such a burden o' work on Philip he's kept right close to the parsonage. Come Sunday mornin' an' time to hold service, his consumptive gambler is that far gone the parson figgers he dassent leave him alone, so he ambles down Amethyst Avenoo to Jake Russell's shanty.

He's aimin' to ask Jake's wife to step up to the parsonage an' play nurse while he's holdin' services; but Jake Russell's wife she meets him with such a dignified front compared to former receptions that he ain't got the heart to state his errand, an' merely says he hopes she'll be on hand to lead in the singin'—which this same female has a voice like a desert canary—an' moseys along to Tom Cahill's cabin. Tom's wife don't attend Philip's church, an' not havin' one of her own in Panamint, her Sundays is free to her; so Philip figgers she'll oblige him, which she does, an' he goes down to the church an' mounts the pulpit.

I'm in church that mornin' myself; for I been hearin' some gossip, an' I'm there out o' curiosity to see what's goin' on. The first thing Philip notices when he turns round to preach his sermon is what I've noticed— an' that is that the male attendance this mornin' has increased fifty percent, an' the percentage o' women has dwindled no little.

The next thing he notices is that Chappie Ellerton is settin' up in the front row, but he don't notice somethin' else, which I do—and that's Bud Deming an' Sunflower Sadie a-settin' away over in a dark corner an' lookin' an feelin' outer place.

Well, son, the parson chooses for his text that mornin' the story about the shepherd that loses a sheep, which he leaves the rest o' the flock an' goes back lookin' for the lost sheep till he finds him; an' how there was more joy in heaven over one sinner that repenteth than ninety-nine just men that need no repentance.

He ain't noways pertinent an' particular in his remarks; but, all the same, Chappie knows the parson means him, an' he's plumb interested right off. Philip gradually works away from the text an' pretty soon he's off on his fav'rite rampage, a-pleadin' for a broader viewp'int in ree-ligion an' more charity an' humanity toward sinners; then he sees Chappie's eyes just a-poppin' with interest, an' he gets worked up an' plumb inspired, an' tears loose regardless. If I'm a ree-ligious man at the time—which I ain't never been an' never will—it's even money he brings tears to my eyes with that sermon.

It shore did lay over anythin' you ever heard tell of, though a-lookin' back at it now it ain't so much what he says as the way he says it. He's that sincere I'm for givin' three cheers, and I guess I'd 'a' done it if Philip don't stop about then an' kneel down for the closin' prayer.

After the congregation files out, Chappie Ellerton's settin' where he is, an', of course, everybody's next to who Philip's been alludin' in his prayer. A lot of us is hangin' round outside, an' when Philip an' Chappie comes out together I jine them, an' we all three walk up Amethyst Avenoo together to the hotel. I'm for backin' the parson's play an' gettin' him an' Chappie well acquainted; so I've invited 'em both up to the hotel to take Sunday dinner with me.

Does Philip talk ree-ligion to Chappie at that feed? No, sir. Philip's smart enough to know any man on earth can get enough of a good thing, an' he just nachelly proceeds to forget he's a preacher an' act natural an' talk natural. As I recall it now Philip was tellin' us about the boy that run the first Marathon race 'way back in B.C., when a barkeep from Bud Deming's place comes runnin' into the dinin'-room.

"Reverend," he says to Philip, "a drunken Greaser's knifed Bud Deming an' Bud's askin' to see you before he kicks the bucket."

Well, son, when me an' Philip an' Chappie gets down there, pore ol' Bud's lyin' on a billiard table, with Sunflower Sadie holdin' his hand an' takin' on pretty hard. There's mebbe twenty men standin' round the table, waitin' for Bud to pass out. But, he smiles when Philip bends over him.

"Parson," he says, a-reachin' out for Philip's hand, "a drunken Greaser has knifed me for fair, but I want to tell you he never got drunk in your place. No, sir. Ever since I been your manager I been runnin' this place respectable; an' when this drunk comes in an' wants a drink I'm sorry, but he can't have no more. I'm for sendin' him on his way peaceable, but he won't go; an' in the mix-up he slips a dirk into me."

Philip, he paws Bud over an' sees he's cut pretty bad; so he ups and tells Bud he'd better get his house in order.

"House!" says Bud, who don't get what Philip's drivin' at. "Why, what are you talkin' about, parson? It ain't my house. You won it fair, though I ain't said nothin' to nobody about it till now." He raises himself up on his elbow. "Boys," he says, "listen to me; I'm dyin', an' I'm tellin' the truth. This house an' everything in it, includin' the bank roll, belongs to the best sky-pilot ever. Last Wednesday night the parson here busts the bank at roulette, an' I staked the business agin the cash, an' lost. I been his manager ever since, an' the book'll show it. Chappie here will bear me out. Now all you fellers, 'cept Chuckwalla an' Chappie an' the help, run along an' leave me alone with my boss, because him an' me has the details o' the business to settle up."

When they're all gone Bud says to Philip:

"Parson, I'm goin' to ask you, for ol' sake's sake, to look after Sadie. She's a good girl, parson. If there's anything wrong with Sadie I'm the responsible party. She's just loved me enough to leave a respectable home an' lose her reputation; an', parson, when I'm gone, for Gawd's sake help her to start in all over again. Sadie, ol' girl, the boss'll look after you when I'm gone; an' you be guided by him, because he'll be the one best, true friend you ever had.

"An' say, boss, you don't want no deadfall like this. No! No! It ain't becomin' to you. Only last night"—Bud is pretty far gone by this time an' talkin' hard—"a feller died o' minin'-camp pneumonia—settin' right up in that chair. An', comin' home from church, me an' Sadie—we got talkin' it over—an' Sadie suggests a plan—parson, we was goin' to—to go up to—the parsonage an' talk—it over with you—this place bein' devoted

—to helpin' folks—instead o' ruinin' 'em—a hospital, you know, parson. An' the restauraw mebbe supports—the hospital; an' you got—a forty-thousand dollar bank roll to start. Chappie said he was goin' to church, an' me an' Sadie—we went too. Me an' Sadie an' Chappie—we're them lost sheep—you was talkin' about—ain't we? Parson, pray for me! I'm goin'—tell the boys not—to—lynch—the Greaser. He ain't responsible. No, parson; it's fellers like me—that kills—people—with whisky—"

"Bud," says our parson, "I give you the word of Almighty Gawd there's going to be more rejoicin' among the angels in heaven when you get there than over the arrival o' ten thousand preachers."

An' then him an' Sunflower Sadie an' Chappie get down on their knees by the billiard table an' pray for Bud Deming's soul. Me, I ain't ree-ligious. I ain't never learned to pray, so I can't j'in in.

In about five minutes ol' Bud's over the river, an' I take charge, while Philip escorts Sunflower Sadie home to the shanty her an' Bud occupied. Sadie's takin' on somethin' awful, an' Philip has her by the arm, tryin' to comfort her; but he can't. An' you want to remember, son, that this is Sunday, in the main street o' Panamint, an' every woman in hearin' dis-tance o' Sunflower Sadie's sobs comes to her door or her winder an' has a look at the procession.

Son, I suppose you've lived long enough in this world to know that the wicked don't amount to nothin'; so nobody worries over 'em. It's only the pure an' the clean that can be reached by scandal. The bigger a man is the more we expect o' him; the heavier he is, the harder he falls. An' it's that way with Philip. This is how the deal figgers out:

The night he's playin' the wheel with Chappie Ellerton, one o' Bud's barkeeps sees him make his killin' an' walk out, leavin' the money behind him. When he asks Bud about it later Bud's some irritated an' fires him for bein' too almighty curious about other people's business. As this barkeep's goin' out he meets Jake Russell comin' in. So nachelly he un-loads his grief on Jake; an', on account o' blamin' the parson for the loss of his job, he tells Jake the parson's been playin' the wheel an' won thousands o' dollars.

Jake, he's plumb surprised, but a little inquiry convinces him the parson *has* been playin' the wheel; so when he goes home that night he tells his wife. Mebbe Jake, bein' human, adds a few trimmin's to suit his fancy, an' his wife jumps to conclusions. She ain't got no more brains than a sage hen nohow; so she runs an' tells her neighbor what the pastor's been up to.

"Like as not," says this female, "he's worth watchin'. Jake says how he calls them awful women down there by their first names!"

Son, before sunset that night there's gossip a-flyin' round Panamint to the effect that the Reverend Mr. Pharo's a terrible gambler; also, that he drinks now an' then, for more'n once he's been seen downtown feelin' pretty jolly; an' mebbe liquor had somethin' to do with it. The next we know he's been drinkin' an' has been seen throwin' gold pieces round like a hardened offender.

On Friday the story's growed, an' the women is smackin' their lips an' wallin' their eyes, an' sayin': "It's such a pity he's that way!" It seems by this time the parson's been leadin' a double life ever since he come into the camp, a-consortin' with the scum o' Panamint by night an' a-preachin' the Gospel by day.

By Saturday it's common knowledge that Philip is the outcast o' his family, an' has only entered the ministry as a sort o' blind, after years o' hell-raisin' an' debauchery, which is most likely why the bishop sends him to Panamint anyhow—to get shet of him. My part in bringin' him is raked over an', as I'm regarded as honest, but desperate on slight provocation, my friendship for Philip don't help him any. With repetition, son, that story's growed so that when the finished product comes back to Mrs. Jake Russell she fails to recognize her own brain child, but takes it all as fresh evidence agin the parson; an' away she goes, spreadin' the news round the camp. Mrs. Russell is one o' these here Christian women that holds she's got a sacred duty to perform by stirrin' things up an' savin' the church from scandal.

Of course, son, you see what happens? When the parson escorts Sunflower Sadie home to her shack, after Bud cashes in, Mrs. Jake Russell sees him. She knows who Sadie is; but, even if she don't, it ain't no trouble to guess what she is—an' right then an' there the parson's damned! That afternoon the ladies o' Panamint swarms like bees. Mrs. Jake, she's the queen bee; an', as there's a lot o' old he-drones swarmin' with them, it all makes considerable of a buzz.

Of course Philip's that busy preparin' for Bud's funeral he don't get a whisper of it. We don't have no ice in Panamint; an', as it's July an' a hundred an' twelve in the shade, an' no shade, we've got to plant Bud in a hurry, which his funeral's billed for ten o'clock next morning.

The first intimation I get that affairs has reached a climax is when the druggist an' the postmaster an' ol' Silvertip calls on me on the hotel porch to consult about the scandal. They don't get far after I find out what they're after.

"Silvertip," I says, "me an' you've fell out once before on account o' you stickin' your nose into the parson's affairs, an' now we've fallen out forever an' for aye, as the poet says. You come down to the bank Monday mornin' an' I'll settle up with you. As for you other two skunks," I says, "you come, too, an' bring checks for your promissory notes."

"Oh, I guess not," says Silvertip. "Several of us has got together an' bought up a little block o' that bank stock from a friend o' your'n and now you're controllin' about forty-eight percent of it instead o' fifty-one. Ed Penrose, who allers votes his stock with you, right or wrong, got hard up an' we bought him out."

Well, son, I can see Silvertip's tellin' the truth, or he dasn't have the nerve to come an' talk that way to the daddy o' Panamint; so I wait, a-cussin' Ed Penrose, to see what kind of proposition Silvertip's got to unload. I don't have to wait long.

"You're responsible for this unworthy parson," he says; but I stopped him with a little Scripture I got up my sleeve. I learn it from Philip.

"Jedge not," I says, "lest ye be jedged!"

"Never mind about that," he says. "We're here, out o' deference to you as the leadin' citizen o' this camp, to give you the quiet tip to get shet o' the Reverend Philip Pharo, or the vestry holds a meetin' an' fires him without notice."

Son, I'm all broke up. I know they mean it, an' yet it don't lay in me to take program from them ol' women. I'm seein' red an' reachin' for my weepons to kill the coyotes, when I happened to recollect I'm the mayor o' Panamint an' standin' for law an' order.

[Old Chuckwalla Bill rolled out of his blankets and stood erect; his voice rose shrilly as he lived once more this outrage of thirty years agone; he trembled with the scourge of it.]

Son [he went on] they have me cornered! Me, I've gave more'n ten thousand dollars toward that church, an' now they're tellin' me I got to slip Philip the word he ain't wanted! I've got to take that boy aside, just when he's up to his ears in the work he loves, an' tell him he ain't makin' good! Me, the daddy o' Panamint! Me, Chuckwalla Bill Redfield, the first an' last mayor this camp ever has! Son, I'm all choked up. I can't say nothin'—can't even cuss ol' Silvertip. I just set there like a fool an' commence to cry—'cause I ain't never been licked before. The elders stand there gloatin' at me, as I discover the minute I can see clear ag'in; an' then it comes over me that I got to set those tarantulas in their place if I go to jail for it for life.

"Gentlemen," I says, "which that word is a mere figger o' speech an' not meant, you-all can quit the Reverend Pharo's church if you feel like it; but me, I'm the biggest subscriber to the funds that built that church an' furnished it, an' I'm goin' to take possession an' maintain the parson in his job, if I have to kill every elder in the flock. This here's a free country, an' Philip Pharo stays in the camp while I'm mayor; an' Gawd have mercy on them that hurts his feelin's or a hair o' his head."

"We'll dispute that in the courts, sir," says Silvertip. The ol' lizard ain't bluffed a little bit; but he sees I'm dangerous, an' him an' his gang pulls their freight without further argyment.

Now, Philip, he 'lows as how he's goin' to have services over Bud in the church, an' has asked me to round up a quartet that's appearin' in the Panamint Variety Theater, an' to make sure the organist is there to play the funeral march an' all. I land the quartet all right, but when I go after the salaried organist I find the elders have been there before me an' the organist's on strike. Yes, sir! It appears that ingrate has scruples an' is arrayed agin the parson; so I give him a slappin' for bein' fresh, an' I 'low, by Judas! I'll play that organ myself if it comes down to it.

I been takin' lessons on the pianner up at the hotel, which I like to amuse myself that-a-way when I go into a dance hall. I don't know one note from the other, but I've took a lot o' finger exercises an' learned how to pump out a fair bass, an' play by ear. Music is a second nature to me, an' if I hear a tune oncet I got it, though, accordin' to Philip, this ain't nothin' remarkable. He says: "There is a chord in every human heart which, if it can be touched, will bring forth sweet music." Still, I've knowed a lot o' people that couldn't sing a lick or play a tune through, though their folks spends a bar'l o' money on teachers for 'em.

However, I ain't put to no such extremity as havin' to play the organ myself. Buckskin Liz is back in town ag'in, favorin' one foot an' lookin' none too robust; but she's the prime pianner tickler o' that country. An' when I approach her with a proposition to play at Bud's funeral she's there a mile—providin' they don't throw her out o' the organ loft.

The funeral leaves Bud's shanty at ten o'clock next mornin'. I'm one o' the pallbearers an' Chappie Ellerton follers the coffin, with Sunflower Sadie on his arm as chief mourner. I've ordered out the Fire Department, but the skunks have struck on me an' won't parade. Most o' Bud's friends is on hand, however; an' all in all, it's a pretty imposin' funeral as we march to the church, which when we get there we find the elders standin' on the front steps an' the door padlocked top an' bottom. Philip's standin' among 'em, lookin' all broke up, an' I see they've been pickin' on the boy.

Well, son, I'm mayor o' Panamint, an' thirty year ago I'm that settled in my convictions I don't abdicate 'em none too easy. I give my handle o' the coffin to one o' Bud's barkeeps an' I walk up the stairs. I'm full o' dignity.

"Gentlemen," I says, "what appears to be the trouble?"

Ol' Silvertip steps for'd.

"Mr. Mayor," he says, "the pastor o' this church havin' disgraced his congregation, himself, an' the house o' Gawd, the vestry has seen fit to remove him from office, an' we don't aim to permit further degradation o' our place o' worship by admittin' this funeral. It's a-makin' a mockery o' ree-ligion," he says.

"All right, Silvertip," I says. "Have it your own way; but I want you to bear in mind the vestry didn't build this church an' equip it. I reckon I ought to be consulted. Open that door—an' be damn quick about it!"

"I got an order from the jestice o' the peace, restrainin' you an' John Doe an' Richard Roe an' William Black an' Thomas Green from usin' this church in any way," says Silvertip. "It's a public buildin', built by public subscription."

"Well," I says, "I'll tend to that jestice o' the peace after the funeral. Meantime let's proceed with these here obsequies." An' I reach under my long-tailed Sunday coat an' produces a pair o' thirty-eights on forty-four frames—the sweetest guns I ever owned. "If there's an elder in sight in one minute," I says, "we're goin' to have another funeral tomorrow mornin'—an' mebbe two or three."

I come up the stairs an' they backed away from me. I seen they didn't have the nerve of a lot o' field-mice; so I shoots the padlocks offen the doors an' throw 'em wide open. Buckskin Liz ducks in an' up into the organ loft first thing; an' when the music starts they lug Bud in an' set him on two chairs up in front near the pulpit. Me, I stand at the door, an' every soul that goes into that church has to state to me whether he's for or agin Philip; an' when they're all inside I got the grandest collection o' thieves, gamblers, bums, rascals, an' low-down men an' women I ever see together at one time before or since. The only respectable persons in the church, from the standp'int o' the righteous, is me an' Philip. Me, I'm no sweet young thing at that, but I'm regarded as a man, more or less. No sir; I didn't even let them elders in to hear the quartet, which is some deeprivation, for they shore sang somethin' beautiful.

I don't suppose I'm ever goin' to forget Philip's oration over Bud Deming. It seems the elders had him to themselves for about half an hour before the funeral come, an' they give him a pretty exact bill o' particulars. Philip seemed to realize mebbe this would be the last sermon he'd preach in Panamint, an' in his openin' remarks he took occasion to refer to the charges agin him. He don't show no bitterness, but quotes from the Scriptures an' says: "Father, forgive them; for they know not what they do!"

Then he says if he can't explain his conduct to their satisfaction, mebbe the Lord can, an' he opens up the Bible an' reads a piece. I learned it by heart afterward. It's from the Gospel o' Saint Matthew, chapter nine, from the tenth to the thirteenth verses:

"And it came to pass, as Jesus sat at meat in the house, behold, many publicans and sinners came and sat down with Him and His disciples.

"And when the Pharisees saw it, they said unto His disciples, Why eateth your Master with publicans and sinners?

"But when Jesus heard that, He said unto them, They that be whole need not a physician, but they that are sick.

"But go ye and learn what that meaneth, I will have mercy, and not sacrifice; for I am not come to call the righteous, but sinners to repentance."

Son, ain't that logic? Them elders had accused him o' keepin' company with sinners an' publicans—Bud Deming, he was the publican; an' in particular they're wild because he went an' sat down to a banquet with the scum o' the camp! Christ did that an' got criticized for it; an' Philip makes the mistake o' thinkin' times has changed! He figgers he can foller in his Master's footsteps an' convince his flock he ain't doin' it for evil pleasure an' base profit.

The Lord could have set down with Bud Deming an' his kind without takin' any resks—and so could Philip. He's constitooted so it ain't no trouble or danger for him to walk through sin an' come out clean every time. There's something about that boy that makes anybody respect him an' his cloth; an' while he's around sinners behave. They know the danger he's runnin', because they've been through it ahead of him; an', instead o' draggin' him down to their level, they're for protectin' him.

That day Philip has the kind o' congregation that big, broad human heart o' his is allers cravin'—the kind o' folks that needs him. No, he didn't come to Panamint to call the righteous to repentance, because they're able to care for themselves; but his big heart naturally expands with love for the unfortunates he sees settin' on the seats in front of him at Bud Deming's funeral, an' he talks to 'em like a brother, just a-drawin' a little object lesson from Bud's life—an' death. He don't have one hard word to say agin them doggone elders that's nigh broke his heart, but there ain't a soul in church that don't know he's sufferin'; an' we're all mentally reachin' out to pat him on the shoulder an' say: "Never you mind, Philip! We're for you, an' don't you forget it!"

I reckon that sermon o' Philip's that day nets the heaviest crop o' converts ever harvested with one preacher. I been a minin'-camp millionaire twice, an' busted both times as sudden as kickin' the ladder out from under a painter—an' I laughed an' called all hands to have a drink. That's all I care for misfortune; but when the world riz up an' busted in two the friend I'd have gone to hell for, I feel almighty bad. I'm full up an' can't join in the singin', an' me—I'm right fond o' music too.

Does Philip ever get back into the church after Bud's funeral? No, sir; he don't. The word's gone out that he owns a gamblin' house an' a dance hall; an' there's no disputin' that, for ain't twenty men heard Bud Deming proclaim it before he dies? Pore Bud! He thinks he's doin' Philip a favor, when every word he says damns the parson deeper'n ever.

An' ain't Philip been seen gamblin'?—which he don't deny it; only they won't take his excuse. They'd have lied out of it themselves; so they figgered Philip was doin' the same thing.

It's a hard hand to beat. Philip's got too much explainin' to do; an', as he tells me privately, he's none too good at explainin' to Pharisees. I'm for buildin' him another church to save trouble an' law-suits, because I know he'll cram it with his newly acquired congregation every Sunday; but he won't stand for that.

"No, Chuckwalla," he says; "that's my church that was built for me, an' I'll have to fight this thing out. The vestry has preferred charges agin me with the bishop; an' until I'm cleared o' them charges it ain't ethics for me to defy my congregation. You'll oblige me, Chuckwalla, by not takin' sides in this controversy."

Him tyin' my hands that way, what could I do? However, my sentiments is so well known that whenever one o' the opposition sees me comin' he takes the other side o' the street. Besides, I'm mayor; an' as mayor I can't foller the dictates o' my ambition, which is to kill Silvertip as a warnin' to all elders.

Philip writes a long letter to the bishop. Me an' Chappie Ellerton, an' Buckskin Liz an' Sunflower Sadie, an' a lot o' non-churchgoers, sends our sworn affidavits, an' on that Philip rests his case. He 'lows as how he's not defendin' himself—only explainin'; an' cites the Bible as his authority. Also he declines to lower his self-respect by appearin' before the Conference for trial; an' while awaitin' the jedgment he's my guest up at the hotel. While's he's under fire I won't permit him to occupy the parsonage.

Well, son, when Philip's trial comes up the elders are on hand an' Philip isn't; an' whatever rannikiboo business they put up on the Conference I dunno. All I know is the Conference finds Philip guilty an' heaves him out o' the church for bein' unworthy.

When Philip gets notice he ain't a preacher no longer it busts him up something awful, but still he don't complain. He lets me read the official kick-out, an' then he takes me by the arm an' me an' him has a long walk up on the malpais, where we sets for about half a day lookin' down on Panamint, an' neither of us sayin' a word. Finally he takes out the bishop's letter an' tears it into little pieces.

"Chuckwalla," he says, "I hope I ain't rebellious, but me an' you met in a fight, an' we been fightin' side by side ever since. This is your fight as much as mine in some ways—an' I ain't goin' to lay down on you. Pana-mint needs me an' I'm goin' to stay. I got a church o' my own—Bud Deming's gambling hall—an' I got a congregation with a good touch o' the devil in it, which is the only kind o' congregation I want anyhow; so I'm goin' into the soul-savin' business on my own account. I got a restauraw runnin' full blast; an', with Chappie managin' that, I can be self-supportin' an' have time to do the work I want to do. I'm a born preacher—I can't never be nothin' else; an' this here's my vineyard. I'm goin' down-town an' git to work."

I shook hands with him. His consideration o' my feelin's that-a-way teched me deep. That night he gives the bulk o' Bud Deming's bank roll to Sunflower Sadie, an' the next day she starts home to her folks back East. She vows she's goin' to be a good girl the rest o' her life, an' I hope she kept her word.

Then Philip gives all the other misfortunates a little road stake, cleans out the stock o' liquors an' gamblin' layouts, an' rigs up what he calls the Panamint Mission. Chappie takes charge o' the restauraw, which Buck-skin Liz is cashier on week days an' organist in the Mission on Sundays an' evenings.

Crabapple Thompson moves Philip's things out o' the parsonage an' follers to the Mission; an' Silvertip an' his crowd import a new preacher, as slick an' smooth as a mouse-colored mule knee-deep in green feed. He measures up to their ideals an' makes the church just what they wanted—a nice, quiet, family affair. He gives 'em what they want an' everybody is happy.

Well, son, Philip was happy, too, even if he was an outlaw, because he got satisfactory results. Also, he's got somethin' else—from that consump-tive gambler he'd cared for until the feller died; an' in about two years I see he's failin'. I get the best doctors an' send him away for three months; but he ain't happy an' comes back. He says he's better off in the desert an' a high altitude, an' I guess he is; but, at that, the disease has him for fair an' in the long run it gets him. He's holdin' my hand when he goes.

I ain't mayor no more, for the church party has busted me wide open;

but I've stuck by him in honor an' in disgrace an' I'm stickin' by him to the grave. He's the biggest man that ever comes to Panamint, an' he's never bigger in my heart than he is the day he's lyin' in state in the Mission.

An' that orthodox parson from Philip's old church comes down an' offers his services to preach our Philip's funeral sermon. I ain't got no quarrel with this new parson an' I'm feelin' too bad to insult him even if I wanted to; so I just says: "No, thank you, parson. I guess we'll use our home talent"—an' we do! Chappie Ellerton officiates.

Hank Bartlett gets out an extra o' the Panamint Nugget, with big black borders an' heavy black type. The entire issue is devoted to Philip, an' it brings every man, woman an' child in Panamint to Philip's funeral. Even ol' Silvertip's there, with the other elders. I'm for orderin' 'em out o' the cemetery—when I see Silvertip's broke up somethin' awful. I dunno what made me do it, but I walk up an' tap him on the shoulder; an' when he looks round at me I hold out my hand.

"Randall," I says, "I thought I hated you; but I find I don't. I guess I've been round Philip too long. I can't disgrace him now by holdin' a grudge agin you."

Pore ol' Silvertip breaks down an' cries like a child.

"We crucified him!" he says. "We crucified him, Mr. Redfield, an' we never knew it!"

"He never held it agin you," I says. "His last words was, 'Chuckwalla, I am content. No crown without a cross!' "

Then I steps over to Silvertip's parson. Chappie has just finished readin': "I am the resurrection an' the life"—an' I know he can't go on without breakin' down. So I says to Silvertip's parson:

"Mebbe you'd be so kind as to forget I was a little stiff yesterday, an' render the closin' prayer?"

"I should be honored," he says, an' done it beautiful.

Son, Panamint divided over Philip, but it come together over him in the finish; an' I was satisfied. They'd licked us oncet, but Philip triumphs in the end; an' all the bitterness in Panamint goes into the grave with him an' stays there.

Old Chuckwalla Bill bit into his chewing tobacco and munched quietly for several seconds. Finally he glanced at me across the camp-fire.

"Son," he said, "would you like to visit the parsonage?"

I nodded assent and in a few minutes we were picking our way across the desert valley. Presently we ascended a gentle slope to a little mesa and

Chuckwalla Bill led the way to a tall granite shaft rising out of the sagebrush. As he stooped and uprooted the sage that covered the "parsonage," I flashed a pocket electric torch on the face of the monument and read the epitaph of the parson of Panamint:

HERE LIES THE BODY

OF

PHILIP PHARO

A Minister of the Gospel of

Jesus Christ

On July 20, 1884, he saved two men and a woman from everlasting fire, receiving burns from which he never recovered. He went to his reward on September 22, 1887.

Erected by the Citizens of Panamint

For the Sinners and Publicans

WILLIAM E. REDFIELD

For the Scribes and Pharisees

ABSALOM RANDALL

"I allers make it a p'int to circle back this way every coupler years an' keep the sage from growin' up round him," the old prospector explained. "I don't like that he should think I'm forgettin' him."

He stood gazing down into the valley, which was bathed in moonlight; and a coyote, catching the manscent borne to him on the hot zephyr that floated up through Panamint, gave tongue on a distant butte. In an open space below us a jack rabbit hopped leisurely about his affairs, crickets whirred, and a little night bird chirped sleepily; but old Chuckwalla Bill neither heard nor saw, for he was gazing over the roofs of pine shanty and tenthouse in the city of his dreams; he was watching again the old, glorious, ruinous rout of fortune surging up and down Amethyst Avenue; he was listening again to Buckskin Liz tickling the ivory, and forgetting much that had come between. Presently he sighed and pointed into the valley.

"Son," he said plaintively, "I was mayor o' that city oncet."

The Caballero's Way

BY O. HENRY

(The Cisco Kid)

William Sydney Porter (1862–1910) was born in North Carolina, migrated to Texas in 1882, and followed a varied career as a cowboy, journalist, and bank teller. In 1898 he was tried and convicted of embezzlement committed during his years as an employee of an Austin bank, and it was while serving a three-year prison sentence that he began writing short stories for the popular magazines under the pseudonym O. Henry. Among the collections of his superb stories is Heart of the West *(1904), which contains some of the most authentic Western tales ever penned. In addition to "The Caballero's Way," two other O. Henry stories were adapted into notable Western films: "A Double-Dyed Deceiver" (see* The Reel West*), which was made into* The Texan *(1930), one of Gary Cooper's early films; and "The Passing of Black Eagle" (see* The Second Reel West*), which became* Black Eagle *(1948).*

The Cisco Kid had killed six men in more or less fair scrimmages, had murdered twice as many (mostly Mexicans), and had winged a larger number whom he modestly forbore to count. Therefore a woman loved him.

The Kid was twenty-five, looked twenty; and a careful insurance company would have estimated the probable time of his demise at, say, twenty-six. His habitat was anywhere between the Frio and the Rio Grande. He killed for the love of it—because he was quick-tempered—to avoid arrest—for his own amusement—any reason that came to his mind would suffice. He had escaped capture because he could shoot five-sixths of a second sooner than any sheriff or ranger in the service, and because he rode a speckled roan horse that knew every cow-path in the mesquite and pear thickets from San Antonio to Matamoras.

Tonia Perez, the girl who loved the Cisco Kid, was half Carmen, half Madonna, and the rest—oh, yes, a woman who is half Carmen and half Madonna can always be something more—the rest, let us say, was hummingbird. She lived in a grass-roofed *jacal* near a little Mexican settlement at the Lone Wolf Crossing of the Frio. With her lived a father or grandfather, a lineal Aztec, somewhat less than a thousand years old, who herded a hundred goats and lived in a continuous drunken dream from drinking *mescal.* Back of the *jacal* a tremendous forest of bristling pear, twenty feet high at its worst, crowded almost to its door. It was along the bewildering maze of this spinous thicket that the speckled roan would bring the Kid to see his girl. And once, clinging like a lizard to the ridgepole, high up under the peaked grass roof, he had heard Tonia, with her Madonna face and Carmen beauty and hummingbird soul, parley with the sheriff's posse, denying knowledge of her man in her soft mélange of Spanish and English.

One day the adjutant-general of the state, who is *ex officio* commander of the ranger forces, wrote some sarcastic lines to Captain Duval of Company X, stationed at Laredo, relative to the serene and undisturbed existence led by murderers and desperadoes in the said captain's territory.

The captain turned the color of brick dust under his tan, and forwarded the letter, after adding a few comments, per ranger Private Bill Adamson, to ranger Lieutenant Sandridge, camped at a water hole on the Nueces with a squad of five men in preservation of law and order.

Lieutenant Sandridge turned a beautiful *couleur de rose* through his ordinary strawberry complexion, tucked the letter in his hip pocket, and chewed off the ends of his gamboge moustache.

The next morning he saddled his horse and rode alone to the Mexican settlement at the Lone Wolf Crossing of the Frio, twenty miles away.

Six feet two, blond as a Viking, quiet as a deacon, dangerous as a machine gun, Sandridge moved among the *jacales*, patiently seeking news of the Cisco Kid.

Far more than the law, the Mexicans dreaded the cold and certain vengeance of the lone rider that the ranger sought. It had been one of the Kid's pastimes to shoot Mexicans "to see them kick": if he demanded from them moribund Terpsichorean feats, simply that he might be entertained, what terrible and extreme penalties would be certain to follow should they anger him! One and all they lounged with upturned palms and shrugging shoulders, filling the air with *"quien sabe"*'s and denials of the Kid's acquaintance.

But there was a man named Fink who kept a store at the Crossing—a man of many nationalities, tongues, interests, and ways of thinking.

"No use to ask them Mexicans," he said to Sandridge. "They're afraid to tell. This *hombre* they call the Kid—Goodall is his name, ain't it?—he's been in my store once or twice. I have an idea you might run across him at —but I guess I don't keer to say, myself. I'm two seconds later in pulling a gun than I used to be, and the difference is worth thinking about. But this Kid's got a half-Mexican girl at the Crossing that he comes to see. She lives in that *jacal* a hundred yards down the arroyo at the edge of the pear. Maybe she—no, I don't suppose she would, but that *jacal* would be a good place to watch, anyway."

Sandridge rode down to the *jacal* of Perez. The sun was low, and the broad shade of the great pear thicket already covered the grass-thatched hut. The goats were enclosed for the night in a brush corral near by. A few kids walked the top of it, nibbling the chaparral leaves. The old Mexican lay upon a blanket on the grass, already in a stupor from his *mescal,* and dreaming, perhaps, of the nights when he and Pizarro touched glasses to their New World fortunes—so old his wrinkled face seemed to proclaim him to be. And in the door of the *jacal* stood Tonia. And Lieutenant Sandridge sat in his saddle staring at her like a gannet agape at a sailorman.

The Cisco Kid was a vain person, as all eminent and successful assassins are, and his bosom would have been ruffled had he known that at a simple exchange of glances two persons, in whose minds he had been looming large, suddenly abandoned (at least for the time) all thought of him.

Never before had Tonia seen such a man as this. He seemed to be made of sunshine and blood-red tissue and clear weather. He seemed to illuminate the shadow of the pear when he smiled, as though the sun were rising again. The men she had known had been small and dark. Even the Kid, in spite of his achievements, was a stripling no larger than herself, with black, straight hair and a cold, marble face that chilled the noonday.

As for Tonia, though she sends description to the poorhouse, let her make a millionaire of your fancy. Her blue-black hair, smoothly divided in the middle and bound close to her head, and her large eyes full of the Latin melancholy, gave her the Madonna touch. Her motions and air spoke of the concealed fire and the desire to charm that she had inherited from the *gitanas* of the Basque province. As for the hummingbird part of her, that dwelt in her heart; you could not perceive it unless her bright red skirt and dark blue blouse gave you a symbolic hint of the vagarious bird.

The newly lighted sun-god asked for a drink of water. Tonia brought it from the red jar hanging under the brush shelter. Sandridge considered it necessary to dismount so as to lessen the trouble of her ministrations.

I play no spy; nor do I assume to master the thoughts of any human heart; but I assert, by the chronicler's right, that before a quarter of an hour had sped, Sandridge was teaching her how to plait a six-strand rawhide stake-rope, and Tonia had explained to him that were it not for her little English book that the peripatetic *padre* had given her and the little crippled *chivo*, which she fed from a bottle, she would be very, very lonely indeed.

Which leads to a suspicion that the Kid's fences needed repairing, and that the adjutant-general's sarcasm had fallen upon unproductive soil.

In his camp by the water hole Lieutenant Sandridge announced and reiterated his intention of either causing the Cisco Kid to nibble the black loam of the Frio country prairies or of haling him before a judge and jury. That sounded businesslike. Twice a week he rode over to the Lone-Wolf Crossing of the Frio, and directed Tonia's slim, slightly lemon-tinted fingers among the intricacies of the slowly growing lariat. A six-strand plait is hard to learn and easy to teach.

The ranger knew that he might find the Kid there at any visit. He kept his armament ready, and had a frequent eye for the pear thicket at the rear of the *jacal*. Thus he might bring down the kite and the humming-bird with one stone.

While the sunny-haired ornithologist was pursuing his studies, the Cisco Kid was also attending to his professional duties. He moodily shot up a saloon in a small cow village on Quintana Creek, killed the town marshal (plugging him neatly in the center of his tin badge), and then rode away, morose and unsatisfied. No true artist is uplifted by shooting an aged man carrying an old style .38 bulldog.

On his way the Kid suddenly experienced the yearning that all men feel when wrongdoing loses its keen edge of delight. He yearned for the woman he loved to reassure him that she was his in spite of it. He wanted her to call his bloodthirstiness bravery and his cruelty devotion. He wanted Tonia to bring him water from the red jar under the brush shelter, and tell him how the *chivo* was thriving on the bottle.

The Kid turned the speckled roan's head up the ten-mile pear flat that stretches along the Arroyo Hondo until it ends at the Lone Wolf Crossing of the Frio. The roan whickered; for he had a sense of locality and direction equal to that of a belt-line street-car horse; and he knew he would soon be nibbling the rich mesquite grass at the end of a forty-foot stake-rope while Ulysses rested his head in Circe's straw-roofed hut.

More weird and lonesome than the journey of an Amazonian explorer is the ride of one through a Texas pear flat. With dismal monotony and startling variety the uncanny and multiform shapes of the cacti lift their twisted trunks and fat, bristly hands to encumber the way. The demon plant, appearing to live without soil or rain, seems to taunt the parched traveler with its lush gray greenness. It warps itself a thousand times about what look to be open and inviting paths, only to lure the rider into blind and impassable spine-defended "bottoms of the bag," leaving him to retreat, if he can, with the points of the compass whirling in his head.

To be lost in the pear is to die almost the death of the thief on the cross, pierced by nails and with grotesque shapes of all the fiends hovering about.

But it was not so with the Kid and his mount. Winding, twisting, circling, tracing the most fantastic and bewildering trail ever picked out, the good roan lessened the distance to the Lone Wolf Crossing with every coil and turn that he made.

While they fared the Kid sang. He knew but one tune and sang it, as he knew but one code and lived it, and but one girl and loved her. He was a single-minded man of conventional ideas. He had a voice like a coyote with bronchitis, but whenever he chose to sing his song he sang it. It was a conventional song of the camps and trails, running at its beginning as near as may be to these words:

> *Don't you monkey with my Lulu girl*
> *or I'll tell you what I'll do—*

and so on. The roan was inured to it, and did not mind.

But even the poorest singer will, after a certain time, gain his own consent to refrain from contributing to the world's noises. So the Kid, by the time he was within a mile or two of Tonia's *jacal*, had reluctantly allowed his song to die away—not because his vocal performance had become less charming to his own ears, but because his laryngeal muscles were aweary.

As though he were in a circus ring, the speckled roan wheeled and danced through the labyrinth of pear until at length his rider knew by certain landmarks that the Lone Wolf Crossing was close at hand. Then, where the pear was thinner, he caught sight of the grass roof of the *jacal* and the hackberry tree on the edge of the arroyo. A few yards farther the Kid stopped the roan and gazed intently through the prickly openings. Then he dismounted, dropped the roan's reins, and proceeded on foot, stooping and silent, like an Indian. The roan, knowing his part, stood still, making no sound.

The Kid crept noiselessly to the very edge of the pear thicket and reconnoitered between the leaves of a clump of cactus.

Ten yards from his hiding place, in the shade of the *jacal,* sat his Tonia calmly plaiting a rawhide lariat. So far she might surely escape condemnation; women have been known, from time to time, to engage in more mischievous occupations. But if all must be told, there is to be added that her head reposed against the broad and comfortable chest of a tall red-and-yellow man, and that his arm was about her, guiding her nimble small fingers that required so many lessons at the intricate six-strand plait.

Sandridge glanced quickly at the dark mass of pear when he heard a slight squeaking sound that was not altogether unfamiliar. A gun-scabbard will make that sound when one grasps the handle of a six-shooter suddenly. But the sound was not repeated; and Tonia's fingers needed close attention.

And then, in the shadow of death, they began to talk of their love; and in the still July afternoon every word they uttered reached the ears of the Kid.

"Remember, then," said Tonia, "you must not come again until I send for you. Soon he will be here. A *vaquero* at the *tienda* said today he saw him on the Guadalupe three days ago. When he is that near he always comes. If he comes and finds you here he will kill you. So, for my sake, you must come no more until I send you the word."

"All right," said the ranger. "And then what?"

"And then," said the girl, "you must bring your men here and kill him. If not, he will kill you."

"He ain't a man to surrender, that's sure," said Sandridge. "It's kill or be killed for the officer that goes up against Mr. Cisco Kid."

"He must die," said the girl. "Otherwise there will not be any peace in the world for thee and me. He has killed many. Let him so die. Bring your men, and give him no chance to escape."

"You used to think right much of him," said Sandridge.

Tonia dropped the lariat, twisted herself around, and curved a lemon-tinted arm over the ranger's shoulder.

"But then," she murmured in liquid Spanish, "I had not beheld thee, thou great, red mountain of a man! And thou art kind and good, as well as strong. Could one choose him, knowing thee? Let him die; for then I will not be filled with fear by day and night lest he hurt thee or me."

"How can I know when he comes?" asked Sandridge.

"When he comes," said Tonia, "he remains two days, sometimes three, Gregorio, the small son of old Luisa, the *lavandera*, has a swift pony. I will write a letter to thee and send it by him, saying how it will be best to come upon him. By Gregorio will the letter come. And bring many men with thee, and have much care, oh, dear red one, for the rattlesnake is not quicker to strike than is '*El chivato*,' as they call him, to send a ball from his *pistola*."

"The Kid's handy with his gun, sure enough," admitted Sandridge, "but when I come for him I shall come alone. I'll get him by myself or not at all. The Cap wrote one or two things to me that make me want to do the trick without any help. You let me know when Mr. Kid arrives, and I'll do the rest."

"I will send you the message by the boy Gregorio," said the girl. "I knew you were braver than that small slayer of men who never smiles. How could I ever have thought I cared for him?"

It was time for the ranger to ride back to his camp on the water hole. Before he mounted his horse he raised the slight form of Tonia with one arm high from the earth for a parting salute. The drowsy stillness of the torpid summer air still lay thick upon the dreaming afternoon. The smoke from the fire in the *jacal*, where the *frijoles* bubbled in the iron pot, rose straight as a plumb line above the clay-daubed chimney. No sound or movement disturbed the serenity of the dense pear thicket ten yards away.

When the form of Sandridge had disappeared, loping his big dun down the steep banks of the Frio crossing, the Kid crept back to his own horse, mounted him, and rode back along the tortuous trail he had come.

But not far. He stopped and waited in the silent depths of the pear until half an hour had passed. And then Tonia heard the high, untrue notes of his unmusical singing coming nearer and nearer; and she ran to the edge of the pear to meet him.

The Kid seldom smiled; but he smiled and waved his hat when he saw her. He dismounted, and his girl sprang into his arms. The Kid looked at her fondly. His thick, black hair clung to his head like a wrinkled mat. The meeting brought a slight ripple of some undercurrent of feeling to his smooth, dark face that was usually as motionless as a clay mask.

"How's my girl?" he asked, holding her close.

"Sick of waiting so long for you, dear one," she answered. "My eyes are dim with always gazing into that devil's pincushion through which you come. And I can see into it such a little way, too. But you are here, beloved one, and I will not scold. *Qué mal muchacho!* not to come to see your *alma* more often. Go in and rest, and let me water your horse and stake him with the long rope. There is cool water in the jar for you."

The Kid kissed her affectionately.

"Not if the court knows itself do I let a lady stake my horse for me," said he. "But if you'll run in, *chica*, and throw a pot of coffee together while I attend to the *caballo*, I'll be a good deal obliged."

Besides his marksmanship the Kid had another attribute for which he admired himself greatly. He was *muy caballero*, as the Mexicans express it, where the ladies were concerned. For them he had always gentle words and consideration. He could not have spoken a harsh word to a woman. He might ruthlessly slay their husbands and brothers, but he could not have laid the weight of a finger in anger upon a woman. Wherefore many of that interesting division of humanity who had come under the spell of his politeness declared their disbelief in the stories circulated about Mr. Kid. One shouldn't believe everything one heard, they said. When confronted by their indignant menfolk with proof of the *caballero*'s deeds of infamy, they said maybe he had been driven to it, and that he knew how to treat a lady, anyhow.

Considering this extremely courteous idiosyncrasy of the Kid and the pride that he took in it, one can perceive that the solution of the problem that was presented to him by what he saw and heard from his hiding place in the pear that afternoon (at least as to one of the actors) must have been obscured by difficulties. And yet one could not think of the Kid's overlooking little matters of that kind.

At the end of the short twilight they gathered around a supper of *frijoles*, goat steaks, canned peaches, and coffee, by the light of a lantern in the *jacal*. Afterward, the ancestor, his flock corralled, smoked a cigarette and became a mummy in a gray blanket. Tonia washed the few dishes while the Kid dried them with the flour-sacking towel. Her eyes shone; she chatted volubly of the inconsequent happenings of her small world since the Kid's last visit; it was as all his other homecomings had been.

Then outside Tonia swung in a grass hammock with her guitar and sang sad *canciones de amor*.

"Do you love me just the same, old girl?" asked the Kid, hunting for his cigarette papers.

"Always the same, little one," said Tonia, her dark eyes lingering upon him.

"I must go over to Fink's," said the Kid, rising, "for some tobacco. I thought I had another sack in my coat. I'll be back in a quarter of an hour."

"Hasten," said Tonia, "and tell me—how long shall I call you my own this time? Will you be gone again tomorrow, leaving me to grieve, or will you be longer with your Tonia?"

"Oh, I might stay two or three days this trip," said the Kid, yawning. "I've been on the lodge for a month, and I'd like to rest up."

He was gone half an hour for his tobacco. When he returned Tonia was still lying in the hammock.

"It's funny," said the Kid, "how I feel. I feel like there was somebody lying behind every bush and tree waiting to shoot me. I never had mullygrubs like them before. Maybe it's one of them presumptions. I've got half a notion to light out in the morning before day. The Guadalupe country is burning up about that old Dutchman I plugged down there."

"You are not afraid—no one could make my brave little one fear."

"Well, I haven't been usually regarded as a jackrabbit when it comes to scrapping; but I don't want a posse smoking me out when I'm in your *jacal*. Somebody might get hurt that oughtn't to."

"Remain with your Tonia; no one will find you here."

The Kid looked keenly into the shadows up and down the arroyo and toward the dim lights of the Mexican village.

"I'll see how it looks later on" was his decision.

At midnight a horseman rode into the rangers' camp, blazing his way by noisy "hallo"s to indicate a pacific mission. Sandridge and one or two others turned out to investigate the row. The rider announced himself to be Domingo Sales, from the Lone Wolf Crossing. He bore a letter for Señor Sandridge. Old Luisa, the *lavandera*, had persuaded him to bring it, he said, her son Gregoro being too ill of a fever to ride.

Sandridge lighted the camp lantern and read the letter. These were its words:

Dear One: He has come. Hardly had you ridden away when he came out of the pear. When he first talked he said he would stay three days or more. Then as it grew later he was like a wolf or a fox, and walked about without rest, looking and listening. Soon he said he must leave before daylight when it is dark and stillest. And then he seemed to suspect that I be not true to him. He looked at me so strange that I am frightened. I swear to him that I love him, his own Tonia. Last of all he said I must prove to him I am true. He thinks that even now men are waiting to kill him as he rides from my house. To escape he says he will dress in my clothes, my red skirt and the blue waist I wear and the brown mantilla over the head, and thus ride away. But before that he says that I must put on his clothes, his *pantalones* and *camisa* and hat, and ride away on his horse from the *jacal* as far as the big road beyond the crossing and back again. This before he goes, so he can tell if I am true and if men are hidden to shoot him. It is a terrible thing. An hour before daybreak this is to be. Come, my dear one, and kill this man and take me for your Tonia. Do not try to take hold of him alive, but kill him quickly. Knowing all, you should do that. You must come long before the time and hide yourself in the little shed near the *jacal* where the wagon and saddles are kept. It is dark in there. He will wear my red skirt and blue waist and brown mantilla. I send you a hundred kisses. Come surely and shoot quickly and straight.

> *Thine Own Tonia*

Sandridge quickly explained to his men the official part of the missive. The rangers protested against his going alone.

"I'll get him easy enough," said the lieutenant. "The girl's got him trapped. And don't even think he'll get the drop on me."

Sandridge saddled his horse and rode to the Lone Wolf Crossing. He tied his big dun in a clump of brush on the arroyo, took his Winchester from its scabbard, and carefully approached the Perez *jacal*. There was only the half of a high moon drifted over by ragged, milk-white gulf clouds.

The wagon-shed was an excellent place for ambush; and the ranger got inside it safely. In the black shadow of the brush shelter in front of the *jacal* he could see a horse tied and hear him impatiently pawing the hard-trodden earth.

He waited almost an hour before two figures came out of the *jacal*. One, in man's clothes, quickly mounted the horse and galloped past the wagon-shed toward the crossing and village. And then the other figure, in skirt, waist, and mantilla over its head, stepped out into the faint moonlight, gazing after the rider. Sandridge thought he would take his chance then before Tonia rode back. He fancied she might not care to see it.

"Throw up your hands," he ordered loudly, stepping out of the wagon-shed with his Winchester at his shoulder.

There was a quick turn of the figure, but no movement to obey, so the ranger pumped in the bullets—one—two—three—and then twice more;

for you never could be too sure of bringing down the Cisco Kid. There was no danger of missing at ten paces, even in that half moonlight.

The old ancestor, asleep on his blanket, was awakened by the shots. Listening further, he heard a great cry from some man in mortal distress or anguish, and rose up grumbling at the disturbing ways of moderns.

The tall, red ghost of a man burst into the *jacal*, reaching one hand, shaking like a *tule* reed, for the lantern hanging on its nail. The other spread a letter on the table.

"Look at this letter, Perez," cried the man. "Who wrote it?"

"*Ah, Dios!* it is Señor Sandridge," mumbled the old man, approaching. "*Pues, señor*, that letter was written by '*El chivato*,' as he is called—by the man of Tonia. They say he is a bad man; I do not know. While Tonia slept he wrote the letter and sent it by this old hand of mine to Domingo Sales to be brought to you. Is there anything wrong in the letter? I am very old; and I did not know. *Valgame Dios!* it is a very foolish world; and there is nothing in the house to drink—nothing to drink."

Just then all that Sandridge could think of to do was to go outside and throw himself face downward in the dust by the side of his hummingbird, of whom not a feather fluttered. He was not a *caballero* by instinct, and he could not understand the niceties of revenge.

A mile away the rider who had ridden past the wagon-shed struck up a harsh, untuneful song, the words of which began:

> *Don't you monkey with my Lulu girl*
> *Or I'll tell you what I'll do—*

Raiders Die Hard

BY JOHN M. CUNNINGHAM

(Day of the Bad Man)

High Noon *(1951), winner of four Academy Awards and the hearts of film buffs everywhere, is widely considered to be the quintessential Western film. Not enough fans of* High Noon *know that it was based on a powerful short story by John M. Cunningham—"The Tin Star," first published in* Collier's *in 1947 (and included in* The Reel West). *Two other Cunningham stories were also adapted for notable films:* Day of the Bad Man, *from the novelette which follows; and* The Stranger Wore a Gun *(1953), a 3-D Western featuring Randolph Scott and Claire Trevor and based on the story "Yankee Gold" (included in* The Second Reel West).

Someone was standing at the window behind Judge Ogilvie. He straightened from his rosebush, and turned.

Sam Wyckoff was standing there, staring at the man he had served ever since he had met Ogilvie in the Army of the Republic.

The expression on Wyckoff's face surprised Judge Ogilvie. For the first time in their long career together, Wyckoff was gazing at his employer with poorly-hidden resentment, and with a kind of sadness.

"You going to santance this man today? This Hayes?" Wyckoff asked.

"Yes."

"To hang?"

"Yes. What else?"

"Is going to be trouble."

Ogilvie smiled a little. "There's always trouble when you try to hang a popular killer in this Territory. Only this time he's going to hang. Maybe it'll be the beginning of some real peace around these parts."

There was a pause. "You still going to sat the date for you wadding, too?" the burly man standing at the window demanded.

Ogilvie frowned. "I said I would. What's the court business got to do with that?"

"You ain't locky, Jodge. Better you wait to ask Miss Lampson."

"Keep your pagan superstitions to yourself."

"Don't cot no more rosses, Jodge. Miss Lampson will wait another day."

The judge bent over his rose bushes again. "She's waited two years already. I can't keep her bluffed forever. Wrap up that Bible I bought her and get out the horses. Court opens in fifteen minutes."

In some of the roses there was still a trace of dew, hidden deep inside, tiny silver specks, delicate and chill. The old pair of surgical scissors, U. S. Army, 1860, poked their blunt nib between the little green leaves and one by one the red roses fell, the long stems toppling aside into the palm of Ogilvie's crippled hand. He held the fingers of his withered arm like a little cup, laying the stems one by one in a newspaper.

He cut ten in the quiet garden above the creek, and then stopped to listen. There were horses in the creek bottom, hidden by the yellow cottonwoods, coming up the slope toward the garden. He could hear them blowing and grunting as they heaved, saddle-leather squeaking and groaning, the beasts panting loudly as they came up the steep bank.

The first rider was a plump, pleasant-looking man with a small, sharp, beak-like nose in a large, smooth, red face.

He smiled, his black eyes twinkling brightly. "Good morning, Judge. Picking flowers, I see."

The judge stood silent, straight and black. "Good morning, Charles. How are all the Hayes brothers?"

The three were armed according to custom; one pistol each, the usual accoutrement. Each also had, tucked under a knee, slanting down the saddle skirt, a rifle in a boot.

Charles touched his horse's mouth with the bit and it halted at the little picket fence at the rear of the garden. The other two ranged up alongside. One rolled a cigarette and struck a sulphur match, and behind a cloud of smoke which rose in the sun, he puffed and sighed. The other individual was like a shadow, slipping up on a lean dun jade.

The judge's shears relaxed open and he looked careless. "How are you, Jake? And you, Howard? I saw your kid brother, Rudy, in the jail last night, and he seemed splendid."

"We're all fine," Charles said. "It's a fine morning."

"Get to the point."

"All right, Ogilvie, I will," Charles said. "There ain't much to it. You been in our county about five years now. You've been a bright young man and a sharp lawyer with what law there is, I mean water rights and so on. But since you was appointed judge, there's been talk you're going to try to boss us people around. That you're going to make this county law-abiding, as you call it."

Ogilvie said, "Go on."

"We heard that you're saying you're going to make an example of Rudy. In fact, hang him."

"He's guilty of murder. The jury said so."

"Hell, yes, he's guilty! But that ain't the point. The point is, you can't just hang Rudy. Why, I wouldn't have even bothered to come here and bother you, Ogilvie, except for this talk, and you being a little different from them other judges. What they always done was order people out of the county, or give them a suspended sentence. Hell! Maybe six months in jail. But hanging's out around here. Understand?" He smiled and nodded at the roses. "Darn pretty flowers."

"They're called roses. Well, Charles, I know how you've been running things around here, one way or another, and I know it hurts your pride to have your brother hanged just for getting caught—but I say he's going to hang, Charles."

"I guess you don't understand, Judge," Charles said. "This ain't a case like in a lawbook."

The smoker blew out a long stream and said, profoundly, "Talk is cheap."

"Shut up, Jake. Judge—"

"Why don't we do it now?" Jake went on. "Why argue?"

"Shut up," the fat one said. "Judge, don't be ornery. That Pole of yours is a good man, but there's only one of him, and there's three of us."

"I guess you don't count me," the judge said.

The shadow on the dun plug laughed. "That Pole."

"I think he's a Hungarian," Ogilvie said. "A gentleman from Central Europe."

"How did you train him, Judge?" Howard asked. "With cheese?"

"A dirty coward," Jake said, puffing steadily. "A dirty coward sitting on a bench judging a real man."

"Shut up, I told you," the fat one said. "You and Howard keep quiet, now."

Howard—the shadow—said, "A lousy cripple."

The fat one turned sharply in the saddle and looked down at Howard.

Howard's mouth dropped open like a gopher hole and he backed his horse away. "I'm sorry, Charles," he said in a small voice.

Charles turned back to the judge, "You don't have to hang Rudy, Judge. You can banish him. Banish him, Judge. I'm not ornery. I don't say let him go. Banish him."

The judge looked up. "Banish?"

"It's an old custom in this territory. The miners' courts started it. Banish. Get out. Don't come back. You can do it."

"Feudal," the judge said, smiling at the roses beside his feet. "Rudolph, thou hast forfeited thy fief. I banish thee forever from my realm. How long do they stay banished, Charles?"

"Beside the point," Charles said. "Often used in cases of doubt—or for other reasons."

"Reasons involving the judge's hide, I suspect."

Charles smiled again.

"But not involving the Federal law, which governs this territory, and to uphold which I am sworn. Charles, thou has forfeited thy fief. I banish thee forever from my garden."

Charles stopped smiling. "Listen. I never had to go this far before—for a long time. I'm warning you."

The screen door behind the judge twanged slowly open, the spring screeching and stretching in its rust.

"You don't have to took this, Jodge," Wyckoff said from the doorway. He held a Government .45-70 carbine, cocked, in his right hand, hip-leveled, and held the screen door open with the other. He had a head like a chopping block and hair like that of an old badger. "If you say the word, you don't have to took this."

The three on their horses slumped a little, their right hands finding their way to resting places more convenient to their armament.

"I'm not 'taking' anything, in the sense you mean, Sam. Have you met these gentlemen? The Hayes brothers—those of them at liberty, that is. Since we are being feudal this morning, I shall introduce them as Charles the Fat. Jake the Slow and Howard the—what shall I say? Howard is the quaint young gentleman with the hare lip. Or is that an old shaving wound, Howard?"

Howard said, "Did you hear that, Charles? Did you hear what he said? He's talking about my moustache!"

"Got out," Wyckoff said. "Got out of here, you boms."

"Don't be so rough," the judge said quietly. "They are merely approaching me with a bribe."

"Not a bribe," Charles said. "You're not getting paid a dime. This is an order. You banish Rudy."

Ogilvie snipped the shears twice, examining the juncture of the cutting edges.

Charles gathered up his reins and lifted them. "Whoever has anything to do with hanging Rudy is going to get himself killed. That ain't in the Federal law either, but it'll work better."

"You should wear a rose behind your ear, Charles. Here, have a free rose."

Charles looked at him for a moment. He lifted his reins gracefully, swaying his plump horse around, and trotted away. The others lined out after him. The cottonwood trash rustled and cracked as they disappeared behind the yellowing foliage.

"What gall," the judge said, picking at a speck of rust on one blade of the scissors. "I expected they might try something, but hardly that they'd announce it."

Wyckoff spat off the end of the porch away from the judge. "Why are we always fiding? Already we made free the Negroes. Who now?"

The judge looked down at the roses and smiled. He slipped the scissors back into his pocket, and stooping, began rolling the roses up in the damp newspaper. His right hand was nimble, his left hung idle, a withered little cup like a child's hand.

"Let's forget the Hayes boys and think of—love. Ah, Wyckoff, isn't it wonderful? You see, it is her gift, that I can love her freely, happily, without embarrassment, her particular genius. It is a wonderful thing."

Wyckoff looked down at him, his heavy mouth a crease among a field of heavy creases, and watched the judge wrap up the roses. "Wonnerful," he said. "You always riding poattry, everything for poattry. It is a wonderful thing, poattry."

"Don't be silly. This is no sentimental thing." The judge stood up, smiling, holding his sheaf of roses neatly wrapped. "I perceive her true beauty in the light of sound reason, Sam. Certainly her love is sound and real, if it can ignore such defects in a man. Such defects as—as I have. And who is a harder judge of a man than a woman? And so who on earth can be happier than I am? Who has a right to be? I have passed the judgment of a queen, I hold a heart more precious than the sun. Why shouldn't I be happy?"

"More poattry. You made up you mind you sat the date today?"

"That's it."

"Then I got some bad news for you, Captain. I mean Jodge."

"What?"

"I wasn't going to tell you, but I got to now, if you going to sat the date today."

"Well, what is it?"

"She don't love you no more."

The judge looked at him in silence. "Is that a Hungarian joke? Why on earth would you say a thing like that?"

Wyckoff slowly blushed.

"What made you say a thing like that? Obviously, if she didn't, she would—oh, what am I talking about?"

Wyckoff stood frozen. "I'm sorry, Jodge."

The judge looked away. "Go get her presents—the book and the rings."

Wyckoff's right hand moved up and down in a kind of fumbled salute, and he turned abruptly. The judge followed, the roses like a child in the hollow of his crippled arm.

CHAPTER TWO

Before the Trial

There was a clump of yellow alders at the end of the deserted street of the town, where the saloons tapered off toward the creek. Wyckoff and the judge crossed the plank bridge, the hoofs of their horses rumbling, and turned up a short road toward the mountains. At the head of the road was a meadow crowded with horses and vehicles of all kinds, and in the middle, a white frame church with a log addition on the back.

Horses were tied everywhere; to the rail before the church, to the spokes of wheels, to the hanging limbs of trees. Wagons had been driven under the small windows of the church, and men stood on the sideboards, peering in. A few had brought ladders and boards, and had built trestles. A large group sat on the steps, ears turned toward the opened front doors.

There was a young woman on the side of the road, at the edge of the meadow, waiting under the yellow arch of leaves. Her firm, dark eyes peered from under a poke bonnet. Ogilvie saw her and a smile came up over his face. He swung down and walked forward, leading his horse. She was smiling back, standing with her hands held together, somewhat timidly.

He took off his hat, slipping the reins up his arm, and walked toward her, stopping a good five feet away. "Hello," he said gently. His eyes went over her face. "How are you? My God, you're lovely. I have something for you—to show you. The present I told you about." He grinned. "The time has come—we can set the date. I've bought the ranch. Will you come around in the back of the church, before I open the court? I'll show them to you."

"Scott—" she began, her smile gone, and her gaze dropping.

He waited. "Yes?" he asked gently.

She looked quickly at Wyckoff, appealingly.

"Yes?" the judge asked. "Well, what are you looking at Sam for? What's Sam done?"

She bent a little, one shoulder dropping, her hands still together. "Scott . . . I beg—"

"Why, what's the matter, darling?"

She shook her head.

"Come and tell me about it in the back, in two minutes," Ogilvie said. "Sam, come on. Bring the present." He led his horse past her. "You come and tell me all about it, darling."

She smiled at him again, stiffly. He turned and started to mount.

"Der rosses," Wyckoff said heavily.

Ogilvie stopped and looked down at the newspaper in the crook of his bad arm. He laughed. "I forgot." He tried to shove them at her with his bad arm, and caught himself, confused. He took them hurriedly in his right hand and extended them to her again, and the looped rein on his arm caught him back. He stood helpless, smiling stiffly at her with the roses extended.

She stepped forward and took them, and the paper fell away. The roses lay fresh and brilliant. "Oh," she said.

"Two years since I planted them," Ogilvie said. "Two years since we got engaged, and now they're ready, really good. And we're ready, finally. Come on back, darling. Just give me a minute to set up the exhibition."

She stood looking down at the roses, and he hurried away.

She looked up at Wyckoff, and said sadly, "You didn't tell him."

"I tried. Why would he believe me?"

The edges of her eyes shone with tears. "Yes, I know. I just thought maybe you could kind of—"

"Wait," Wyckoff said. "Don't tal him today. Not now. He got to santance this man Hayes. Since Hayes was caught Wiley is scared his brothers will break him out of jail, and they got to do something in a hurry."

"But he wants to set the date today! I'll have to tell him."

Wyckoff looked away. "Miss Lampson, this Wiley, maybe he is only a passing thing. Wait a little more."

She looked down.

"I understand," he said. "Wiley is a big, handsome, pretty man, he is strong—got both arms. Big, fat arms to squeeze a woman. That's true, no?"

She flushed. "If you please."

"So is a bear got big arms. Look, I go to the woods, I got you a bear. Why don't you marry a bear? I tal you something, Miss Lampson—"

"You've said enough," she said in a small voice, her face red.

"Only this. The jodge, he will love you when you are old and full of wringles and your teeth you put in a glass-water. Ain't that something? But Wiley, even now he is always looking from the side of his eye."

"How dare you!" she said, her head up straight. "How dare you talk to me like that—you *peasant!*"

He smiled. "Yas, that's me, a peasant."

"Barney is big and strong and—capable. He can protect me."

"What makes you think," Wyckoff said. "The jodge can't protect you? Too skinny? Don't eat enoff? I suppose a woman got to prove it. And that's still poattry."

She looked down. "Nothing you will say will do any good."

"I know it. A woman got to prove everything. I must go to the jodge." He got down off the horse, led it around her, and when at a polite distance, took off his hat, bowed, and remounted. He crossed the meadow at a canter.

A voice called, "We going to hang him today, Scott?" The man was among the crowd on the front steps of the church. The judge rode on, face front, down the side of the building.

"Where's your bodyguard at, Ogilvie?" somebody else shouted from the top of a wagon.

"We're all waiting, Scott."

The prisoner was in a closely-covered wagon, which was backed up near the plank door to the little log addition in the rear of the church. There were half a dozen men loitering around the door, all heavily armed, and two sat on the high wagon seat in front. The team was neatly pegged out on the meadow nearby, grazing contentedly.

The sheriff was leaning against a wheel of the wagon.

"Your prisoner still there, Barney?" the judge asked.

Sheriff Wiley unhooked a high heel from a wagon spoke and smiled lazily, straightening up. "Where else? Or do you still think Sam should have won the election?"

"Not that, Barney. I never claimed you weren't good enough to be sheriff. I just said Sam would be better. More polite to put it that way." He looked in the back of the wagon. The tarp was white, and in the interior it was light and warm, trapping the heat of the weak sun. The man at the other end of the wagon bed drew on a cigarette as the judge looked in and spewed out a long stream of smoke in his direction. The smoke curled around Ogilvie's face.

"Going to sentence me today, Judge?" he asked, smiling gently. He flipped a little ash off the end of his smoke. "That's all right, Judge. You can go ahead and do it. I know the law's got to go through the motions." He smiled again, composed and friendly.

Wiley said, "Scott, I want to talk to you for a moment."

"Come inside," Ogilvie said, turning away from the wagon and ducking into the building. Wiley followed him in and shut the door. The place was half-dark, lighted by two bullseye windows, damp and smelling of rotting logs and the damp earth floor. On one side of the room were cupboards and a stack of old benches.

"Myra's coming here in a couple of minutes, so make it snappy. It's going to be kind of private."

Wiley looked at him carefully. The judge was smiling, dusting off the top of a table and the best of the chairs. "I saw you down there with her by the bridge."

"You sound a little critical. How come?"

"Nothing, nothing, Ogilvie." He cleared his throat. "Listen, Scott, I know you've had it in for me ever since I beat Sam in the election, but—" He stopped, looking away uncomfortably.

"Well, what is it? A favor? As it happens, the elections had no effect on my opinions. What do you want?"

Somebody knocked on the door and pushed it open. One of the guards stood there with his Winchester pointed politely down. "There's a few dozen people or so here to see you, Scott," he said. "The Hayes brothers. And Mrs. Quarry."

"How nice," Ogilvie said. "Will you ask them to wait? Tell the Hayes family I shall be busy for the next few years, and if they have anything important to do— Tell Mrs. Quarry to come in."

"No," Wiley said sharply.

Ogilvie turned. "Why not?"

"Not just yet."

Ogilvie swung to the door. "Ask her to wait, and shut the door. All right, what's the matter?"

"I just want to check," Wiley said in a low voice. "There's a little talk going around about—about you banishing Rudy instead of hanging him. I just wanted to make sure."

"Banishing?"

"Yeah. The old law. The one the vigilantes and the miners' courts used when they were up the creek. It was going around last night."

"Is that so? Last night."

Wiley looked at him steadily. "I just wanted to be sure. You know what it'll mean to me, if you do pull such a thing."

"What, exactly?"

"I'll get killed. Exactly."

"I'm not much up on the old customs. Tell me."

"If you banish him, he'll have to leave town by a certain time. If he hangs around I've got to enforce the sentence."

"Well, so what? You ran for the job."

"Listen, there'll be Rudy and the other three. Four of them, hanging around town. Four of them, Scott."

"What's the matter? Aren't you the people's hero? Can't you take care of a little thing like four bushwhackers?"

Wiley said nothing.

"What's the matter, Barney? Weren't you the best man after all? You're big and strong, Wiley. You're a pretty good shot. You won the turkey shoot last year, didn't you?"

"Turkey shoot," Wiley said.

"Why couldn't you just pretend that the Hayes brothers were a lot of turkeys?" Ogilvie said. "You could get one of the boys down in the saloon to make a gobbling noise. That would complete the illusion, and you'd be steady as a rock."

"Listen," Wiley said in the same low voice, "you can't cross me up like this. Just on account of that election."

"What do you think I am?" Ogilvie asked. "If I did cross you up, you could only blame yourself for giving me the idea. No, Blarney—I mean

Barney, sorry—I won't cross you up. You know, there's another rumor that the Hayes boys are going to kill anybody that has anything to do with hanging Rudy, too. Well, I won't even ask you to hang him locally. I intend to sentence him to hang in the Territorial prison, where the job will be done anonymously. You can take your posse of stalwarts outside and drive Rudy up to the railroad by five this afternoon, and catch the train." He looked at Wiley's large, handsome face. "Your color is coming back, Barney. Can you go forward now with your head held high?"

"You think you're so damned smart," Wiley said, moving toward the door. "I have to ask you a favor and you rub it in. I'd like to see you hold down my job for a while." He let his eyes run down Ogilvie's bad arm to the wizened hand, smiled, and went out.

The judge looked down at the palm of his left hand. He could flex the biceps of the arm, and he could lift it toward the front a little. He made these movements, tentatively, and then stood quiet, regarding the atrophied fingers. He tried to move one of them. Nothing happened.

The door opened, admitting a dark bulk, and closed again. Mrs. Quarry came into the dim light from the bullseye windows and stood with her arms folded, each hand nestled in the other sleeve, across her large stomach. She wore a black shawl around her shoulders, a man's blue shirt, and a long, full skirt of black cotton with small white dots. She looked used to work.

"Sit down, Mrs. Quarry," the judge said, turning a chair around for her with his good hand, holding the other one slightly behind him. "How are you getting along?"

"That's it," she said. "Just getting along. Our foreman's good. I mean mine. Thank God for that, he's a good man. I can't ride, but I can keep the branding irons hot, and that's a help. Besides, I'm learning to handle them. I don't like burning them animals. But then—"

The judge nodded and smiled. "Don't be too independent now, Mrs. Quarry. You know how it is, out here in the country. People'll feel hurt if you don't let 'em help you, even if you don't need it. You let 'em help you. You don't want to hurt anybody's feelings."

She sniffed and looked down and sniffed again, trying to keep her tears up her nose. "Judge," she croaked.

"Yes?"

"I want you to do me a favor."

"Every day I do at least one favor. What is it?"

"I want you to hang him. No mistake."

His eyebrows went up slightly.

"That's why I come. You won't let me down?"

"It'll all be taken care of properly. It's all taken care of in the law, Mrs. Quarry. It isn't personal."

"It was personal when that weasel murdered Joe. That was personal."

"I know how you feel. You can depend on the law."

"That's it. I can't. We depended on the law, Joe did, from the beginning. And when them weasels stole our cows, where was it? Barney Wiley come out and looked for tracks just once in six months. As far as I know, the rest of the time he was down on main street—keeping the peace in the saloons. That's him. That's his job, Judge. Keeping the peace in town on Sunday morning."

The judge looked down. From beneath the edge of her full black skirt, one shoe-toe peeked out, a small, black, wrinkled toe. She probably had on high laced shoes under those petticoats. Morning after morning she would lace up those high shoes of hers and put on those tons of petticoats, when she was nearly too old to move. She wore modesty like the shield of her soul.

"We must uphold the law, Mrs. Quarry."

"You mean Barney Wiley? He shouldn't have even been sheriff, Judge. Sam Wyckoff should have been sheriff. Sam would have told Joe and the others what to do to surround them weasels, and nobody would have got kilt. Instead of Joe," she said bitterly, "trying to outshoot that pack of varmints, that shooting was all they knew. Well," she finished, "Joe's dead. And I'm going to hear that dog's neck pop, that Rudy Hayes, with my own two ears." A white fire leaped up in the back of her eye. "And if it don't, I'm going to shoot that no account sheriff myself, and nobody's going to blame me."

She looked down to see that her invisible toes did not trespass on anything unfitting. She got up and labored out on her flat feet.

CHAPTER THREE

To Kill a Sheriff . . .

Wiley and two guards came to the door and went through, leading the prisoner into the courtroom.

"You'd better put the rest of your men around in the courtroom," Ogilvie said.

Wyckoff came in with the wrapped-up book in his hand. The judge took it and went to the door.

Myra was sitting in a neat little buggy, the reins in her hands. Ogilvie put his hand in his coat pocket and took hold of something. "Come on, I've waited long enough, I'm free—the court can wait a minute."

She came through the door, brushing past Wyckoff. She shut the door on Wyckoff and faced the judge. "Scott—"

"That was beautiful. Say it again." He smiled at her and took a paper from his pocket. "Every time you say my name, I get dizzy. Am I still in love, Myra, after two years? Is that it?" He laid the paper on the table, and took a little box from another pocket.

"Scott, wait—"

"What for? All morning people have been asking me to do things for them, making me wait. I'm sick of waiting. You are too. We both are. We've waited so long, we've got the waiting habit."

He unwrapped the book and laid it on the table beside the paper and the box. "There it is. That's our future. Here's us, and the future. Forgive the drama," he said. "I had to celebrate it—announce it—legalize it? Anything so important as us, deserves a ceremony. Let me show you."

She was looking at the things on the table, her hands tight together in front of her, the way she had been on the bridge.

"Here's your book. A white Bible," he said, smiling. "That's customary for the bride, isn't it? The box contains two wedding rings, one for you and one for me, and the paper is the deed to our ranch."

"No, Scott," she said.

He looked at her intently. "What do you mean, no?"

She stood up straight and took a deep breath. "All right," she said, "I didn't know it would be so difficult—"

He looked at her dumbly. "I'm beginning to get the idea," he said after a moment. "Something bad has happened. Good and bad. I mean about our marriage."

She swallowed.

"Do you mind if I sit down?" he asked. He sat in the clean chair and laid his good arm on the table. His wrist trembled. "What in God's name is it?" he broke out, his fist tightening against the tremble.

"Scott—we can't get married."

"We can't?" he asked tightly. "Why not? Are we first cousins or something?"

"I've fallen in love."

"What?"

"I'm sorry. I'm in love."

"Weren't we always in love?"

"I mean—with somebody else."

He sat quiet. "Somebody else. Not me? What are you talking about?"

"I'm sorry, Scott. Especially," she said, gesturing at the things on the table, "especially," she said, beginning to cry and putting her hand over her eyes, "after you did all this—"

"Myra, for Heaven's sake, I beg you, do not cry, let's keep it rational," he said in the same, tight, small voice. "You mean," he asked carefully, like a lawyer approaching an exceedingly subtle point, "you mean to say, you do *not* love me—after all. You mean that it was a delusion."

After a moment, he went on. "It's peculiar, I had no notion of this till today. God knows you're not deceitful. How could I be so stupid?" He closed his hand around the ring-box, hiding it. "Tell me," he said. "Was there a time when you did love me? In the beginning? A little while?"

"Scott," she said, "Scott, why couldn't I have been some other woman? Scott, I do love you—in a way—I don't want to hurt you. . . . You are so dear, so kind, so loving—have been so kind to me, why, every day there has been some little thing; the flowers, the unexpected things, all this time, you have made all my days so sweet. Scott, how can I repay you? It's so difficult. I do love you, in a way—but something has come up—"

"It's the long wait," he said, looking at the window. "The long wait." He smiled. "Who is the honored gentleman who has taken my place? Or shall I say, who has taken that which I pre-empted so long, hardly mine— presuming on a young girl's ignorance of men, let us say. Working on the young girl's sensibilities to make gratitude—"

"Please, Scott—"

"—to make gratitude and sentiment a substitute for love. Shall we say?" He stood up. "Who is the worthy gentleman? He must be a hero, a stalwart, a perfection of a man— Or why? Maybe he is just a man, a whole man, with two arms. Why should he, after all, have to be more than that? Just one, ordinary man—why would it take any more to wake up a young girl's heart? After all, who was I—after all."

She stood looking at him across the table. "It's Barney. Barney Wiley."

He looked up, above her head. "Wiley?" His eyes moved around as though he were trying to assemble a composition, making up a picture. "You mean the sheriff?"

"Yes. Barney Wiley."

"That's odd," he said quietly. "That I should have had no hint of it at all. Why, surely this thing must have had some kind of beginning. But he knew we were engaged. Surely you don't mean to say, he approached you —that you permitted him to approach. . . . No, hardly you."

"It was an accident. He helped me one day, out riding. An accidental meeting." She looked sadly at the dirt floor. "A kind of friendship. You have been so busy, Scott—riding around all over the country on your circuit, hunting up our ranch—the ranch."

"That was my job, of course. I could hardly be accused of neglecting you. Unless it could be argued that a two-year engagement is, in fact, a kind of neglect of nature. I have presumed too much upon the human element."

She stood alone in the dim light, humble.

"So you want to go," he said.

"Yes," she said faintly.

"How funny. This was to be the occasion, a celebration. How funny, that it should turn out this way. All right. Good-bye."

She turned toward the door, and when she had reached it, turned again and smiled at him. "Good-bye, Scott."

"There's a man in there waiting for his sentence. I really shouldn't keep him waiting."

"Scott, I wish—I wish I had never met Barney. If I had not, we would have been happy."

"You mean," he said, smiling, "*I* would have been happy. Good-bye."

She turned and disappeared from the bright doorway.

Wyckoff came in, heavily and humbly. "You better go in there. They think you scared to hang him."

Ogilvie had the ring box in his hand.

"Did you hear her? What she said?"

"A liddle. She told me before."

Ogilvie flung the box in the corner.

Wiley opened the courtroom door and stuck his head in. "What's the matter? Everybody's waiting."

Ogilvie looked at him for a moment. "I hear there is a kind of an understanding between you and Myra."

Wiley stood silent for a moment, his hand on the edge of the door. He tried a smile. "I'm glad she told you. There isn't any understanding between us. There couldn't be, as long as she was engaged."

"Exactly. That was the understanding—that nothing would be understood until she had broken the engagement. The essence of an understanding is that nothing is said. But enough was said to reach the understanding. How did you do it? You must be pretty clever along some lines, Barney. It's pretty hard to make advances to a woman without their being advances."

Wiley said nothing. He stood blinking slowly in the doorway. "What do you mean?"

"I mean you have been courting her behind my back. It has dawned upon me slowly. In fact, you are a thief, and she does not know that she's been stolen."

"That's a lie."

"You are the liar."

They stood silent, their eyes locked.

"Or do you," the judge said, advancing slowly, "take me for a fool? Any first-year law student could read this back to the facts. I know the kind of underhanded play it was—you were so friendly and helpful, such a cheerful companion, you helped fill the dull hours when I was away on circuit, riding with her. Nothing open, nothing to make an issue, always just a friend, working on her. And now you've got the gall to stand there and try to look hurt."

Wiley smiled. He said, "All right, Scott, whatever it was, it's happened. As far as I'm concerned you can go climb the old elm tree. I've got her."

Ogilvie moved forward a step, his head sinking and his jaw sticking out a little. "Don't underestimate me, Wiley. I'm legal only just so far."

Wiley smiled openly. "You and Wyckoff. The almighty pair. What have you got now? I've got his job and your girl and from now on, as far as I'm concerned, I don't see why I even have to look friendly." He started to shut the door.

"Wait," the judge said.

Wiley watched him carefully. "You think you've got her," Ogilvie said. "You think I'm going to let you break her heart? Go on in there and call the court to order."

"What do you mean?"

"Do as you're told."

Wiley shut the door slowly and Ogilvie smiled at Wyckoff.

"What's the matter with you?" Wyckoff said. "Why you looking so happy?"

"Helena is too far. There's too much chance of Rudy's getting away. Don't you think? Besides, a local hanging would have a better effect as a public example. I'll set it for a week from today. He'll have to do it alone.

They'll be laying for him. Maybe they'll kill him first and bust the jail. That's more likely."

"Supposing they get you first?"

"Supposing I take a long vacation? Beginning this afternoon."

Wyckoff looked at him carefully. "I think this is murder."

"It's the duty of the county sheriff to carry out the sentences, isn't it?"

"You can't get away with it," Wyckoff said softly. "Not inside you. It's legal, but it's murder. You got to take the chance. Wiley don't got to, unless you make him."

"It's his duty," Ogilvie said.

"What hoppened to you?"

The judge's head gave a spasmodic, trembling shake. "You think I'm going to let him get away with this? I'll kill him. I'll kill him from the bench."

"Is that what she wants?"

"He deserves it," Ogilvie said.

"By whose law?" Wyckoff nodded at the little white Bible. "You giving her a Bible, and then this. That's a laugh."

Ogilvie grabbed the book in his good hand.

"Put it down," Wyckoff said. "No matter who you are, you throw that book, you're finished."

Ogilvie dropped it on the table. "Get out," he said.

"Listen," Wyckoff said. "You think she wouldn't know? Who would you be fooling? You'd be a murderer. They hear about you engagement broking—then this. Everybody would know the truth. You think she love you then? The dogs would not even bite you—you would stink so."

"Get out," Ogilvie said. "Why should I take it? All my life I've been taking it. Then I find her, and now this dirty—this devil twists her mind. Why should I take it? Let him take it!"

Wyckoff said. "Some people is made to take it. Maybe you got to take it."

"Not any more. This time I'll write my own damn law." He smiled slowly. "It's going to be good, too. That slob. He looks so big and fine, and underneath he's such a sneaking little baby. Wait 'til they pull down on him. They'll make him cry first, he'll blubber and cry, like those little rebel troopers we caught that time."

"You're the devil. You're so sweet on top. Rosses. Flowers. I thought she got you gentled. But you still a devil underneath. I seen it before, you remember. I stop you once before. You remember the rebel troopers we took with the sharpened sabers, and you were going to cot them to pieces with them, for chopping up your arm."

"Get out of here."

Wyckoff took a step toward him. "Maybe I knock you out," he said in a low voice. "Knock you cold and break up the trial and go to jail. It would be better."

Ogilvie's arm flicked out and he flipped the gun out of Wyckoff's holster. He held it steadily on Wyckoff's chest. "Get out," he said.

Wyckoff looked down at the gun, and then at the face above it. "Please."

"I'd as soon kill you as not. Get out of here and keep out of my way."

Wyckoff's hand dropped. "All right. All right, Captain. I know. I understand." He turned away.

Ogilvie laid the gun on the table and went toward the court room door. "Listen," Wyckoff said.

Ogilvie turned with his hand on the latch.

"If you going to do it," Wyckoff said, "don't be a fool about it. You lose her for good, this way, I would rather shoot Wiley myself, for you."

"You heard what I said," Ogilvie said coldly. "I'll do as I please and I'll do it my own way. I said this morning I'd set the date of my wedding today, hanging or no hanging. What makes you think I won't?"

"But now," Wyckoff said, "you are no good. No—good."

CHAPTER FOUR

The Judgment

She was sitting on the middle aisle seven rows back from the sanctuary rail, upon which Charles and Jake Hayes were resting their heels, their spurs dangling on the court side. Her face was the first thing Ogilvie saw in all that small sea of faces, his eyes going home there at once. She was smiling, looking toward one of the south windows, through which the sun was coming, full of the golden light of alder leaves outside.

She was smiling at Wiley, who was standing with his deputies in back of the prisoner's chair, leaning against the wall next to the window, his arms folded, one heel tucked up behind him against the wall.

It was a pair of smiles, intimate and tender on her part, and on his, pleased, confident and amused. Ogilvie looked away.

Mrs. Quarry was sitting in the front row across the aisle from the Hayes brothers.

Ogilvie walked across the low platform in the front of the church. The crowd hushed and then began to buzz louder than ever. They had taken the pulpit out and put a small table in instead. He sat down at it. Jake Hayes saw him and took his feet down, and Charles touched his arm. Jake slowly put his feet back up.

Ogilvie rapped sharply on the table with a carpenter's hammer. The crowd shut up the way a flock of birds suddenly freezes in a tree. Ogilvie opened the drawer of the table and adjusted the pistol which was lying inside so that it was convenient to his right hand.

He addressed the courtroom at large. "Yesterday, you heard the jury return a verdict of guilty. There never was any doubt of this. Rudy Hayes killed Joe Quarry in the sight of half a dozen men. That is, Quarry's riders, while they were surrounding Hayes, who was then in the act of stealing some of Quarry's cattle. This was murder in the first degree. I will now sentence the prisoner. Hayes, have you got anything to say?"

Rudy Hayes sat with his arms folded, not looking at the judge. He was smiling at his brother. Charles Hayes' little owl-beak nose was sharp as a talon in the middle of his fat pink face.

"Hell, no," Rudy Hayes said casually, "why should I say anything?"

"In that case I—"

"Your honor," Charles Hayes said, standing up, "may I plead with the court," he said gently, "in consideration of the youth of the prisoner, to banish him, rather than hang him?"

Somebody outside the windows began clapping and shouted, "Hurray!" A small chorus took up the cheer and kept at it for a few seconds.

"Your honor is a man with a kind heart," Hayes said gently. "I beg you to banish my brother from the territory, and I guarantee that he will start a new life elsewhere. He is young and rash, your honor. You are a generous man, a big man, a kind man. You won't hang him. You'll show him mercy." The same number of hands began clapping, and precisely the same number of voices shouted with mechanical zeal, "Hurray, hurray, hurray!"

"You hear what the local citizens want, your honor."

"Sit down," Ogilvie said. "I never heard of anything more preposterous."

"Your honor," Mrs. Quarry said from her seat just beyond the rail, "I ask you to banish him too. For pity's sake. It was my husband he killed, after all. I was the one hurt most of all."

A woman in the back of the court began to sob and gulp. Ogilvie started to rap with the hammer, and another woman began to blubber. He sat quiet.

"I don't understand this, Mrs. Quarry," he said. "I would rather expect you to insist on the full sentence."

Mrs. Quarry said, quietly and calmly, "No, Mr. Ogilvie, not so. It would be better to banish him. The poor young feller."

The clapping and cheering began again, and this time was joined by many more hands. Charles Hayes smiled at the judge.

"After all, Judge," Mrs. Quarry went on in her quiet, clear voice, "if I am willing to forgive Rudy Hayes his awful deed, why ain't you? If anybody has rights here, ain't it me? Your honor, *I* forgive him, and I plead with you, to leave him go."

A whole chorus of sobbing broke out in the rear of the church.

"Banish him!" the organized voices yelled from outside. And then hands in the courtroom began clapping, breaking out here and there, and rising to a roar. Cheers rose, and men began stomping their feet.

Ogilvie sat impassively, waiting. Charles Hayes smiled pleasantly at him. The cheering and the sobbing continued. Mrs. Quarry, looking pleased with herself, sat down. The clapping began to die out and Ogilvie rapped moderately.

"A recess," he said. "For a few minutes only. Mrs. Quarry, I would like to speak to you privately in the back room—if you will be so kind." He stood up, shutting the table drawer, and went out.

They came around together, Charles Hayes and Mrs. Quarry, dignified and self-possessed. Hayes let her in, past Wyckoff, and shut the door behind himself. Ogilvie held a chair for her. She didn't take it.

"Congratulations, Charles," Ogilvie said. "You have an able pupil, but what is that without a gifted teacher? You were most appealing, Mrs. Quarry."

Mrs. Quarry looked modestly at her toes. "Mr. Hayes is a sincere man. I'm sure he is a sincere man. He asked me to forgive his brother." She looked up, smiling.

"Let's cut out the lying," Ogilvie said quietly.

Mrs. Quarry looked blank.

"Come, Mrs. Quarry. I know you want Rudy dead."

Mrs. Quarry sniffed. "Wiley said you was going to send that Hayes to Helena to hang next month and give Wiley a vacation for a while. I told you I wanted him hanged here, Judge. I told you why. I can't make no trip to Helena next month." Her eyes opened wide. "But it ain't that so much. Mr. Hayes here give me the idea, to banish him, and I see the point. Not Mr. Hayes's point, exactly. I want you to banish him, you set the time and then let them fight it out, and I hope they're both killed. That Hayes and Wiley both."

She swung around on Charles. "So there!" she spat. "You and your, 'Have mercy. Please!' says you, 'Forgive my brother, banish him.' All right, banish him, and let him and Wiley fight it out down town. Let them have mercy on each other. I'll be around and I think I'll bring a gun to the ball too." She smiled and her eyes were full of tears. "I'll teach them hounds for killing my Joe, them stinking dogs."

Wiley open the courtroom door and stood looking in. "What's going on?" he asked suspiciously. "Ogilvie, what are you doing?"

"Him," Mrs. Quarry said, jerking an elbow at Wiley. "Look at him. He's the one at fault. *He* let the rustling go on and on."

Wiley came down slowly into the room.

"They want me to banish Rudy," Ogilvie said to him. "It'll be up to you to expel him from town, if he doesn't leave properly. How do you like that, Barney?"

Wiley looked at Hayes' gentle smile, and then at Ogilvie. "You're going to throw it all onto me. Is that it? Is that your revenge?"

"My apologies for Mr. Wiley," Ogilvie said, smiling at Barney, "he's a trifle upset. What revenge, Barney? Don't be silly. Nobody wants revenge. I'm a judge of the law. Mrs. Quarry has asked for mercy, and so has Rudy's brother. Aren't they entitled to consideration? Am I above mercy? Should I not show mercy? Why should *you* object to a show of mercy?"

"Mercy!" Wiley said. "It's a dirty murder, that's what it is, I can see it in your faces. Why don't you do what you should?"

They stood silent. A woodrat rustled in one of the corners. Hayes said, "I told the judge, he would be unhappy later if he hanged Rudy. He'd feel remorse. You see, Wiley, it's in everybody's interest to show mercy this way."

"Indeed it is," Ogilvie said. "And I know you'll do a good job, Barney. Nobody likes a coward. Not even a woman, a woman in love. They like cowards least of all. Do you suppose, Charles, Rudy would put a fight?"

"Well," Charles said, "Rudy likes it around here."

Wiley looked bitterly at the three of them. "Wait'll I tell about this."

"Tell what?" Ogilvie asked. "That we're showing mercy? Go on, you lousy coward, and watch your charge."

They watched Wiley go back through the door, moving heavily and slowly.

"Thank you, Judge," Mrs. Quarry said. She went out.

Hayes said, "You're a smart man, Judge. I always knew you were. You can get Wyckoff elected—in fact, you can appoint him to take Wiley's place, can't you? I mean, well, if things don't work out right for him. And besides, why can't you and I be friends, anyway? We can do each other a lot of good." He smiled. "All you have to do is sentence Rudy to banishment, like I said—remember—and you'll be the best-liked man in the county."

"Really?" Ogilvie said. "Already I'm beginning to have a dirty feeling in my mouth. There's no point in this. What does it do? To kill that fool. If I could keep on killing him, and see him die forever—but once he's dead, what's left? Just plain nothing. Nothing but you, and Mrs. Quarry—oh, she and I would have a great time grieving together, muttering and mumbling over our woes. Nothing left but her and you and murder in my mouth to suck on till I slid into the pit. Get out, you fat slob, get out."

"Remember!" Charles said loudly warningly. "I'll take your cussing—but remember."

He went out. Ogilvie stood in the dim room. "Mercy," he said to himself. He looked at the white Bible.

She came in without knocking, soft in the dim light, a small figure slipping in and standing there, looking up at him.

"I heard some people talking," she said. "They said that man will never leave town. They said Barney would have to fight him, and Barney would be killed. They said that man's brothers would help him, and together they'd all kill Barney. Did you know that?"

"It's funny, when you come near, how everything changes—the light brightens, everything grows clear. Without you, there is—nothing, darkness, confusion. But now you're here," he said, looking down at her and smiling. "Yes. I know what they'll do to Barney."

"I ask you—knowing how you feel—but Scott. I depend on your generosity—your nobility. You wouldn't let anything happen to Barney, would you? You'll send him away with that prisoner, up to Helena, won't you? The way he said you would? We planned—he planned to take me with him, on the train. We would get married in Helena."

"In Helena?" he asked blankly. "Married? You and him?"

"You'll do what you said, won't you?"

"What would you do if I refused?" he asked, looking away from her.

"Would you refuse?" she asked gently.

He thought for a long moment. Then he said, smiling, "No, if you ask me, I will give it to you. I have to, anyway. It's my duty—a thing I never forgot until this afternoon."

"Thank you, Scott. I will always be grateful to you."

"That's something."

She turned to go. "I will always owe you my happiness, after all, won't I?"

"Accept it as a kind of gift; it is free. I'm not asking you for anything. To marry, and not to marry, to have you, or to be refused by you—what difference does it make? I still love you—you are still the same. Nothing that you ever did, caused me to love you, nothing you can do can cause me to stop loving you."

"Good-bye, Scott."

"Good-bye, darling. And don't worry about losing your precious Barney."

He took her to the door. He stood and watched her going back up along the side of the church.

Wyckoff leaned against the wagon wheel, watching him calmly. Ogilvie said, "I want your rifle. Not the Springfield. The Winchester. Leave it on the table in there."

"You want my pistol too, Jodge?"

"The one in the drawer's enough."

"You want me, Jodge? Here I am. Here I am, Jodge."

"Watch after her."

He went back into the tiny courtroom, sat down at the table and pulled out the drawer again. He rapped on the table with the hammer and said in the silence, "I sentence you, Rudolph Hayes, to death by hanging in the Territorial Prison not later than thirty days from this date."

Nobody in the courtroom said anything. He ignored the fixed eyes of Charles Hayes and Mrs. Quarry, and said, matter-of-factly, "The request for banishment is denied, as an improbable and certainly outmoded solution to the worst problems of this territory. There cannot be any mercy until there has been justice, which begins with a respect for law. It is the duty of this court to assist in the firm establishment of justice in this territory. The court is dismissed."

Nobody moved.

He turned to Wiley and said in the same crisp, matter-of-fact voice, "Sheriff, you will take the prisoner and travel immediately to the railroad and board the five o'clock train eastbound to Helena."

"That's a hell of a thing," somebody shouted outside.

"That's all," Ogilvie said. "Go home."

They went, slowly and grudgingly at first, and then the courtroom was empty, except for three people, the two Hayes men and Mrs. Quarry, sitting in the front row, looking steadily at Ogilvie.

Wiley and his eight men herded the prisoner out through the back door into the shack behind.

Mrs. Quarry dropped her eyes and looked at her knees. A rattle of tug chains being hooked came faintly through open doors from the wagon outside. Voices rose and fell in brief argument. A faint breeze coming through the church swept down the aisle, lifting a piece of newspaper and coasting it down toward the door.

Mrs. Quarry took a corner of her shawl and held it to her eyes, hiding her face, and getting to her feet, went slowly down the aisle after the newspaper.

Howard Hayes appeared at the main door. "Charles," he said down the length of the aisle, "they're getting ready to pull out. They got Rudy tied up in there. Charles, what's going to happen to Rudy?"

Charles stood up. "So long, Judge," he said. "We'll be seeing you later."

Ogilvie took the pistol out of the drawer and pointed it at Charles' chest. "It would convenience me greatly if you gave me occasion to kill you now, Charles." Charles sat down. "But I guess you won't. We'll wait here a while."

CHAPTER FIVE

One Less for Helena

Howard ducked out of view beyond the door. They heard the short shout of the driver and the crack of a whip. Wheels groaned and harness clicked. The creak of hubs went past below the windows, and the rapid pummel of ridden horses. Dust rose in a thick cloud, and the sounds quickly faded. Distantly, the trotting horses pounded across the wooden bridge, and silence came back.

"Charles?" Howard called from outside somewhere. "You want me to chase them?"

"No," Charles said calmly.

"You want me to try a shot through the window, Charles?" Howard asked again.

"No, Howard," Charles said patiently. "Just wait a while."

They sat in silence. The shadows moved across the floor.

"You going anywhere this afternoon, Judge?" Charles asked casually. "Anywhere special?"

"Yes," Ogilvie said. "I'm going up to my ranch. I bought the old Bar WX, you know, Charles. You know the way? Up the bench, then straight up toward the mountains. You can't miss it."

Charles said, "Those sure were pretty roses you had down in your garden, Ogilvie. You remember? I keep remembering them, somehow."

The judge sat silent for a little while. "Yes," he said, looking down the long aisle, "I remember."

After a while, Ogilvie said, "All right, beat it."

They got up under the gun and went out, unhurried. He watched them go, and waited till the sound of their horses' hoofs had died. Then he closed the table drawer, shoved the pistol into his pants and went out the back door.

He took the rifle lying on the table in his good hand and clutching the stock with his elbow, awkwardly worked the lever, partly opening the breech. There was a cartridge already in the chamber.

He went out and stopped, seeing Sam Wyckoff sitting on the ground with the reins of his horse drooping handy. Myra was sitting in her buggy nearby.

"What are you here for, Myra?" Ogilvie asked.

"Barney," she said. "He said he'd get them started, and then come back for me, and we'll go in the buggy."

"Such is devotion to duty," Ogilvie said. He got his horse an mounted it, carrying the rifle across his pommel Indian style.

"Where you going, Jodge?" Wyckoff asked.

"For a little ride, Sam."

"Can I come?"

"I told you once," Ogilvie said. "Watch out for her." He rode on.

Wyckoff stood up and slowly slapped the dust off the seat of his pants. "Good thing I listen at the winder sometimes, or I'd never know nothink. Miss Lampson, I'm going to tal you a things. Something is going to happen very soon. I prove to you, a woman, that your Barney is a big coward. I do it so you don't make no mistakes."

She looked at him quietly, as though she were tired. "If you mean you're going to try to beat him up, don't bother. I know you're bigger. Nothing you could do would make any difference. I love him."

"You love him," Wyckoff said. "What you know about love? For you it is all guitars and grape juice, dancing in the moon. Why don't you young women ever learn that love is giffing things up? Love is a fighter, she is harder than nails, she is old, she got a face like a ham sandwich, she smiles when she hurts, she is loyal, she is good, she bears lots and lots children. She loves a real man, not a pritty one. Look, here comes your pritty one right now, young woman."

He pointed his chin across the meadow. Wiley loped his horse toward them. He pulled up, ignoring Wyckoff. "Come on, darling."

"Listen," Wyckoff said. "All these Hayes boms are laying for the jodge. Now. He is got to fight them. Why? For you, Miss Lampson, so you will be happy with prittyboy here? More poattry." He grinned. "Prittyboy, you come and help me in this fight."

"Cut it out," Wiley said heavily. "Come on, Myra. I'll leave my horse in town and—"

"Wait, Wiley," she said. "Sam, are you making this up?"

"Myra, darling. I said, come on—"

"Shot opp, young fellow," Sam said. "Miss Lampson, this morning they told the jodge they kill him and everybody that helped with hanging their brother. Why you think the jodge sent prittyboy here up to Helena, instead of hanging Rudy here? Now the jodge is staying here—he got to taking it for all of you."

He looked at Wiley. "I say to you, prittyboy, come on with me and help him. I took a chance in waiting this long."

"I don't believe it," Wiley said. "It's some kind of trick of his, some kind of lawyer sneak trick. Nobody ever fights three to one. They run."

"You don't coming?"

"No. I've got go take care of my prisoner."

Wyckoff smiled. "He won't shoot you, anyway." He turned his horse. "Miss Lampson, I hope you are very happy with this dirty coward, all your life. Good-bye."

She put down her reins. "I think you'd better go with Sam, Barney."

He looked at her and said, "I'm sure it's just a story."

"Please go. Isn't it your duty?"

"My first duty," he said, looking away, "is to my prisoner. Come on, we have to make the train." He added, "I hope you won't make it necessary for me to drive you."

She looked at him in silence.

He said, dismounting and tying his horse to the back of the buggy,

"Move over, Myra. I see I'll have to take over." He climbed in and took the reins. "So long, Wyckoff," he said.

"I'm sorry," she said. She climbed out and mounted his horse, untying it from the buggy. "Good-bye, Barney. Have a good time in Helena."

She turned her horse toward Wyckoff. "Sam, please, where are the rings? The ones he bought for us? I know there isn't much time—but please—*our* rings?"

The first shot was careful and deliberate, as Ogilvie had supposed it would be, but it came sooner than he had expected, at the moment when he was sighing with relief at emerging from the thickets of the canyon that ran up the bench onto the rough plateau above. It came—the sharp crack of the bullet passing, much like the pop of a whip, then the crack of the rifle itself, from behind, down the canyon.

He dropped forward over the horn and stabbed the mare with his spurs. She jumped out like a jackrabbit and made three bounds into a dead run.

He heard the second bullet whack into her head and as she slid forward and he went down, he saw the blue smoke above a boulder ahead and to the left.

He went off over her head and landed flat on his belly, sliding in the gravel. The pistol fell out of his pants. He left it and ran to the right, into the cover of the boulders, away from the rifle ahead.

A third one opened up ahead, a little to the left of his new direction, and even as he ducked and began crabbing through the boulders he knew he was being simply herded back toward the first rifle.

He went back to the edge of the bench, fifty yards from where the road came up out of the canyon, and waited behind a rock. Howard came up on foot, his rifle in his hand. He stood looking around. Charles called something to him.

Ogilvie steadied his rifle against the rock and dropped Howard neatly in the road.

He left his rock and found three others, making a kind of nest, protected on two sides. He cranked another cartridge into his rifle and as he got into his rock nest, he saw Jake stand up from behind a boulder and aim. He threw his rifle up and squeezed off just as Jake's bullet hit him in the left forearm, breaking one of the bones. He looked up from the hole in his coat sleeve and saw Jake lying face down across his boulder, arms hanging down, like an empty shirt drying in the sun. His rifle lay in the open, thrown ten feet away.

He could hear Charles calling to Jake, the voice moving around among the boulders. He sat, dizzy, and as the pain in his arm grew and the sweat began to come out hard, Charles began to curse, the sound coming from behind Jake's boulder.

Charles stuck his head up like a prairie dog. Ogilvie swung his rifle, slowly, the weight of it seeming to drag. Charles saw him and snapped a shot at him. He cursed and as Ogilvie threw himself sideways, down behind one of his rocks, he snapped two more at him.

Charles cursed him slowly in the silence from behind his dead brother. He began firing deliberately against Ogilvie's side rock. The ricochets splattered down, pellets of broken lead stinging into Ogilvie's face, drops of blood forming up.

"Come out," Charles said, his voice choked with fury. "Come out." He fired fast, bouncing bullets down into Ogilvie's hole, and Ogilvie lay still, his arm over his face. He heard the dry snapping of Charles' hammer fall on the empty gun, and threw himself up out of the hole onto his feet.

Charles stared at him openmouthed, a fresh cartridge in one hand, the opened rifle in the other. Ogilvie said, "Drop it," and held his rifle on him.

Charles dropped it, and made a leap across his boulder for Jake's rifle, lying on the ground. He got it, but not before Ogilvie was on him, holding his own gun on Charles' back as Charles knelt over the full gun.

"Get up, Charles," Ogilvie said. "I dislike all this bloodshed intensely. Just get up and be quiet. You're under arrest."

Charles stood up slowly, his fists clenched, his fat face bursting. He looked from side to side desperately, and suddenly turned and ran. Ogilvie swung up his rifle, one-armed, trying to line him up.

Another rifle fired, a deeper, heavier, shorter blast, and Charles fell, still running. Wyckoff came up over the edge of the bench, the Government carbine smoking. Charles lay still, panting.

"I heard what you said, Captain," Wyckoff said. "I mean, Jodge. He ain't dead. Only upsat a little."

"I'm obliged," Ogilvie said, lowering the Winchester. "In Barney's absence, do you think you could take him into your gracious custody, Sam?"

"I think," Myra said, looking over the edge of the bench, "Barney's absence will last for quite a while. Please, Scott, will you forgive me? Oh, my God, you're hurt." She scrambled up the bank and ran toward him, her hair awry, her dress rumpled and mussed. She stood looking up at his face.

"A few old shaving wounds," he said. "They always reopen when I smile too wide."

"Oh, Scott, why was I such a fool? Rub it in. I deserve it, rub it in. My head was full of foolishness."

Ogilvie sat down on a stone. He looked at Charles, groaning and wiggling.

"Sam," he said wearily, "remove that. And kindly dump Jake behind some rock out of sight. I want to welcome home my wife in a fitting manner, and these people are ruining the setting. A kiss is what I need, one simple kiss to make it well."

"Am I hearing poattry again? Jodge, you brains is foggy. I think you need a drink. Why don't you just take you wife and ride home with her to the rose garden? I stay here and clean up the robbish."

Myra smiled. "I brought the rings. Our rings," she said.

"That's all I want to hear," he said. "The way you say that. *Our* rings." He took her arm and led her to the road.

Mission with No Record

BY JAMES WARNER BELLAH

(Rio Grande)

*Director John Ford was a great admirer of James Warner Bellah's power-
ful and historically accurate military fiction. All three films in Ford's acclaimed "cavalry trilogy" featuring the talents of John Wayne, among other
big-name stars, were based on* Saturday Evening Post *stories by Bellah:*
Fort Apache *(1948), on "Massacre" (see* The Reel West*); She Wore a
Yellow Ribbon (1949), on "Command" and "Big Hunt" (see* The Second
Reel West*); and* Rio Grande, *on the story which follows. In 1960 Ford also
filmed Bellah's SEP serial* Sergeant Rutledge, *with Woody Strode giving a
brilliant performance in the role of a black cavalry sergeant court-martialed
for murder.*

The Officer of the Guard heard the sound of many wagon wheels echoing
up from the Sudro Road. It was almost four in the morning and the dawn
wind that carried the sound husked across the Fort Starke parade ground,
pelting sand at the pine boards of the Officers' Picket Quarters, lashing
the taut halyards in a frenzied tattoo against the flagpole.

The O.G. started running—those wagons were the replacement detail,
almost a day ahead of time. He skirted the parade ground and took the
short cut past Colonel Massarene's isolated quarters, back toward the
guardhouse. Then he stopped stock-still in his tracks, his head cocked to
the soft call of a violin— "Samanthe . . . while the moon doth shine
. . . Samanthe." Through the lighted window of the C. O.'s quarters, he
could see the slender silhouette of Colonel Massarene, head bent, arm
crooked to the bow, drawing out a gentle song of lost years and of forgotten candlelight and of jasmine on the night air—"Samanthe——"

For a second, the Officer of the Guard stood listening and staring in
utter disbelief. A frigid shadow of a man, D. L. Massarene, living in

Capuchin solitude with one chair, one cot, one table. Ruling the West and the regiment with it, with the iron hand of duty. Never a meal with another officer. Never a word of praise or a word for laughter. Alone there and friendless, with the grisly sobbing of his violin to lift the lost years from his soul and give him surcease.

Suddenly to the O.G., it was as if he were peeping—as if he had sneaked into another man's privacy and desecrated it, for in some strange fashion there was the honor of a woman in that song . . . and bitter tears and lonely desperation. In quick embarrassment, he turned and ran again, toward headquarters and the guardhouse and the slow, rocketing sound of the wagon convoy that was rolling onto the post now from the Sudro Road.

The O. G. came up behind Sergeant Shattuck, and the sergeant swung around. "Recruit replacement from Jefferson Barracks, Mr. Topliff; eighteen hours ahead of schedule. General Sheridan rode in with 'em from Elkhorn. He's in post headquarters. A runner's gone for the colonel." D'Arcy Topliff took the headquarters veranda in two long strides. Philip Henry Sheridan, his back to the hanging lamp, was flicking the damper, toeing open the draft, throwing in post oak until the stove roared like a river boat.

"Sheridan, mister"—in a bleak York State twang—"what about coffee?"

"Topliff, Officer of the Guard, sir," and D'Arcy put the duty coffeepot on.

Sheridan stretched out his hands to thaw their numbing chill. He must have looked pinched and blue this way, the morning he galloped in from Winchester to smash Jubal Early, for it can be cold in the early mornings in October in the Shenandoah Valley.

Colonel Massarene, running along the headquarters duckboards, struck the veranda once, lightly, and pushed open the door with a quick insistence that flowed through him easily from head to clicked heels, to voice, "Good morning, general."

Sheridan said, "Seven years, isn't it, Massarene, since we last had coffee together?"

"Seven, sir. Even. On the fifteenth of next month."

Tall, Massarene. Spare, almost to a whisper of pain, but a magnificent animal turned like a fine tool to his job. Colonel of cavalry and nothing more, for there was nothing left to him beyond that. Nor for Sheridan either. But with Sheridan there was a flamboyant touch in mustache and chin whisker, of no depth in their gesture, that the saber blade of his fine nose didn't throw the laugh to.

He said, "Massarene, I'm bringing you an order. I'm giving it to you personally. I'm sending you across the Rio Grande after the Lipans, Kickapoos and the Apaches. I'm tired of hit and run, and diplomatic hide and seek. Cross the border and burn 'em out, and to high hell with the Department of State!"

"Mr. Topliff," Massarene said, "you didn't hear that . . . except officially. Which is not hearing it at all."

Outside, the recruits from Jefferson Barracks were unloading baggage with the dogged sullenness of early morning, thumping it down to the ground, cursing softly, getting the job done, but with no joy in it.

"Do I have a written order for the mission, general?" Massarene asked.

"No." Phil Sheridan shook his head. "Grant and I will take personal responsibility in Washington, but we want no official paper record to exist. My job is to protect Texas. You cross the Rio Grande and smash 'em, Massarene, as Mackenzie smashed 'em!"

Outside, with the wagon train unloaded and the gray first light loping across the prairie like the shadow of a gaunt wolf, Sergeant Shattuck began calling the roll of the replacement detail, "Andrews, Blake, Cattlett, Fink——"

Inside, General Sheridan said, "Too bad about your son, Massarene."

"I beg your pardon, sir?"

"Being found, I mean. Dismissed from the Academy."

"——Heinze, Hooker, Ives, Jacobs——"

"I still don't understand you, general."

"Your son was dismissed from West Point two months ago. Hadn't you heard?"

Headquarters was cold suddenly with the tomb's breath, and the years that had passed over the colonel began to flow suddenly back toward him.

He said, "I have had no news of my son, general, since he was three years old. And I never expect to hear anything about him again——"

"——Lowry, Lutz, Marble, Massarene——"

No one of the three in headquarters moved an eye but it was as if the living fiber of Colonel Massarene had been belly-kicked—as if a shadow, fast moving, had flicked him with physical force.

After a moment, he said, "I shall move out with the regiment, general, at reveille, the day after tomorrow. . . . Mr. Topliff, knock out the adjutant at once." But the sound that hung in the room was the echo of that name "Massarene," like a dead man's coat on a peg.

The news ran through the regiment before morning stable call: "One of the new recruits from Jefferson is the Old Man's son! He failed in mathematics and they kicked him out of the Academy. He enlisted the same day at Highland Falls." And at breakfast in the bachelor officers' mess: "His mother was one of the Fahnestock sisters. Unbelievably beautiful. And the youngster is as handsome as sin, with the Old Man's wiriness. She couldn't take the life, they say. Had her own money. Left Massarene years ago, when he was a lieutenant."

When D'Arcy Topliff spotted the paymaster's wagon and inspected the escort for Sheridan's trip to Elkhorn, the general thanked him.

Then as he climbed in, he turned his head. "You married, mister?"

Topliff smiled. "That's hard to come by out here, general."

"When you come by it," Sheridan said, "see that it's an Army girl. One that can cook, sew, ride, shoot, breed and keep her complexion. And remember, I told you, mister."

The men joked about putting chevrons on at Starke with hooks and eyes. They hated Colonel Massarene because he hewed so close to the line that no humanity ever got between, only an immaculate military justice that was machine-made, and as icy as the fingers of death. They hated him because he was ever right, and they hated him because they knew they could never love him. "God, I hope the boy has steel; for the Old Man will break him in his two hands, if he hasn't!"

When Colonel Massarene inspected the recruit detail, he looked straight into his son's eyes, but there was no recognition in either man, no wavering.

"I hope the blood of every one of you ran thick down your legs in the Jefferson riding ring," the Old Man said to the detail. "I hope you're all dry of it, except in your hearts. Desert . . . and I'll find you and rope you and bring you back. Go slack in your duties . . . and I'll stiffen your spines against escort-wagon wheels. In this regiment, it is harder to make corporal than it is for a Hindoo to get into heaven. You're for company duty as of today. . . . Dismiss the detail." And he turned on his heel and walked off.

After guard mount, when Topliff marched off as O.G., the Old Man sent for him to come to headquarters. "Mr. Topliff," he said, "only you and I know where the regiment is going. That's enough tongues to leak it. So we'll have no more tongues—not even the adjutant's—in on it. Chart me three alternate routes. Roughly, I want to move southwest from Starke to the Tablelands, as a diversion, and I want to cross the border somewhere between Peco and San Jacinto by forced night march, leaving the escort wagons behind. The moon is dark in nine days. I'll cross then and I'd like very well to have the regiment think it was crossing the Querhada River, rather than the Rio Grande. . . . until the last possible minute. I suppose you understand you may resign your commission? Should General Sheridan die in the midst of this, you'll lose it, and I'll lose mine . . . and everyone else."

"You don't intend to offer resignation to the other officers, sir. You only mention it to me because I was present and know the mission?"

"An order, Mr. Topliff, is an order. I cannot offer it to the others until the Rio Grande is crossed, and then I will not."

Working out the lines of march, D'Arcy Topliff was in the outer office of headquarters when Private Massarene came in. He heard the interview, and it was like the pounding of short in-blows through the partition.

"You sent for me, sir?"

"I did." And a long pause that writhed in the air as the eyes of those two met and whipped at each other like knives. "I sent for you to put it to you straight. That you are my son is merely a matter of official record. For years you have undoubtedly lived with a concept of me, as I have of you. I shall give you my concept of you. It is not pleasant. There are two blood streams coursing in you. One is deeply ingrained in a way of soft and moneyed living—so deeply that pride of oath and commitment is secondary to its continued necessity. That is on your record."

Outside, Topliff could feel in his own cheeks the hot rush of angry blood darkening the boy's handsome face until the lips became white as a new scar. And in his mind Topliff whispered frantically, *Don't answer him. Don't talk back.*

"And it is on your record, too, that you have failed at West Point and have turned out as unfit for a commission. So you have enlisted, in a dramatic gesture, to lacerate yourself by showing your carbine to men you have hazed. Neither the failure nor the attempt to atone for it impresses me. Your other blood stream is mine, but your concept of that is a concept of plumes, parades and band music. Following the lie of their lure, you have rashly and thoughtlessly placed your living upon the table top, and the cards are dealt. I put it to you flatly, that the royal straight flush of glory never comes up in life, and that only fools hope for it. My father shot, for cowardice, at Chapultepec, the officer son of a United States senator with his own hand. I shall not bedevil you, but what comes to other men will only come to you in this regiment through a meticulous, immaculate performance of duty up to the last detail. You have chosen my way of life; I shall see that you attain to it unto its deepest essence or leave your bones to bleach under the prairie moon!"

. Topliff, outside, realized that his own hands were clenched so tightly that his arms ached to the elbows. It was the boy's voice—low, even and controlled, like flicked gloves.

"Do I . . . have the privilege of speaking, sir . . . or do I not?"

"Within the strict limitations of decorum."

"I didn't ask to be sent to this regiment, sir, but I wouldn't have it otherwise, now that I'm here. Except for one thing."

"And what is that one thing?"

Young Massarene said, "That there might be any faint thought in your mind, sir, that I came to this regiment ever to call you 'father.' "

Jasper! What life can do to people at times, and so uselessly, so wholly without reason.

Young Massarene went to C Company for duty—Lieutenant Cohill's company—but as the way is with things like that, once you've been let in on the inside track, D'Arcy Topliff kept crossing the boy's trail. A lean youngster, lithe and flat in the hips, deep-chested. Loading the regimental escort wagons behind the commissary corral. On the ammunition detail. Post fatigue detachments. Stables. And Topliff watched him closely to see what was there, for there could have been many wrong things.

Because Topliff had gone over to the youngster's side instinctively, when the colonel had flayed him, he stayed over. And without knowing quite how, a part of him got into young Massarene's mind, just as a part of him had got into the colonel's mind when he had heard that violin at four in the morning.

The regiment moved out on schedule and took the long trail down into the southwest country. And sometimes in the days that followed, D'Arcy Topliff rode as young Massarene. Sometimes he rode as the colonel. He was young Massarene when they found the burned-out wagon train and the dead wagoners, with one strapped face downward to a wagon shaft with his tongue out, but still alive to the horror of writhing ants. Young Massarene, with the bitter bile in his throat, swallowing as he dug the long grave, swallowing eternally to keep his food down against the green corruption in his nostrils. *White gloves and pipe-clayed cross belts. Varnished boots and brass buttons in the Hudson River sunlight.* Another world away from Sergeant Shattuck, drawing his revolver carefully and putting it in the wagoner's agonized hand. Picking it up again from where it whipped to, in jerking recoil, from the lone shot that brought peace.

But Topliff was the colonel in his mind, when the smoke was high beyond the head of the column, when they rode slowly down into Corinth Wells to the burned-out houses. Women were dead in the yards, and there was a twelve-year-old girl with her mind gone completely and forever to her torn nakedness. "Someone please give me a drink of water and tell me a funny story."

"Cohill," Colonel Massarene said, "take the pursuit. I'll give you twelve hours. Twenty men. Meet me"—he put his finger on his map—"here, at San Jacinto." And Topliff felt it in Colonel Massarene's mind before the colonel said it. Felt it for what the colonel's thinking was, for it is easy to steady recruits with action, but it is the hard way to make them see, and not lash back. It is easy to temper their anger with hot carbines, but it is merciless to hold them in close restraint. And nothing is worse than burying women the Apaches have worked over; nothing is worse than an insane girl digging down again to her mother's dead face in the starlight.

"Don't take the detail from C Company, Mr. Cohill. Take the pickets. And under no circumstances cross the Rio Grande," the colonel said.

Cohill didn't run the hostiles down. They were across the Rio Grande before he hit the river line. Across, as they always were now, safe in formal protocol, reeking with drying blood in the green smoke of their villages, under the theoretic protection of a wreck of empire that had sprawled in disorder since the breeze of Queretaro whipped at the blue smoke of the firing party's rifles and ruffled the blond beard of Maximilian von Habsburg, dead in the dust that rose about his riddled body. "Don't take the detail from C Company, Mr. Cohill."

So it was for days, as Massarene moved the regiment steadily along. Then presently the regiment was a bad joke to itself—a slow-moving buffoon with the clowns who got the laughs, slapsticking in behind it to strike and dashing up ahead to grimace in derision. Almost they seemed to watch from the other side, time the regiment's march and plan their forays to fit the pattern.

Anger burned deep as bowel pain, and still Massarene held the regiment in his two gray hands, watching it as a surgeon watches sickness, listening to its faintest curse and the wire-pulled shadow of anger in faces. It was as if the regiment were a single man to him—Topliff's mind again—a man he would condition by withholding water, by making him sweat in the forced night marches, by shortening rations to empty his belly for the scalpel, by toning his animal instinct to face the shock of the cutting edge. "Under no circumstances will you cross the Rio Grande."

The regiment went cold and silent under the treatment, sullen to a point of meticulous fury in performance. Quick animal fights in the bivouacs, put down quickly with harder fists; and the horses had it, too, in their souls—hoof lashings on the picket ropes, soft and angry screams. And still, like a surgeon, Massarene watched it to the final moment. Then he rolled up his sleeves and strapped on his rubber apron and reached for the scalpel.

He bivouacked that afternoon at three-thirty and grazed wide on the picket pins. He inspected personally—like a pup lieutenant on his first detail to the guard. He fed a hot meal at four-thirty. He made a double ammunition issue, and one short ration and a cantle-roll oat issue, and suddenly, through the command, the thinking was like the cocking of a piece on a frosty night—a leaping question—a cold threat—a resurgence that turned the anger from white to crimson.

When the first darkness came down, Colonel Massarene stood to horse, on passed voice order. No water, except on officer order. No unauthorized eating or feeding. No advance guard. No flank guards. No trumpet calls. Nothing but a long column closely knit, cased in discipline, poised for a javelin cast into the night.

"Mount."

A quick reversal of the day's direction of march, a quick doubling-back at a tangent toward the south and east, and at half past eleven that night: "Jasper!"—through the column—"This ain't the Querhada! This is the Rio Grande!" And there it was, with its saffron waters cutting the dust of the march like a double-bitted ax blade, holding it high over the United States while the regiment forded across, in the cold inertia of its movement—forded across and stood sweat-dank under the stars while the Old Man called in his officers.

"Gentlemen," he said, "the direction of march is south by west, magnetic, to Santa Maria. I'm burning out everything in my path—everything Kickapoo, Lipan and Apache, and anything else that the darkness fails to distinguish. I'm going through like a scourge—in column at the gallop, so that the next five hours will be remembered for twenty years to come. If I'm opposed by troops, I'm still going through, for a recrossing at Paredes at six A.M. You will leave your dead, shoot wounded horses and lash your wounded in their saddles. There will be no dismounted action." And then he said the one thing he had to say while his hatred of the necessity twisted across his gray face and left its bitter taste upon his lips: "Gentlemen, I am operating under orders. You are operating under my orders. You need, therefore, have no thought for the consequences of tonight's work. That will be thrashed out thousands of miles away by men who wear clean clothing and sit in comfortable offices." And then he did it, as coldly as the drawing of a saber: "Mr. Cohill, screen me to the southward at a thousand yards' distance and cut me a pathway. Mr. Cohill, take C Company."

There it is. No easy first commitment, no racing fight in daylight across your own terrain with reserves behind you and surgeons to stop your bone-broken screaming. No, you'll watch that from the sidewalk. But this is different. If your mount goes down on this, you're done to get back, unless you catch a free mount. You're out ahead, in this fight, for first contact in darkness, for ambush and barricades and a burst of tearing fire from shadows. If you're hit, you're done, unless a bunkie ties you on. If you break, Cohill will shoot you like a dog. And if you are a hero, no one will see it in the darkness for a cheap reward. "Mr. Cohill, screen me to the southward at a thousand yards' distance and cut me a pathway. Mr. Cohill, take C Company." But the words Topliff seemed to hear were not those words; they were the other ones: "or leave your bones to bleach under the prairie moon."

Strangely, as C Company moved out under Flint Cohill's low word of command, there were hot hoofs and creaking leather in it, not shirt sweat and horse dung, but the faint rustle of silken shirts and jasmine on the night air, and the quiet sobbing of a woman, echoing down the lost years.

Topliff saw young Massarene's face as he passed by in the darkness, for there was starlight in the river wash—saw it briefly. Handsome as sin, but a man's face, and a man's body moving in easy oneness with his mount. Only between that and the colonel's face there was a subtlety of difference that was more than years—linen cuffs instead of wool. The turned-up collar of the duelist instead of gray eyes along open sights. Laughter warming the cold word, for humanity. The stamina of insouciance to face a mistake with a fillip and work it down the hard way to a rightful place once more, on the wings of ancient blood.

Harder that way by far, than the ruthless runway of a lifetime of discipline. *Don't try too hard, boy,* Topliff's mind whispered. And the knowledge was on Topliff that there are ways of life for all of us and no man dare criticize another for the pathway that fits his feet, for it is a lonely journey always, and God speaks many tongues.

"Lead out!"

Well, it is in the books—impersonally, with the date and the fact—but it is left there suspended in midair, for two laws crossed each other and diplomacy is manner, not morality. But see the reprisal raid for a red beast in the night, clawing on a forty-seven mile arc of the world like the devil in white-hot armor. See the spoor of dead in its pathway, hacked open and gaping, and the crimson flowers of flame that burst against the darkness and gutted in the echo of ruthless hoofs.

The breathing in men's throats was drawn wire, tearing at membranes, and there were fear and murder and hope in their minds until they were as raw as clawed flesh.

But one mind wasn't. "Topliff, get after Pennell to close up! Close up!" One mind frozen to the machine, one mind holding it to the job. Even if it vibrated from its bed, it wouldn't cast loose. Lash it. Hold it true. Grab it and keep it functioning even if it tears the fingers from your hands. "Tell Pennell, I'll try him. Tell him I'll shoot him, damn him, if he separates. Keep the column closed up—closed up!"

Seven villages they burned out—Lipan, Kickapoo and Apache—hitting them out of the night on the exact positions the colonel's authenticated information had placed them. Coming down like an avalanche from the darkness, leaving nothing behind but the wall of savage women, halting each time to reform briefly and take up the inexorable march at the walk, and then presently at the trot, and then again, "Right front into line! Gallop! Yo!" all the way to Escobedo, and there in the last darkness and the cold river mists—with the end of it in sight—the word had gone on ahead on the wings of the flames behind or on instinct, and C Company hit the barricade and the running fire that defended it. Horses were down, shrieking in agony, and the command bunched in on itself in the roadway and a ricochet sent the chapel bell tolling briefly overhead. Flames burst high and made the whole thing clear for just a second—not actually to see at the time, but to remember long afterward.

Red knife cuts laced across the night and 'dobe dust spat from the lashed walls. The regiment crushed in on C Company, debouching right and left around the chapel to keep its momentum, dividing—"Go through, Cohill! Damn you, go through!" And Cohill, with his face covered with blood in the flames and white-streaked in dust, a centaur on his bunched horse, leaped over and screamed to C to follow him.

Someone was thrashing in the roadway, his horse down, flaying at him with pain-crazed hoofs—thrashing and screaming, "Mother! Mother!" as they will.

Topliff was knee to knee with the colonel when the other rider cut in front of them, bent low at the gallop and grabbed the man's thrown-up arm, wrenching him to his dragging feet, pulling him to his pommel, just as his own horse pitched forward, throwing both of them to the chapel steps, head over. With one hand young Massarene still held the man he had rescued. With the other he began to fire steadily into the firing, like a man on the pistol range, squeezing off evenly, his handsome lips drawn back in the firelight.

Colonel Massarene threw up his own mount, turned him on his heels and raced back into the murderous firing to a free horse—raced back to the chapel steps.

"Mount, Donald, you fool!" and his son threw on, dragging his bunkie up again.

"Thank you, sir"—as cold as a word passed at whist, not studied, not controlled, but the voice of the man himself—of a competent journeyman, working well at his trade.

Then it was, as the three of them galloped knee to knee, that Topliff heard the bullet strike the Old Man like a rock hurled into mud. Then it was also that he saw young Massarene's shoulder and upper arm torn clean open to the white bones, for the mesquite bushes stood outlined now against the racing dawn.

The colonel was down close to his mount's neck, sweat-drenched and worn thin and broken with pain, but he kept at the gallop until he reached the head of the column and halted it to reform. Then he said, "Mr. Topliff, I can't dismount. Rope me in the saddle."

Topliff tied one of his feet and young Massarene passed the halter under his horse and tied the other foot.

"You're hurt," the colonel said to the boy, and suddenly Topliff knew that the lost years no longer stood between those two like grinning beggars with their hungry hands held out for alms. The essence of affinity was there, as it had always been. The handsome face beside the gray one—that was like a finer metal stamped from the same coin press.

"That doesn't matter, does it, sir?"

And in the broad light of day there was the feeling of soft white hands on D'Arcy Topliff—hands touching him gratefully for his understanding, because what D'Arcy heard was: *I'm sorry, but all my life I knew I would have to show you someday that she wasn't as wrong as you cared to believe her; that I'd have to come out here and prove it to you in the only way you could ever understand, father.*

And the reason Topliff heard those words was that young Massarene grinned when he said, "That doesn't matter, does it, sir?"

The regiment recrossed the Rio Grande at Paredes at six A.M. Colonel Massarene was the last man over, riding between his son and Lieutenant Topliff, lashed still in his saddle.

"Mr. Topliff, pass the word to Major Allshard to take over command. Donald, turn in to the regimental surgeon for that arm, and rejoin your company. When the surgeon is finished with the wounded, send him along. I'll wait here for the escort wagons. Untie me and let me down."

Topliff untied the halter and slid the colonel out of his saddle. Young Massarene, half-circling his mount on the forehead, saluted with his bridle hand, for the other arm was useless, and bowed slightly into the salute. There was infinite grace in the gesture and a gentleness of finer living.

The colonel, one hand pressed tightly into his torn side, returned the courtesy, and whatever stain lay between those two was washed clean. The years they had lost were forgotten and the debt was paid in full.

The Hanging Tree

BY DOROTHY M. JOHNSON

(The Hanging Tree)

"The Hanging Tree" was conceived and written as a novel, but when Dorothy M. Johnson (1905–1984) was rather astonishingly unable to find a publisher for it, she painstakingly whittled it down to its present novella size for publication in her 1957 collection The Hanging Tree and Other Stories. *The film version with Gary Cooper and Maria Schell, released two years later, is one of three films made from her award-winning short fiction. The others are* The Man Who Shot Liberty Valance *(1962), starring James Stewart and John Wayne and based on the short story of the same title (included in* The Reel West); *and* A Man Called Horse *(1970), also adapted from a story of the same title (included in* The Second Reel West) *and starring Richard Harris.*

I

Just before the road dipped down to the gold camp on Skull Creek, it crossed the brow of a barren hill and went under the out-thrust bough of a great cottonwood tree.

A short length of rope, newly cut, hung from the bough, swinging in the breeze, when Joe Frail walked that road for the first time, leading his laden horse. The camp was only a few months old, but someone had been strung up already, and no doubt for good cause. Gold miners were normally more interested in gold than in hangings. As Joe Frail glanced up at the rope, his muscles went tense, for he remembered that there was a curse on him.

Almost a year later, the boy who called himself Rune came into Skull Creek, driving a freight wagon. The dangling length of rope was weathered and raveled then. Rune stared at it and reflected, If they don't catch you, they can't hang you.

Two weeks after him, the lost lady passed under the tree, riding in a wagon filled with hay. She did not see the bough or the raveled rope, because there was a bandage over her eyes.

Joe Frail looked like any prospector, ageless, anonymous and dusty, in a fading red shirt and shapeless jeans. His matted hair, hanging below his shoulders, would have been light brown if it had been clean. A long mustache framed his mouth, and he wore a beard because he had not shaved for two months.

The main difference between Joe Frail and any other newcomer to Skull Creek was that inside the pack on his plodding horse was a physician's satchel.

"Now I wonder who got strung up on that tree," remarked his partner. Wonder Russell was Joe Frail's age—thirty—but not of his disposition. Russell was never moody and he required little from the world he lived in. He wondered aloud about a thousand things but did not require answers to his questions.

"I wonder," he said, "how long it will take us to dig out a million dollars."

I wonder, Joe Frail thought, if that is the bough from which I'll hang. I wonder who the man is that I'll kill to earn it.

They spent that day examining the gulch, where five hundred men toiled already, hoping the colors that showed in the gravel they panned meant riches. They huddled that night in a brush wickiup, quickly thrown together to keep off the rain.

"I'm going to name my claim after me when I get one," said Wonder Russell. "Call it the Wonder Mine."

"Meaning you wonder if there's any pay dirt in it," Joe Frail answered. "I'll call mine after myself, too. The Frail Hope."

"Hell, that's unlucky," his partner objected.

"I'm usually unlucky," said Joe Frail.

He lay awake late that first night in the gulch, still shaken by the sight of the dangling rope. He remembered the new-made widow, six years ago, who had shrieked a prophecy that he would sometime hang.

Before that, he had been Doctor Joseph Alberts, young and unlucky, sometimes a prospector and sometimes a physician. He struck pay dirt, sold out and went back East to claim a girl called Sue, but she had tired of waiting and had married someone else. She sobbed when she told him, but her weeping was not because she had spoiled her life and his. She cried because she could not possess him now that he was rich.

So he lost some of his youth and all his love and even his faith in love. Before long he lost his riches, too, in a fever of gambling that burned him up because neither winning nor losing mattered.

Clean and new again, and newly named Frail—he chose that in a bitter moment—he dedicated himself to medicine for a winter. He was earnest and devoted, and when spring came he had a stake that would let him go prospecting again. He went north to Utah to meet a man named Harrigan, who would be his partner.

On the way, camped alone, he was held up and robbed of his money, his horse and his gun. The robbers, laughing, left him a lame pinto mare that a Digger Indian would have scorned.

Hidden in a slit in his belt for just such an emergency was a twenty-dollar gold piece. They didn't get that.

In Utah he met Harrigan—who was unlucky, too. Harrigan had sold his horse but still had his saddle and forty dollars.

"Will you trust me with your forty dollars?" Joe Frail asked. "I'll find a game and build it bigger."

"I wouldn't trust my own mother with that money," Harrigan objected as he dug into his pocket. "But my mother don't know how to play cards. What makes you think you do?"

"I was taught by an expert," Joe Frail said briefly.

In addition to two professions, doctor and miner, he had two great skills: he was an expert card player and a top hand with a pistol. But he played cards only when he did not care whether he won or lost. This time winning was necessary, and he knew what was going to happen—he would win, and then he would be shattered.

He found a game and watched the players—two cowboys, nothing to worry about; a town man, married, having a mildly devilish time; and an older man, probably an emigrant going back East with a good stake. The emigrant was stern and tense and had more chips before him than anyone else at the table.

When Doc sat in, he let the gray-haired man keep winning for a while. When the emigrant started to lose, he could not pull out. He was caught in some entangling web of emotions that Doc Frail had never felt.

Doc lost a little, won a little, lost a very little, began to win. Only he knew how the sweat ran down inside his dusty shirt.

The emigrant was a heavy loser when he pulled out of the game.

"Got to find my wife," was his lame excuse. But he went only as far as the bar and was still there, staring into the mirror, when Doc cashed in his chips and went out with two hundred dollars in his pockets.

He got out to the side of the saloon before the shakes began.

"And what the hell ails you?" Harrigan inquired. "You won."

"What ails me," said Doc with his teeth chattering, "is that my father taught me to gamble and my mother taught me it was wicked. The rest of it is none of your business."

"You sound real unfriendly," Harrigan complained. "I was admiring your skill. It must be mighty handy. The way you play cards, I can't see why you waste your time doctoring."

"Neither can I," said Doc.

He steadied himself against the building. "We'll go someplace and divide the money. You might as well have yours in your pocket."

Harrigan warned, "The old fellow, the one you won from, is on the prod."

Doc said shortly, "The man's a fool."

Harrigan sounded irritated. "You think everybody's a fool."

"I'm convinced of it."

"If you weren't one, you'd clear out of here," the cowboy advised. "Standing here, you're courting trouble."

Doc took that as a challenge. "Trouble comes courting me, and I'm no shy lover."

He felt as sore as raw meat. Another shudder shook him. He detested Harrigan, the old man, himself, everybody.

The door swung open and the lamplight showed the gray-haired emigrant. The still night made his words clear: "He cheated me, had them cards marked, I tell you!"

Salt stunk unbearably on raw meat. Doc Frail stepped forward.

"Are you talking about me?"

The man squinted. "Certainly I'm talking about you. Cheating, thieving tin horn—"

Young Doc Frail gasped and shot him.

Harrigan groaned, "My God, come on!" and ducked back into darkness.

But Doc ran forward, not back, and knelt beside the fallen man as the men inside the saloon came cautiously out.

Then there was a woman's keening cry, coming closer: "Ben! Ben! Let me by—he's shot my husband!"

He never saw her, he only heard her wailing voice: "You don't none of you care if a man's been killed, do you! You'll let him go scot free and nobody cares. But he'll hang for this, the one who did it! You'll burn in hell for this, the lot of you—"

Doc Frail and Harrigan left that place together—the pinto carried both saddles and the men walked. They parted company as soon as they could get decent horses, and Doc never saw Harrigan again.

A year or so later, heading for a gold camp, Doc met the man he called Wonder, and Wonder Russell, it seemed to him, was the only true friend he had ever had.

But seeing him for the first time, Joe Frail challenged him with a look that warned most men away, a slow, contemptuous look from hat to boots that seemed to ask, "Do you amount to anything?"

That was not really what it asked, though. The silent question Joe Frail had for every man he met was "Are you the man? The man for whom I'll hang?"

Wonder Russell's answer at their first meeting was as silent as the question. He smiled a greeting, and it was as if he said, "You're a man I could side with."

They were partners from then on, drifting through good luck and bad, and so finally they came to Skull Creek.

They built more than one wickiup in the weeks they spent prospecting there, moving out from the richest part of the strike, because that was already claimed.

By September they were close to broke.

"A man can go to work for wages," Wonder Russell suggested. "Same kind of labor as we're doing now, only we'd get paid for it. I wonder what it's like to eat."

"You'll never be a millionaire working someone else's mine," Doc warned.

"I wonder how a man could get a stake without working," his partner mused.

"I know how," Joe Frail admitted. "How much have we got between us?"

It added up to less than fifty dollars. By morning of the following day, Joe Frail had increased it to almost four hundred and was shuddering so that his teeth chattered.

"What talent!" Wonder Russell said in awe. He asked no questions.

Four days after they started over again with a new supply of provisions, they struck pay dirt. They staked two claims, and one was as good as the other.

"Hang on or sell out?" Joe Frail asked.

"I wonder what it's like to be dirty rich," Wonder mused. "On the other hand, I wonder what it's like to be married?"

Joe Frail stared. "Is this something you have in mind for the immediate future, or are you just dreaming in a general kind of way?"

Wonder Russell smiled contentedly. "Her name is Julie and she works at the Big Nugget."

And she already has a man who won't take kindly to losing her, Joe Frail recollected. Wonder Russell knew that as well as he did.

She was a slim young dancer, beautiful though haggard, this Julie at the Big Nugget. She had tawny hair in a great knot at the back of her neck, and a new red scar on one shoulder; it looked like a knife wound and showed when she wore a low-necked dress.

"Let's sell, and I'll dance at your wedding," Joe Frail promised.

They sold the Wonder and the Frail Hope on a Monday and split fifteen thousand dollars between them. They could have got more by waiting, but Wonder said, "Julie don't want to wait. We're going out on the next stage, Wednesday."

"There are horses for sale. Ride out, Wonder." Doc could not forget the pale, cadaverous man called Dusty Smith who would not take kindly to losing Julie. "Get good horses and start before daylight."

"Anybody'd think it was you going to get married, you're in such a sweat about it," Wonder answered, grinning. "I guess I'll go tell her now."

A man should plan ahead more, Joe Frail told himself. I planned only to seek for gold, not what to do if I found it, and not what to do if my partner decided to team up with someone else.

He was suddenly tired of being one of the anonymous, bearded, sweating toilers along the creek. He was tired of being dirty. A physician could be clean and wear good clothes. He could have a roof over his head. Gold could buy anything—and he had it.

He had in mind a certain new cabin. He banged on the door until the owner shouted angrily and came with a gun in his hand.

"I'd like to buy this building," Joe Frail told him. "Right now."

A quarter of an hour later, he owned it by virtue of a note that could be cashed at the bank in the morning, and the recent owner was muttering to himself out in the street, with his possessions on the ground around him, wondering where to spend the rest of the night.

Joe Frail set his lantern on the bench that constituted all the cabin's furniture. He walked over to the wall and kicked it gently.

"A whim," he said aloud. "A very solid whim to keep the rain off."

Suddenly he felt younger than he had in many years, light-hearted, completely carefree, and all the wonderful world was his for the taking. He spent several minutes leaping into the air and trying to crack his heels together three times before he came down again. Then he threw back his head and laughed.

Lantern in hand, he set out to look for Wonder. When he met anyone, as he walked toward the Big Nugget, he lifted the lantern, peered into the man's face, and asked hopefully, "Are you an honest man?"

Evans, the banker, who happened to be out late, answered huffily, "Why, certainly!"

Wonder Russell was not in the saloon, but tawny-haired Julie was at the bar between two miners. She left them and came toward him smiling.

"I hear you sold out," she said. "Buy me a drink for luck?"

"I'll buy you champagne if they've got it," Joe Frail promised.

When their drinks were before them, she said, "Here's more luck of the same kind, Joe." Still smiling gaily, she whispered, "Go meet him at the livery stable." Then she laughed and slapped at him as if he had said something especially clever, and he observed that across the room Dusty Smith was playing cards and carefully not looking their way.

"I've got some more places to visit before morning," Joe Frail announced. "Got to find my partner and tell him we just bought a house."

He blew out the lantern just outside the door. It was better to stumble in the darkness than to have Dusty, if he was at all suspicious, be able to follow him conveniently.

Wonder was waiting at the livery stable corral.

"Got two horses in here, paid for and saddled," Wonder reported. "My war sack's on one of 'em, and Julie's stuff is on the other."

"I'll side you. What do you want done?"

"Take the horses out front of the Big Nugget. They're yours and mine, see? If anybody notices, we bought 'em because we made our pile and we've been drinking. Hell, nobody'll notice anyway."

"You're kind of fidgety," Joe Frail commented. "Then what?"

"Get the horses there and duck out of sight. That's all. I go in, buy Julie a drink, want her to come out front and look at the moon."

"There isn't any moon," Joe warned him.

"Is a drunk man going to be bothered by that?" Wonder answered. "I'll set 'em up for the boys and then go show Julie the moon while they're milling around. That's all."

"Good luck," Joe Frail said, and their hands gripped. "Good luck all the way for you and Julie."

"Thanks, partner," Wonder Russell said.

And where are you going, friend? Joe Frail wondered. Your future is none of my business, any more than your past.

He staggered as he led the horses down the gulch, in case anyone was watching. A fine performance, he told himself; too bad it is so completely wasted. Because who's going to care, except Dusty Smith, if Julie runs off and gets married?

He looped the lines over the hitch rail so that a single pull would dislodge them. Then he stepped aside and stood in the shadows, watching the door.

Wonder Russell came out, singing happily: "Oh, don't you remember sweet Betsy from Pike, who crossed the big desert with her lover Ike?"

Another good performance wasted, Joe Frail thought. The lucky miner with his claim sold, his pockets full of money, his belly full of whiskey—that was Wonder's role, and nobody would have guessed that he was cold sober.

Wonder capped his performance by falling on the steps and advising them to get out of the way and let a good man pass. Joe grinned and wished he could applaud.

Two men came out and, recognizing Russell, loudly implored him to let some golden luck rub off on them. He replied solemnly, "Dollar a rub, boys. Every little bit helps." They went away laughing as he stumbled through the lighted doorway.

Joe Frail loosened his guns in their holsters and was ready in the shadows. The best man helps the happy couple get away, he remembered, but this time not in a shower of rice with tin cans tied to the buggy and bunting on the team!

Wonder Russell was in the doorway with Julie beside him, laughing.

"Moon ain't that way," Russell objected. "It's over this way." He stepped toward the side of the platform where the saddled horses were.

Inside the lighted room a white-shirted gaunt man whirled with a gun in his hand, and Dusty Smith was a sure target in the light for three or four seconds while Joe Frail stood frozen with his guns untouched. Then the noise inside the saloon was blasted away by a gunshot, and Wonder Russell staggered and fell.

The target was still clear while Dusty Smith whirled and ran for the back door. A pistol was in Joe Frail's right hand, but the pistol and the hand might as well have been blocks of wood. He could not pull the trigger—until the miners roared their shock and anger and Dusty Smith had got away clean.

Joe Frail stood frozen, hearing Julie scream, seeing the men surge out the front door, knowing that some of them followed Dusty Smith out the back.

There were some shots out there, and then he was no longer frozen. His finger could pull the trigger for a useless shot into the dust. He ran to the platform where Julie was kneeling. He shouldered the men aside, shouting, "Let me by. I'm a doctor."

But Wonder Russell was dead.

"By God, Joe, I wish you'd have come a second sooner," moaned one of the men. "You could have got him from the street if you'd been a second sooner. It was Dusty Smith."

Someone came around the corner of the building and panted the news that Dusty had got clean away on a horse he must have had ready out back.

Joe Frail sat on his heels for a long time while Julie held Wonder's head in her arms and cried. One of the little group of miners still waiting asked, "You want some help, Joe? Where you want to take him?"

He looked down at Julie's bowed head.

My friend—but her lover, he remembered. She has a better right.

"Julie," he said. He stooped and helped her stand up. "Where do you want them to take him?"

"It doesn't matter," she said dully. "To my place, I guess."

Joe Frail commissioned the building of a coffin and bought burying clothes at the store—new suit and shirt that Wonder had not been rich long enough to buy for himself. Then, carrying a pick and shovel, he climbed the hill.

While he was digging, another friend of Wonder's came, then two more, carrying the tools of the same kind.

"I'd rather you didn't," Joe Frail told them. "This is something I want to do myself."

The men nodded and turned away.

When he stopped to rest, standing in the half-dug grave, he saw another man coming up. This one, on horseback, said without dismounting, "They got Dusty hiding about ten miles out. Left him for the wolves."

Joe Frail nodded. "Who shot him?"

"Stranger to me. Said his name was Frenchy Plante."

Joe went back to his digging. A stranger had done what he should have done, a stranger who could have no reason except that he liked killing.

Joe Frail put down his shovel and looked at his right hand. There was nothing wrong with it now. But when it should have pulled the trigger, there had been no power in it.

Because I shot a man in Utah, he thought, I can't shoot any more when it matters.

Julie climbed the hill before the grave was quite finished. She looked at the raw earth, shivering a little in the wind, and said, "He's ready."

Joe stood looking at her, but she kept her eyes down.

"Julie, you'll want to go away. You'll have money to go on—all the money for his claim. I'll ride with you as far as Elk Crossing, so you'll have someone to talk to if you want to talk. I'll go with you farther than that if you want."

"Maybe. Thanks. But I kind of think I'll stay in Skull Creek."

She turned away and walked down the hill.

Sometime that night, Julie cut her throat and died quietly and alone.

II

Elizabeth Armistead, the lost lady, came to Skull Creek the following summer.

About four o'clock one afternoon, a masked man rode out of the brush and held up a stage coach some forty miles south of the diggings. Just before this, the six persons aboard the stage were silently wrapped in their separate thoughts, except the stage line's itinerant blacksmith, who was uneasily asleep.

A tramp printer named Heffernan was dreaming of riches to be got by digging gold out of the ground. A whiskey salesman beside him was thinking vaguely of suicide, as he often did during a miserable journey.

The driver, alone on his high seat, squinted through glaring light and swiped his sleeve across his face, where sand scratched the creases of his skin. He envied the passengers, protected from the sand-sharp wind, and was glad he was quitting the company. He was going back to Pennsylvania, get himself a little farm. Billy McGinnis was fifty-eight years old on that last day of his life.

The sick passenger, named Armistead, was five years older and was planning to begin a career of schoolteaching in Skull Creek. He had not intended to go there. He had thought he had a good thing in Elk Crossing, a more stable community with more children who needed a school. But another wandering scholar had got there ahead of him, and so he and his daughter Elizabeth traveled on toward the end of the world.

The world ended even before Skull Creek for Mr. Armistead.

His daughter Elizabeth, aged nineteen, sat beside him with her hands clasped and her eyes closed but her back straight. She was frightened, had been afraid for months, ever since people began to say that Papa was dishonest. This could not be, must not be, because Papa was all she had to look after and to look after her.

Papa was disgraced and she was going with him into exile. She took some comfort from her own stubborn, indignant loyalty. Papa had no choice, except of places to go. But Elizabeth had had a choice—she could have married Mr. Ellerby and lived as she had always lived, in comfort.

If Papa had told her to do so, or even suggested it, she would have married Mr. Ellerby. But he said it was for her to decide and she chose to go away with Papa. Now that she had an idea how harsh life could be for both of them, she was sick with guilt and felt that she had been selfish and willful. Mr. Ellerby had been willing to provide Papa with a small income, as long as he stayed away, and she had deprived him of it.

These two had no real idea about what the gold camp at Skull Creek would be like. The towns they had stopped in had been crude and rough, but they were at least towns, not camps. Some of the people in them intended to stay there, and so made an effort toward improvement.

Mr. Armistead was reasonably certain that there were enough children in Skull Creek for a small private school, and he took it for granted that their parents would be willing to pay for their education. He assumed, too, that he could teach them. He had never taught or done any other kind of work, but he had a gentleman's education.

He was bone-tired as well as sick and hot and dusty, but when he turned to Elizabeth and she opened her eyes, he smiled brightly. She smiled back, pretending that this endless, unendurable journey to an indescribable destination was a gay adventure.

He was a gentle, patient, hopeful man with good intentions and bad judgment. Until his financial affairs went wrong, he had known no buffeting. Catastrophe struck him before he acquired the protective calluses of the spirit that accustomed misfortune can produce.

All the capital they had left was in currency in a small silk bag that Elizabeth had sewed under her long, full traveling dress.

Elizabeth was wondering, just before the holdup, whether her father could stand it to travel the rest of the day and all night on the final lap of the journey. But the stage station would be dirty and the food would be horrible—travel experience had taught her to be pessimistic—and probably it would be better if they went on at once to Skull Creek where everything, surely, would be much, much pleasanter. Papa would see to that. She could not afford to doubt it.

Billy McGinnis, the driver, was already in imagination in Pennsylvania when a masked rider rode out of scanty timber at his right and shouted, "Stop there!"

Billy had been a hero more than once in his career, but he had no leanings that way any more. He cursed dutifully but hauled on the lines and stopped his four horses.

"Drop that shotgun," the holdup man told Billy. He obeyed, dropping the weapon carefully, making no startling movement.

"Everybody out!" yelled the masked man. "With your hands up."

The printer, as he half fell out of the coach (trying to keep his hands up but having to hang on with one of them), noted details about the bandit: tall from the waist up but sort of short-legged, dusty brown hat, dusty blue shirt, red bandanna over his face.

The whiskey salesman stumbled out hastily—he had been through this a couple of times before and knew better than to argue—and wondered why a man would hold up a stage going into a gold camp. The sensible thing was to hold up one going out.

The blacksmith, suddenly wide awake, was the third to descend. He accepted the situation philosophically, having no money with him anyway, and not even a watch.

But Mr. Armistead tried to defend his daughter and all of them. He warned her, "Don't get out of the coach."

As he stepped down, he tried to fire a small pistol he had brought along for emergencies like this.

The bandit shot him.

Billy McGinnis, jerking on the lines to hold the frightened horses, startled the masked man into firing a second shot. As Billy pitched off the seat, the team lit out running, with Elizabeth Armistead screaming in the coach.

She was not in it any more when the three surviving men found it, overturned, with the frantic horses tangled in the lines, almost an hour later.

"Where the hell did the lady go to?" the blacksmith demanded. The other two agreed that they would have found her before then if she had jumped or fallen out during the runaway.

They did the best they could. They shouted and searched for another hour, but they found no sign of the lost lady. At the place where the coach had turned over, there was no more brush or scrubby timber by the road, only the empty space of the Dry Flats, dotted with greasewood.

One of the horses had a broken leg, so the whiskey salesman shot it.

They unhitched the other three, mounted and searched diligently, squinting out across the flats, calling for the lost lady. But they saw nothing and heard no answering cry.

"The sensible thing," the printer recommended, "is to get on to the station and bring out more help."

"Take the canteen along?" suggested the whiskey salesman.

"If she gets back here, she'll need water," the blacksmith reminded him. "And she'll be scared. One of us better stay here and keep yelling."

They drew straws for that duty, each of them seeing himself as a hero if he won, the lady's rescuer and comforter. The blacksmith drew the short straw and stayed near the coach all night, with the canteen, but the lady did not come back.

He waited alone in the darkness, shouting until he grew hoarse and then voiceless. Back at the place of the holdup, Billy McGinnis and Mr. Armistead lay dead beside the road.

Doc Frail was shaving in his cabin, and the boy called Rune was sullenly preparing breakfast, when the news came about the lost lady.

Doc Frail was something of a dandy. In Skull Creek, cleanliness had no connection with godliness and neither did anything else. Water was mainly used for washing gold out of gravel, but Doc shaved every morning or had the barber do it.

Since he had Rune to slave for him, Doc had his boots blacked every morning and started out each day with most of the dried mud brushed off his coat and breeches. He was a little vain of his light brown curly hair, which he wore hanging below his shoulders. Nobody criticized this, because he had the reputation of having killed four men.

The reputation was unearned. He had killed only one, the man in Utah. He had failed to kill another, and so his best friend had died. These facts were nobody's business.

Doc Frail was quietly arrogant, and he was the loneliest man in the gold camp. He belonged to the aristocracy of Skull Creek, to the indispensable men like lawyers, the banker, the man who ran the assay office, and saloon owners. But these men walked in conscious rectitude and carried pistols decently concealed. Doc Frail wore two guns in visible holsters.

The other arrogant ones, who came and went, were the men of ill will, who dry-gulched miners on their way out with gold. They could afford to shoulder lesser men aside.

Doc Frail shouldered nobody except with a look. Where he walked, other men moved aside, greeting him respectfully: "Morning, Doc. . . . How are you, Doc? . . . Here about the trouble down the gulch, Doc?"

He brandished no pistol (though he did considerable target practice, and it was impressively public) and said nothing very objectionable. But he challenged with a look.

His slow gaze on a stranger, from hat to boots, asked silently, "Do you amount to anything? Can you prove it?"

That was how they read it, and why they moved aside.

What he meant was, "Are you the man I'm waiting for, the man for whom I'll hang?" But nobody knew that except himself.

By Skull Creek standards, he lived like a king. His cabin was the most comfortable one in camp. It had a wood floor and a half partition to divide his living quarters from his consulting room.

The boy Rune, bent over the cookstove, said suddenly, "Somebody's hollering down the street."

"That's a fact," Doc answered, squinting in his shaving mirror.

Rune wanted, of course, to be told to investigate, but Doc wouldn't give him the satisfaction and Rune wouldn't give Doc the satisfaction of doing anything without command. The boy's slavery was Doc's good joke, and he hated it.

There was a pounding on the door and a man's voice shouting, "Doc Frail!"

Without looking away from his mirror, Doc said, "Well, open it," and Rune moved to obey.

A dusty man shouldered him out of the way and announced, "Stage was held up yestiddy, two men killed and a lady lost track of."

Doc wiped his razor and permitted his eyebrows to go up. "She's not here. One of us would have noticed."

The messenger growled. "The boys thought we better warn you. If they find her, you'll be needed."

"I'll keep it in mind," Doc said mildly.

"They're getting up a couple posses. I don't suppose you'd care to go?"

"Not unless there's a guarantee I'd find the lady. What's the other posse for?"

"To get the road agent. One of the passengers thinks he'd recognize him by the build. The driver, Billy McGinnis, was shot, and an old man, the father of the lost lady. Well, I'll be going."

The messenger turned away, but Doc could not quite let him go with questions still unasked.

"And how," he inquired, "would anybody be so careless as to lose a lady?"

"Team ran off with her in the coach," the man answered triumphantly. "When they caught up with it, she wasn't in it any more. She's lost somewheres on the Dry Flats."

The boy Rune spoke unwillingly, unable to remain silent and sullen: "Kin I go?"

"Sure," Doc said with seeming fondness. "Just saddle your horse."

The boy closed down into angry silence again. He had no horse; he had a healing wound in his shoulder and a debt to Doc for dressing it. Before he could have anything he wanted, he had to pay off in service his debt to Doc Frail—and the service would end only when Doc said so.

Doc Frail set out after breakfast to make his rounds—a couple of gunshot wounds, one man badly burned from falling into his own fire while drunk, a baby with colic, a miner groaning with rheumatism, and a dancehall girl with a broken leg resulting from a fall off a table.

The posses were setting out then with considerable confusion and some angry arguments over the last of the horses available at the livery stable.

"You can't have that bay!" the livery stable man was shouting. "That's a private mount and I dassent rent it!"

"You certainly dassent," Doc agreed. "The bay is mine," he explained to three scowling men. The explanation silenced them.

Doc had an amusing thought. Rune would sell his soul to go out with the searchers.

"Get the mare ready," Doc said, and turned back to his cabin.

"I've decided to rent you my horse," he told the sullen boy. "For your services for—let's see—one month in addition to whatever time I decide you have to work for me anyway."

It was a cruel offer, adding a month to a time that might be endless. But Rune, sixteen years old, was a gambler. He blinked and answered, "All right."

"Watch yourself," Doc warned, feeling guilty. "I don't want you crippled." The wound was two weeks old.

"I'll take good care of your property," the boy promised. "And the horse too," he added, to make his meaning clear. Doc Frail stood back, smiling a little, to see which crowd Rune would ride with. There was no organized law enforcement in the gravel gulches of Skull Creek, only occasional violent surges of emotion, with mob anger that usually dissolved before long.

If I were that kid, thought Doc, which posse would I choose, the road agent or the lady? He watched the boy ride to the milling group that was headed for the Dry Flats and was a little surprised. Doc himself would have chosen the road agent, he thought.

So would Rune, except that he planned to become a road agent himself if he ever got free of his bondage.

Rune dreamed, as he rode in the dust of other men's horses, of a bright, triumphant future. He dreamed of a time when he would swagger on any street in any town and other men would step aside. There would be whispers: "Look out for that fellow. That's Rune."

Doc Frail's passage in a group earned that kind of honor. Rune, hating him, longed to be like him.

Spitting dust, the boy dreamed of more immediate glory. He saw himself finding the lost lady out there on the Dry Flats in some place where less keen-eyed searchers had already looked. He saw himself comforting her, assuring her that she was safe now.

He was not alone in his dreaming. There were plenty of dreams in that bearded, ragged company of gold-seekers (ragged even if they were already rich, bedraggled with the dried mud of the creek along which sprawled the diggings). They were men who lived for tomorrow and the comforts they could find somewhere else when, at last, they pulled out of Skull Creek. They were rough and frantic seekers after fortune, stupendously hard workers, out now on an unaccustomed holiday.

Each man thought he was moved by compassion, by pity for the lost and lovely and mysterious lady whose name most of them did not yet know. If they went instead because of curiosity and because they needed change from the unending search and labor in the gravel gulches, no matter. Whatever logic moved them, they rode out to search, fifty motley, bearded men, each of whom might find the living prize.

Only half a dozen riders had gone over the sagebrush hills to look for the road agent who had killed two men. The miners of Skull Creek gambled for fortune but, except when drunk, seldom for their lives. About the worst that could happen in looking for the lost lady was that a man might get pretty thirsty. But go looking for an armed bandit—well, a fellow could get shot. Only the hardy adventurers went in that posse.

When the sun went down, nobody had found anybody, and four men were still missing when the rest of the lady's seekers gathered at the stage line's Station Three. The state company superintendent permitted a fire to be set to a pile of stovewood (freighted in at great expense, like the horse feed and water and everything else there) to make a beacon light. The missing men came in swearing just before midnight. Except for a few provident ones, most of the searchers shivered in their broken sleep, under inadequate and stinking saddle blankets.

They were in the saddle, angry and worried, before dawn of the day Elizabeth Armistead was found.

The sun was past noon when black-bearded Frenchy Plante stopped to tighten his cinch and stamp his booted feet. He pulled off a blue kerchief that protected his nose and mouth from the wind-borne grit, shook the kerchief and tied it on again. He squinted into the glare and, behind a clump of greasewood, glimpsed movement.

A rattler, maybe. Might as well smash it. Frenchy liked killing snakes. He had killed two men, too, before coming to Skull Creek, and one since —a man whose name he found out later was Dusty Smith.

He plodded toward the greasewood, leading his horse, and the movement was there—not a rattler but the wind-whipped edge of a blue skirt.

"Hey!" he shouted, and ran toward her.

She lay face down, with her long, curling hair, once glossy brown, dull and tangled in the sand. She lay flat and drained and lifeless, like a dead animal. Elizabeth Armistead was not moving. Only her skirt fluttered in the hot wind.

"Lady!" he said urgently. "Missus, here's water."

She did not hear. He yanked the canteen from his saddle and pulled out the stopper, knelt beside her and said again, "Lady, I got water."

When he touched her shoulder, she moved convulsively. Her shoulders jerked and her feet tried to run. She made a choking sound of fear.

But when he held the canteen to her swollen, broken lips, she had life enough to clutch at it, to knock it accidentally aside so that some of the water spilled on the thankless earth. Frenchy grabbed the canteen and set it again to her lips, staring at her face with distaste.

Dried blood smeared it, because sand cut into the membranes of the nose like an abrasive. Her face was bloated with the burn of two days of sun, and her anguished lips were shapeless.

Frenchy thought, I'd rather be dead. Aloud he said, "No more water now for a minute. Pretty soon you can have more, Missus."

The lost lady reached blindly for the canteen, for she was blind from the glaring sun, and had been even before she lost her bonnet.

"You gotta wait a minute," Frenchy warned. "Don't be scared, Missus. I'm going to fire this here gun for a signal, call the other boys in. We'll get you to the stage station in no time."

He fired twice into the air, then paused. Two shots meant "found dead." Then he fired the third that changed the pattern and told the other searchers, listening with their mouths open slightly, that the lady had been found living.

The first man to get there was tall, fair-haired Rune, aching with sunburn and the pain of his wound, which had pulled open. When Frenchy found the lady, Rune had been just beyond a little rise of barren ground, stubbornly dreaming as he rode.

I should have been the one, he thought with dull anger. I should have been the one, but it's always somebody else.

He looked at the lady, drained and half dead, dull with dust. He saw the frail and anxious hands groping for the canteen, clutching it as Frenchy guided it to her mouth. He saw the burned, blind face. He said, "Oh, God!"

Frenchy managed a friendly chuckle.

"You're going to be all right, Missus. Get you to a doctor right away. That's a promise, Missus. Frenchy Plante's promise."

He put his name on her, he staked his claim, Rune thought. Who cares? She's going to die anyway.

"I'll go for Doc," Rune said, turning his horse toward the stage station.

But he couldn't go for Doc, after all. He took the news to Station Three; he had that much triumph. Then there was vast confusion. The stage line superintendent ordered a bed made up for the lady, and it was done—that is, the stocktender took the blankets off his bunk and gave them a good shaking and put them back on again. Riders began to come in, shouting, "How is she? Who found her?"

By the time Frenchy Plante arrived, with the lady limp in his arms, and an escort of four other searchers who had gone in the direction of his signal shots, it was discovered that nobody at all had started for Skull Creek to get the doctor.

Rune sat on the ground in the scant shade of the station with his head bowed on his knees, as near exhausted as he had ever been in his life. His shoulder wound hurt like fury, and so did his stomach whenever he remembered how the lost lady looked.

Frenchy Plante was the hero again. He borrowed a fresher horse and rode on to Skull Creek.

He found Doc Frail at home but occupied with a patient, a consumptive dancer from the Big Nugget. With her was another woman, who looked up scowling, as Doc did, when Frenchy came striding in.

"Found the lady, Doc," Frenchy announced. "Want you to come right away."

"I have a patient here," Doc said in controlled tones, "as you will see if you're observant. This lady also needs me."

The consumptive girl, who had seldom been called a lady, was utterly still, lying on Doc's own cot. Her friend was holding her hands, patting them gently.

"Come out a minute," Frenchy urged, "so I can tell you."

Doc closed the door behind him and faced Frenchy in the street.

Frenchy motioned toward the door. "What's Luella doing in your place?"

"Dying," Doc answered. "She didn't want to do it where she works."

"How soon can you come? The lost lady's real bad. Got her to the stage station, but she's mighty sick."

"If she's as sick as this one," Doc said, "it wouldn't do her any good for me to start out there anyway."

"Damned if you ain't a hard-hearted scoundrel," commented Frenchy, half shocked and half admiring. "You ain't doing Luella no good, are you?"

"No. Nobody ever has. But I'm not going to leave her now."

Frenchy shrugged. "How long'll it be?"

"Couple hours, maybe. Do you expect me to strangle her to hurry it along?"

Frenchy's eyes narrowed. "I don't expect nothing. Get out there when you feel like it. I done my duty anyhow."

Was that a reminder, Doc wondered as he watched Frenchy ride on to the Big Nugget, that once you did a duty that should have been mine? That you killed Dusty Smith—a man you didn't even know—after I failed?

Doc Frail went back into his cabin.

A few hours later, Luella released him by dying.

It was dawn when he flung himself off a rented horse at the station and stumbled over a couple of the men sleeping there on the ground.

The lost lady, her face glistening with grease that the stocktender had provided, was quiet on a bunk, with a flickering lamp above her on a shelf. Cramped and miserable on his knees by the bunk was Rune, whose wrist she clutched with one hand. Her other arm cradled Frenchy's canteen.

There was a spot of blood on Rune's shoulder, soaked through Doc's neat dressing, and he was almost too numb to move, but he looked up with hostile triumph.

"She let me be here," he said.

"Now you can go back to Skull Creek," Doc told him, stating a command, not permission. "I'll stay here until she can be moved."

Dispossessed, as he had often been before, but triumphant as he had longed to be, Rune moved away, to tell the sleepy, stirring men that Doc had come. He was amused, when he started back to the gold camp a little later, by the fact that he still rode Doc's mare and Doc would be furious when he discovered it.

The searchers who delayed at Station Three because of curiosity were relieved at the way Doc Frail took charge there. The lost lady seemed to be glad of his presence, too. He treated her burns and assured her in a purring, professional tone, "You'll get your sight back, madam. The blindness is only temporary, I can promise you that."

To the clustering men, he roared like a lion: "Clean this place up—she's got to stay here a few days. Get something decent for her to eat, not this stage-line diet. That's enough to kill an ox. Clean it up, I say—with water. Don't raise a lot of dust."

The superintendent, feeling that he had done more than his duty by letting the stocktender feed the search posse, demurred about wasting water.

"Every drop has to be hauled clear from Skull Creek," he reminded Doc, who snapped back, "Then hitch up and start hauling!"

The stocktender was caught between Doc's anger and the superintendent's power to fire him. He said in a wheedling voice, "Gonna make her some good soup, Doc. I shot a jackrabbit and had him in the pot before he quit kicking."

"Get out of here," snarled Doc. He bent again to the burned, anguished lady.

"You will be able to see again," he promised her. "And your burns will heal."

But your father is dead and buried, and Skull Creek is no place for you, my dear.

III

Frenchy Plante was still around when Rune got back to Skull Creek. Frenchy swaggered, as he had a right to do, being the man who had found the lost lady. But he spent only half a day or so telling the details over. Then he went back to the diggings, far up the gulch, to toil again in the muck and gravel. He had colors there, he was making wages with a small sluice, he had high hopes of getting rich. It had happened before.

The curious of Skull Creek left their own labors to stand by and get the story. When Frenchy was out of the way, Rune became the belligerent center of attention. He had just finished applying a bunchy bandage to his painful shoulder when he jumped guiltily at a pounding on Doc's door. He finished putting his shirt on before he went to take the bar down.

"Doc ain't back yet?" the bearded caller asked.

Rune shook his head.

"Expecting him?" the man insisted.

"He don't tell me his plans."

The man looked anxious. "Look here, I got a boil on my neck needs lancing. Don't suppose you could do it?"

"Anybody could do it. Wrong, maybe. Doc could do it right—I guess."

The man sidled in. "Hell, you do it. Ain't he got some doctor knives around, maybe?"

Rune felt flattered to have someone show confidence in him.

"I'll find something," he offered. He did not know the name of the thing he found, but it was thin and sharp and surgical. He wiped it thoroughly on a piece of clean bandage and, after looking over the boil on the man's neck, opened it up with a quick cut.

The patient said, "Wow!" under his breath and shuddered. "Feels like you done a good job," he commented. "Now tie it up with something, eh?"

He stretched out his booted legs while he sat back in Doc's best chair and waited for Rune to find bandaging material that pleased him.

"You was right on the spot when they found her, I hear," he hinted.

"I was second man to get there," Rune answered, pretending that to be second was nothing at all, but knowing that it was something, knowing that the man's boil could have waited, or that anyone could have opened it.

"Heard she's a foreigner, don't talk no English," the man hinted.

"She didn't say nothing to me," Rune answered. "Couldn't talk any language. She's an awful sick lady."

The man touched his bandage and winced. "Well, I guess that fixes it. Your fee the same as Doc Frail's, I suppose?"

As coolly as if he were not a slave, Rune nodded, and the man hauled a poke from his pocket, looking around for the gold scales.

For a little while after he had gone, Rune still hated him, even with the man's payment of gold dust stowed away in his pocket. So easy to get a doctor—or somebody with a knife, anyway—when you had the dust to pay for it! So easy to enter servitude if you were penniless and had to have a shoulder wound dressed and thought you were going to die!

Before the morning was half done, another visitor came. This time it was a woman, and she was alone. The ladies of Skull Creek were few and circumspect, armored with virtue. Rune guessed that this one, wife of Flaunce the storekeeper, would not have visited Doc Frail's office without a companion if she had expected to find Doc there.

But she asked in her prissy way, "Is the doctor in?" and clucked when Rune shook his head.

"Well, I can see him another day," she decided. "It was about some more of that cough medicine he gave me for my little ones."

And what for do they need cough medicine in warm weather? Rune would have liked to ask her. He said only, "He ain't here."

"He's out at the stage station, I suppose, with the poor lady who was rescued. Have you heard how she's getting along?"

"She's alive but blind and pretty sick," he said. "She'll get her sight back afterwhile."

"I don't suppose anyone knows why she was coming here?" the woman probed.

"Was with her pa, that's all I know. He's dead and she can't talk yet," Rune reported, knowing that what Flaunce's wife really wanted to know was, Is she a lady or one of those others? Was he really her father?

"Dear me," she asked, "is that blood on your shirt?"

Another one, then, who did not know his shame.

"I shot a rabbit, ma'am," he lied. That satisfied her, even though a man would not normally carry a freshly killed rabbit over his shoulder.

The woman decided the cough medicine could wait and minced up the deep-rutted street of the gulch, carefully looking neither to the right nor left.

At the store, buying supplies for Doc's account, Rune inquired, "Any news of the other posse? Them that was after the road agent?"

"It's bigger'n it was, now they found the lost lady. Some of the men figure there's got to be a lesson taught."

"If they catch him, that is," Rune suggested, and the storekeeper nodded, sighing, "If they catch him."

In Doc's absence, Rune carried out a project he had in mind, now that there was no fear of interruption by Doc himself. He searched with scrupulous care for the place where Doc hid his gold.

There should be some in the cabin somewhere. Doc had much more than a physician's income, for he had grubstaked many miners, and a few of them had struck it rich. Doc could afford to be careless with his little leather pokes of nuggets and dust, but apparently he wasn't careless. Rune explored under every loose board and in every cranny between the logs, but he didn't find anything. He did not plan to take the gold yet anyway. It could wait until he was free to leave.

And why don't I pull out now? he wondered. Two men that morning had asked if he wanted to work for wages, and he had turned them down.

It was not honor that kept him there—he couldn't afford the luxury of honor. It was not his wound; he knew now he wasn't going to die of that. The reason he was going to stay, he thought, was just because Doc expected him to run out. He would not give his master that much satisfaction.

He was Rune, self-named, the world's enemy. The world owed him a debt that he had never had much luck in collecting.

He thought he was going to collect when he came to Skull Creek in triumph driving a freight team and carrying his whole fortune—eighty dollars in gold—inside a canvas belt next to his skin. He drew his pay, had a two-dollar meal, and set out for the barber shop.

There was music coming from the Big Nugget. He went in to see the source. Not for any other purpose; Rune spent no money that he didn't have to part with. He did not mean to gamble, but while he watched, a miner looked up and said, scowling, "This is a man's game."

He began to lose, and he could not lose, he must not lose, because if you did not have money you might as well be dead.

When he left the saloon, he was numb and desperate and dead.

Toward morning he tried to rob a sluice. He was not yet hungry, but he would be hungry sometime. He had been hungry before and he was afraid of it. He lurked in shadows, saw the sluice had no armed guard. He was scrabbling against the lower riffles, feeling for nuggets, when a shot came without warning. He fell, pulled himself up and ran, stumbling.

Twenty-four hours later he came out of hiding. He was hungry then, and his shoulder was still bleeding. By that time, he knew where the doctor lived, and he waited, huddling outside the door, while the sun came up.

Doc, in his underwear, opened the door at last to get his lungs full of fresh air and, seeing the tall boy crouching on the step, said, "Well!" Noticing the blood-stiffened shirt he stepped back, sighing, "Well, come in. I didn't hear you knock."

Rune stood up carefully, trying not to move the injured shoulder, holding it with his right hand.

"I didn't knock," he said, hating this man of whom he must ask charity. "I can't pay you. But I got hurt."

"Can't pay me, eh?" Doc Frail was amused. "Guess you haven't heard that the only patients who didn't pay me are buried up on the hill."

Rune believed his grim joke.

"You've been hiding out with this for quite a spell," Doc guessed, as he teased the shirt away from the wound, and the boy shuddered. "You wouldn't hide out without a reason, would you?"

He was gentle from habit, but Rune did not recognize gentleness. He was being baited and he was helpless. He gave a brazen answer:

"I got shot trying to rob a sluice."

Doc, working rapidly, commented with amusement, "So now I'm harboring a criminal! And doing it for nothing, too. How did you figure on paying me, young fellow?"

The patient was too belligerent, needed to be taken down a peg.

"If I could pay you, I wouldn't have tackled the sluice, would I?" the boy demanded. "I wouldn't have waited so long to see you, would I?"

"You ask too damn many questions," Doc grunted. "Hold still. . . . Your wound will heal all right. But of course you'll starve first."

Sullen Rune made no answer.

Doc Frail surveyed him. "I can use a servant. A gentleman should have one. To black his boots and cook his meals—you can cook, I hope?—and swamp out the cabin."

Rune could not recognize kindness, could not believe it, could not accept it. But that the doctor should extract service for every cent of a debt not stated—that he could understand.

"For how long?" he bargained, growling.

Doc Frail could recognize what he thought was ingratitude.

"For just as long as I say," he snapped. "It may be a long time. It may be forever. If you bled to death, you'd be dead forever."

That was how they made the bargain. Rune got a home he needed but did not want to accept. Doc got a slave who alternately amused and annoyed him. He resolved not to let the kid go until he learned to act like a human being—or until Doc himself became too exasperated to endure him anymore. Rune would not ask for freedom, and Doc did not know when he would offer it.

There was one thing that Rune wanted from him: skill with a gun.

Doc's reputation as a marksman trailed from him like a tattered banner. Men walked wide of him and gave him courtesy.

But I won't lower myself by asking him to teach me, Rune kept promising himself. There were depths to which even a slave did not sink.

A letter came from Doc Frail the day after Rune returned to Skull Creek. It was brought by a horseback rider who came in from Station Three ahead of the stage.

Rune had never before in his life received a letter, but he took it as casually as if he had had a thousand. He turned it over and said, "Well, thanks," and turned away, unwilling to let the messenger know he was excited and puzzled.

"Ain't you going to read it?" the man demanded. "Doc said it was mighty important."

"I suppose you read it already?" Rune suggested.

The man sighed. "I can't read writing. Not that writing, anyhow. Print, now, I can make out with print, but not writing. Never had much schooling."

"He writes a bad hand," Rune agreed, mightily relieved. "Maybe the store man, he could make it out."

So there was no need to admit that he could not read, either. Even Flaunce, the storekeeper, had a little trouble, tracing with his finger, squinting over his glasses.

Doc had no suspicion that his servant could not read. He had never thought about the matter. If he had known, he might not have begun the letter, "White Sambo."

Hearing that, his slave reddened with shame and anger, but the store man merely commented, "Nickname, eh? 'White Sambo: Miss Elizabeth Armistead will arrive in Skull Creek in three or four days. She is still weak and blind. She must have shelter and care. I will provide the care, and the shelter will have to be in the cabin of the admirable and respectable Ma Fisher across the street from my own mansion.

"'Convey my regards to Mrs. Fisher and make all the necessary arrangements. Nothing will be required of Mrs. Fisher except a temporary home for Miss Armistead, who will of course pay for it.'"

The storekeeper and the messenger stared at Rune.

"I'm glad it ain't me that has to ask Ma Fisher a thing like that," the messenger remarked. "I'd as soon ask favors of a grizzly bear."

Flaunce was kinder. "I'll go with you, son. She wants a sack of flour anyhow, over to the restaurant. I'll kind of back you up—or pick up the pieces."

Ma Fisher served meals furiously in a tent restaurant to transients and miners who were tired of their own cooking in front of the wickiups along the gulch. She seldom had any hired help—too stingy and too hard to get along with, it was said. Her one luxury was her cabin, opposite Doc's, weather-tight and endurable even in cold weather. Most of the population, willing to live miserably today in the hope of a golden tomorrow, housed itself in shacks or lean-to's or caves dug into the earth, eked out with poles and rocks and sods.

Ma Fisher fumed a little when she was informed that the lost lady would be her guest, but she was flattered, and besides she was curious.

"I won't have time to wait on her, I want that understood," she warned. "And I won't stand for no foolishness, either."

"She's too sick for foolishness, I'd say," the storekeeper said soothingly. "Hasn't got her sight back yet. She mighty near died out there, you know."

"Well," Ma Fisher agreed without enthusiasm. "Well."

The first words Elizabeth Armistead spoke in the stage station were, faintly, "Where is Papa?"

"Your father is dead," Doc Frail answered gently. "He was shot during the holdup."

Why didn't she know that? She had seen it happen.

She answered with a sigh: "No." It was not an exclamation of shock or grief. It was a soft correction. She refused to believe, that was all.

"They buried him there by the road, along with the driver," Doc Frail said.

She said again, with more determination, "No!" And after a pause she pleaded, "Where is Papa?"

"He is dead," Doc repeated. "I am sorry to tell you this, Miss Armistead."

He might as well not have told her. She did not accept it.

She waited patiently in darkness for someone to give a reasonable explanation for her father's absence. She did not speak again for several hours because of her weakness and because of her swollen, broken lips.

Doc wished he could give her the comfort of a sponge bath, but he did not dare offend her by offering to do so himself, and she was not strong enough to move her arms. She lay limp, sometimes sleeping.

When he judged that the girl could better bear the trip to Skull Creek in a wagon than she could stand the stage station any longer, he explained that she would stay at Mrs. Fisher's—a very respectable woman, she would be perfectly safe there—until she could make plans for going back East.

"Thank you," the lost lady answered. "And Papa is in Skull Creek waiting?"

Doc frowned. The patient was beginning to worry him. "Your father is dead, you know. He was shot in the holdup."

She did not answer that.

"I will try again to comb your hair," Doc offered. "Tomorrow you can wash, if you want to try it. There will be a blanket over the window, and one over the door, and I will be outside to make sure no one tries to come in."

Her trunk was there, brought from the wrecked coach. He searched out clean clothes that she could put on, and carefully he combed her long, dark, curling hair. He braided it, not very neatly, and wound the two thick braids up over her head.

IV

The wagon was slow, but Doc Frail preferred it for his patient; she could ride easier than in the coach. He ordered the wagon bed well padded with hay, and she leaned back against hay covered with blankets. He had a canvas shade rigged to protect her from the sun. The stage-line superintendent himself was the driver—mightily relieved to be getting this woman to Skull Creek where she would be no more concern of his.

Doc Frail had not looked ahead far enough to expect the escort that accompanied them the last mile of the journey. He sat with the lost lady in the wagon bed, glaring at the curious, silent miners who came walking or riding or who stood waiting by the road.

None of them spoke, and there was no jostling. They only stared, seeing the lady in a blue dress, with a white cloth over her eyes. From time to time, the men nearest the wagon fell back to let the others have their turn.

Once, Doc got a glimpse of the boy, Rune, lanky and awkward, walking and staring with the rest. Doc scowled, and the boy looked away.

For a while, the doctor closed his eyes and knew how it must be for the girl who could hear but could not see. The creak of the wagon, the sound of the horses' hoofs—too many horses; she must know they were accompanied. The soft sound of many men's feet walking. Even the restless sound of their breathing.

The lady did not ask questions. She could not hide. Her hands were clasped tightly together in her lap.

"We have an escort," Doc murmured. "An escort of honor. They are glad to see that you are safe and well."

She murmured a response.

At the top of the hill, where the road dipped down to the camp, they lost their escort. The riders and the walkers stepped aside and did not follow. Doc Frail glanced up as the wagon passed under the great, out-thrust bough of the gnarled tree and felt a chill tingle the skin along his spine.

Well, the fellow deserved the hanging he would get. Doc regretted, however, that the mob that would be coming in from the north would have to pass Ma Fisher's cabin to reach the hanging tree. He hoped they would pass in decent silence. But he knew they would not.

Rune waited near the tree with the other men, torn between wanting to help the lost lady into the cabin and wanting to see the road agent hang. Whichever thing he did, he would regret not having done the other. He looked up at the great bough, shivered, and decided to stay on the hill.

He could see Doc and the stage superintendent help Miss Armistead down from the wagon. As they took her into Ma Fisher's cabin, he could see something else: dust in the distance.

A man behind him said, "They're bringing him in."

Rune had two good looks at the road agent before he died and one brief, sickening glance afterward. The angry miners were divided among themselves about hanging the fellow. The men who had pursued him, caught him, and whipped him until his back was bloody were satisfied and tired. Four of them even tried to defend him, standing with rifles cocked, shouting, "Back! Get back! He's had enough."

He could not stand; men pulled him off his horse and held him up as his body dropped and his knees sagged.

But part of the crowd roared, "Hang him! Hang him!" and shoved on. The mob was in three parts—those for hanging, those against it, and those who had not made up their minds.

Rune glimpsed him again through the milling miners beneath the tree. The posse men had been pushed away from him, their guns unfired, and men who had not pursued him were bringing in a rope.

The black-bearded giant, Frenchy Plante, tied the noose and yanked the road agent to his feet. Frenchy's roar came over the rumbling of the mob: "It's his fault the lost lady pridnear died! Don't forget that, boys!"

That was all they needed. Order came out of chaos. Fifty men seized the rope and at Frenchy's signal "Pull!" jerked the drooping, bloody-backed road agent off the ground. Rune saw him then for the third time, dangling.

A man beside him said knowingly, "That's the most humane way, really —pull him up all standing."

"How do you know?" Rune sneered. "You ever get killed that way?"

With the other men, he walked slowly down the hill. He waited in Doc's cabin until Doc came in.

"You had to watch," Doc said. "You had to see a man die."

"I saw it," Rune growled.

"And the lost lady might as well have. She might as well have been looking, because Ma Fisher kindly told her what the noise was about. And was offended, mind you, when I tried to shut her up!"

Doc unbuckled his gun belt and tossed it on his cot.

"You're going to wait on Miss Armistead," he announced. "I told her you would do her errands, anything that will make her a little easier. Do you hear me, boy? She keeps asking for her father. She keeps saying, 'Where is Papa?' "

Rune stared. "Didn't you tell her he's dead?"

"Certainly I told her! She doesn't believe it. She doesn't remember the holdup or the team running away. All she can remember is that something happened so the coach stopped, and then she was lost, running somewhere, and after a long time a man gave her a drink of water and took the canteen away again."

"Did she say where she's going when she gets her sight back?" Rune asked.

Doc let out a gusty breath. "She has no place to go. She says she can't go back because she has to wait for Papa. He was going to start a school here, and she was going to keep house for him. She has no place to go, but she can't stay alone in Skull Creek. It's unthinkable."

Ma Fisher came flying over to get Doc.

"The girl's crying and it'll be bad for her eyes," she said.

Doc asked coolly, "And why is she crying?"

"I'm sure I don't know," Ma answered, obviously injured. "I wasn't even talking to her. She started to sob, and when I asked her what was the matter, she said, 'Papa must be dead, or he would have been waiting here to meet me.' "

"Progress," Doc growled. "We're making progress." He went out and left Ma Fisher to follow if she cared to do so.

Doc was up before daylight next morning.

"When Ma Fisher leaves that cabin," Doc told Rune, when he woke him, "you're going to be waiting outside the door. If the lady wants you inside for conversation, you will go in and be as decently sociable as possible. If she wants to be alone, you will stay outside. Is that all perfectly clear?"

It was as clear as it was hateful. Rune would have taken delight in being the lady's protector if he had had any choice. (And Doc would, too, except that he wanted to protect her reputation. It wouldn't look good for him to be in the cabin with her except on brief professional visits.)

"Nursemaid," Rune muttered sourly.

Ma Fisher scowled when she found him waiting outside her door, but Miss Armistead said she would be glad of his company.

The lost lady was timid, helpless, but gently friendly, sitting in the darkened cabin, groping now and then for the canteen that had been Frenchy's.

Rune asked, "You want a cup to drink out of?" and she smiled faintly.

"I guess it's silly," she answered, "but water tastes better from this canteen."

Rune kept silent, not knowing how to answer.

"Doctor Frail told me your first name," the lost lady said, "but not your last."

"Rune is all," he answered. He had made it up, wanting to be a man of mystery.

"But everybody has two names," she chided gently. "You must have another."

She was indeed ignorant of frontier custom or she would not make an issue of a man's name. Realizing that, he felt infinitely superior and therefore could be courteous.

"I made it up, ma'am," he told her. "There's lots of men here go by names they wasn't born with. It ain't a good idea to ask questions about folks' names." Then, concerned lest he might have offended her, he struggled on to make conversation:

"There's a song about it. 'What was your name in the States? Was it Johnson or Olson or Bates?' Goes that way, sort of."

The lady said, "Oh, my goodness. Doctor Frail didn't make up his name, I'm sure of that. Because a man wouldn't take a name like that, would he?"

"A man like Doc might," Rune decided. The idea interested him. "Doc is a sarcastic fellow."

"Never to me," Miss Armistead contradicted softly. "He is the soul of kindness! Why, he even realized that I might wish for someone to talk to. And you are kind, too, Rune, because you came."

To get her off that subject, Rune asked, "Was there any errands you'd want done or anything?"

"Doctor Frail said he would send my meals in, but I am already so much obligated to him that I'd rather not. Could you cook for me, Rune, until I can see to do it myself?"

"Sure," he agreed. "But I cook for Doc anyhow. Just as easy to bring it across the street."

"No, I'd rather pay for my own provisions." She was firm about that, with the pathetic stubbornness of a woman who for the first time must make decisions and stick to them even if they are wrong.

"I have money," she insisted. "I can't tell what denomination the bills are, of course. But you can tell me."

Poor, silly lady, to trust a stranger so! But Rune honestly identified the bills she held out.

"Take the five dollars," she requested, "and buy me whatever you think would be nice to eat. That much money should last for several days, shouldn't it?"

Rune swallowed a protest and murmured, "Kind of depends on what you want. I'll see what they got at Flaunce's." He backed toward the door.

"I must be very businesslike," Miss Armistead said with determination. "I have no place to go, you know, so I must earn a living. I shall start a school here in Skull Creek."

Arguing about that was for Doc, not for his slave. Rune did not try.

"Doc's going in his cabin now," he reported, and fled across the street for instructions.

The storekeeper's inquisitive wife got in just ahead of him, and he found Doc explaining, "The lady is still too weak for the strain of entertaining callers, Mrs. Flaunce. The boy here is acting as amateur nurse, because she needs someone with her—she can't see, you know. But it would not be wise for anyone to visit her yet."

"I see," Mrs. Flaunce said with cold dignity. "Yes, I understand perfectly." She went out with her head high, not glancing at the cabin across the street.

Doc thus cut the lost lady off from all decent female companionship. The obvious conclusion to be drawn—which Mrs. Flaunce passed on to the other respectable women of the camp—was that the doctor was keeping the mysterious Miss Armistead. Ma Fisher's stern respectability was not enough to protect her, because Ma herself was strange. She chose to earn her living in a community where no sensible woman would stay if she wasn't married to a man who required it.

When Mrs. Flaunce was gone, Rune held out the greenback.

"She wants me to buy provisions with that. Enough for several days, she says."

Doc's eyebrows went up. "She does, eh? With five dollars? Why, that'd buy her three cans of fruit, wouldn't it? And how much is Flaunce getting for sugar, say?"

"Dollar a pound."

Doc scowled thoughtfully. "This is a delicate situation. We don't know how well fixed she is, but she doesn't know anything about the cost of grub in Skull Creek. And I don't want her to find out. Understand?"

Rune nodded. For once, he was in agreement with his master.

Doc reached into his coat pocket and brought out a leather poke of dust.

"Put that on deposit to her account at the store," he ordered.

"Lady coming in on the stage wouldn't have gold in a poke, would she?" Rune warned.

Doc said with approval, "Sometimes you sound real smart. Take it to the bank, get currency for it, and take the currency to Flaunce's. And just pray that Ma Fisher doesn't take a notion to talk about the price of grub. Let the lady keep her stake to use getting out of here as soon as she's able."

A week passed before he realized that Elizabeth Armistead could not leave Skull Creek.

V

Elizabeth could find her way around the cabin, groping, stepping carefully so as not to fall over anything. She circled sometimes for exercise and to pass the long, dark time and because she did not feel strong enough to think about important matters.

The center of her safe, circumscribed world was the sagging double bed where she rested and the table beside it, on which was the water bucket. She still clung to Frenchy Plante's canteen and kept it beside her pillow but only when she was alone so that no one would guess her foolish fear about thirst. But every few minutes she fumbled for the dipper in the bucket. She was dependent on strangers for everything, of course, but most important of them was Rune, who filled the water bucket at the creek that he said was not far outside the back door.

She had explored the cabin until she knew it well, but its smallness and scanty furnishings still shocked her. Papa's house back East had had nine rooms, and until his money began to melt away, there had been a maid as well as a cook.

She moved cautiously from the table a few steps to the front door—rough planks with a strong wooden bar to lock it from the inside; around the wall to a bench that Rune had placed so she would not hurt herself on the tiny stove; then to the back door.

But the need for decision gnawed at her mind and made her head ache.

"You must go back East just as soon as you can travel," Doctor Frail had said—how many times?

But how could she travel again when she remembered the Dry Flats that had to be crossed? How could she go without Papa, who was dead, they kept telling her?

The cabin was uncomfortably warm, but she could not sit outside the back door, where there was grass, unless Rune was there. And she must not open the door unless she knew for sure who was outside.

She could not go back East yet, no matter what they said. To stay in Skull Creek was, of course, an imposition on these kind people, but everything would work out all right after a while—except for Papa, who they said was dead.

She remembered what Papa had said when his investments were dwindling.

"We do what we must," he had told her with his gentle smile when he made the hard decision to go West. And so his daughter would do what she must.

I must find a place for the school, she reminded herself. Perhaps Mrs. Fisher will let me use this cabin. I must offer her pay, of course, very tactfully so she will not be offended.

It was a relief to keep her mind busy in the frightening darkness, safe in the cabin with an unknown, raucous settlement of noisy men just outside the door. There were women, too; she could hear their laughter and screaming sometimes from the saloon down the street. But ladies did not think about those women except to pity them.

They were very strange, these people who were looking after her—Doc, who sounded strained and cross; Rune, whose voice was sullen and doubtful; Mrs. Fisher, who talked very little and came to the cabin only to groan into bed. Elizabeth was a little afraid of all of them, but she reminded herself that they were really very kind.

There was cautious knocking on the door, and she called out, "Yes?" and turned. Suddenly she was lost in the room, not sure of the position of the door. Surely the knocking was at the back? And why should any of them come that way, where the little grassy plot went only down to the creek?

She stumbled against a bench, groping. The knocking sounded again as she reached the door. But she was cautious. "Who is it?" she called, with her hand on the bar.

A man's voice said, "Lady! Lady, just let me in."

Elizabeth stopped breathing. The voice was not Doc Frail's nor Rune's. But it was cordial, enticing: "Lady, you ever seen a poke of nuggets? I got a poke of gold right here. Lady, let me in."

She trembled and sank down on the floor in her darkness, cowering. The voice coaxed, "Lady? Lady?"

She did not dare to answer. She did not dare to cry. After a long time the pounding and the coaxing stopped.

She could not escape any more by planning for the school. She was remembering the long horror of thirst, and the noise the mob had made, going past to hang a man on a tree at the top of the hill. She hid her burned face in her trembling hands, crouching by the barred door, until a familiar and welcome voice called from another direction, "It's me. Rune."

She groped to the front door, reached for the bar. But was the voice familiar and therefore welcome? Or was this another importunate, lying stranger? With her hand on the unseen wooden bar, she froze, listening, until he called again. His voice sounded concerned: "Miss Armistead, are you all right in there?"

This was Rune. She could open the door. He was not offering a poke of nuggets, he was only worried about her welfare.

"I was frightened," she said as she opened the door.

"You're safer that way in Skull Creek," he said. "Anything you want done right now?"

"You are so kind," she said gently. "No, there is nothing. I have plenty of drinking water in the bucket. Oh—if you go to the store, perhaps there would be some potatoes and eggs?"

After a pause he said, "I'll ask 'em." (A month ago there had been a shipment of eggs; Doc had mentioned it. There had not been a potato in camp since Rune came there.)

"Doc says to tell you you'll have your unveiling this evening, get your eyes open. I got to go find him now, give him a message from the Crocodile."

"The—what?"

"Ma Fisher, I mean." She could hear amusement in his voice.

"Why, it's not nice to speak of her so. She is very kind to me, letting me share her home!"

There was another pause. He said, "Glad to hear it," and "I'll go find Doc now. He went to get a haircut."

Doc's haircut was important. He went often to the barbershop for a bath, because he could afford to be clean, but never before in Skull Creek had he let scissors touch his hair, hanging in glossy waves below his shoulders.

A miner might let his hair and whiskers grow, bushy and matted, but Doc Frail was different. His long hair was no accident, and it was clean. He wore it long as a challenge, a quiet swagger, as if to tell the camp, "You may make remarks about this if you want trouble." Nobody did in his presence.

Except the barber, who laughed and said, "I been wantin' to put scissors to that, Doc. You gettin' all fixed up for the lost lady to take a good look?"

Doc had dignity even in a barber's chair. "Shut up and tend to business," he advised. There was no more conversation even when the barber handed him a mirror.

Rune had too much sense to mention the reformation. The tall boy glanced at him, smiled tightly, and reported, "Ma Fisher wants to see you. She's tired of having the lost lady underfoot."

Doc snorted. "Ma has no weariness or distaste that a poke of dust won't soothe." He turned away, but Rune was not through talking.

"Can I come when you take the bandage off her eyes?"

"No. Yes. What do I care?" Doc strode away, trying to put his spirits into a suitably humble mood to talk business with Ma Fisher.

The girl was a disturbing influence for him, for Rune, for the whole buzzing camp. She must get out in a few days, but she must not be made any more miserable than she already was.

He did not wait for Ma Fisher to attack, from her side of the dirty wooden counter in her tent restaurant. He spoke first: "You would no doubt like to be paid for Miss Armistead's lodging. I will pay you. I don't want you to get the idea that I'm keeping her. My reason for wishing to pay is that I want her to keep thinking the world is kind and that you have welcomed her."

Ma Fisher shrugged. "You can afford it. It's an inconvenience to me to have her underfoot."

Doc put a poke on the counter. "You can heft that if you want to. That's dust you'll get for not letting her know she's unwelcome. You'll get it when she leaves, in a week or so."

Ma lifted the leather sack with an expert touch. "All right."

Doc swept it back again. "One compliment before I leave you, Mrs. Fisher: you're no hypocrite."

"Two-faced, you mean? One face like this is all a woman can stand." She cackled at her own wit. "Just the same, I'd like to know why you're willing to pay good clean dust to keep the girl from finding out the world is cruel."

"I wish I knew myself," he answered.

I'll take off the dressings now, he decided, and let her get a glimpse of daylight, let her see what she's eating for a change.

He crossed the street and knocked, calling, "Doc Frail here." Rune opened the door.

Elizabeth turned her face toward him. "Doctor? Now will you let me see again? I thought if you could take the dressings off now, you and Rune might be my guests for supper."

You and Rune. The leading citizen and the unsuccessful thief.

"I'll be honored," Doc replied. "And I suppose Rune realizes that it is an honor for him."

He removed the last dressings from her eyes and daubed the closed lids with liquid.

"Blink," he ordered. "Again. Now try opening them."

She saw him as a blurred face, close up, without distinguishing characteristics. The one who protected in the darkness, the one who had promised to bring light. The only dependable creature in the world. There was light again, she had regained her sight. She must trust him, and she could. He had not failed her in anything.

But he was a stranger in a world of terror and strangers. He was too young. A doctor should be old, with a gray chin beard.

"Hurts a little?" he said. "You can look around now."

He stepped aside and she was lost without him. She saw someone else, tall in the dimness; that was Rune, and he was important in her life. She tried to smile at him, but she could not tell whether he smiled back.

Doc said, "Don't look in a mirror yet. When your face is all healed, you will be a pretty girl again. Don't worry about it."

Unsmiling, she answered, "I have other things to concern me."

Elizabeth tried to make conversation as they ate the supper Rune had cooked. But now that she could see them dimly, they were strangers and she was lost and afraid.

"It's like being let out of jail, to see again," she offered. "At least I suppose it is. When may I go outside to see what the town is like?"

"There is no town, only a rough camp," Doc told her. "It's not worth looking at, but you may see it tomorrow. After sunset, when the light won't hurt your eyes."

The following day, after supper, when she heard knocking on the front door, she ran to answer. Dr. Frail had changed his mind about waiting until later, she assumed. He must have come back sooner than he had expected from a professional call several miles away.

She swung the door wide—and looked up through a blur into the black-bearded, grinning face of a stranger. Then she could not shut it again. A lady could not do a thing so rude as that.

The man swept off his ragged hat and bowed awkwardly. "Frenchy Plante, ma'am. You ain't never seen me, but we sure enough met before. Out on the Dry Flats."

"Oh," she said faintly. He looked unkempt and she could smell whiskey. But he had saved her life. "Please come in," she said, because there was no choice. She hoped he did not notice that she left the door open. With this man in the cabin, she wanted no privacy.

He remembered to keep his hat in his hand but he sat down without waiting to be invited.

"Figure on doing a little prospecting, ma'am," he said jovially. "So I just dropped in to say good-by and see how you're making out."

Frenchy was well pleased with himself. He was wearing a clean red shirt, washed though not pressed, and he had combed his hair, wanting to make a good impression on the lost lady.

"I have so much to thank you for," Elizabeth said earnestly. "I am so very grateful."

He waved one hand. "It's nothing, lady. Somebody would of found you." Realizing that this detracted from his glory, he added, "But of course it might have been too late. You sure look different from the first time I seen you!"

Her hands went up to her face. "Doctor Frail says there won't be any scars. I wish I could offer you some refreshment, Mr. Plante. If you would care to wait until I build up the fire to make tea?"

Doc Frail remarked from the doorway, "Frenchy would miss his afternoon tea, I'm sure."

There were a few men in the camp who were not afraid of Doc Frail—the upright men, the leading citizens, and Frenchy Plante.

Frenchy had the effrontery to suggest, "Come on in, Doc," but the wisdom to add, "Guess I can't stay, ma'am. Going prospecting, like I told you."

Doc Frail stood aside so as not to bar his progress in leaving. "I thought your claim was paying fairly well."

Frenchy made an expansive gesture. "Sold it this morning. I want something richer."

Elizabeth said, "I hope you'll find a million dollars, Mr. Plante."

"With a pretty lady like you on my side, I can't fail, can I?" replied the giant, departing.

Elizabeth put on her bonnet. With her foot on the threshold, she murmured, "Everyone is so kind." She took Doc's arm as he offered it.

"To the left," he said. "The rougher part of the camp is to the right. You must never go that way. But this is the way you will go to the hotel, where the stage stops. Next week you will be able to leave Skull Creek."

She did not seem to hear him. She trembled. She was staring with aching eyes at the rutted road that led past Flaunce's store and the livery stable, the road that took a sudden sweep upward toward a cottonwood tree with one great out-thrust bough.

"You are perfectly safe," Doc reminded her. "We will not go far this time. Only past the store."

"No!" she moaned. "Oh, no!" and tried to turn back.

"Now what?" Doc demanded. "There is nothing here to hurt you."

But up there where she had to go sometime was the hanging tree, and beyond was the desert. Back all that distance, back all alone—a safe, quiet place was what she must have now, at once.

Not here in the glaring sun with the men staring and the world so wide that no matter which way she turned she was lost, she was thirsty, burning, dying.

But there must be some way out, somewhere safe, the cool darkness of a cabin, if she could only run in the right direction and not give up too soon—

But someone tried to keep her there in the unendurable sun glare with the thirst and endless dizzying space—someone held her arms and said her name urgently from far away as she struggled.

She jerked away with all her strength because she knew the needs of her own anguished body and desperate spirit—she had to be free, she had to be able to hide.

And where was Papa, while this strange and angry man carried her back to the cabin that was a refuge from which she would not venture forth again?

And who was this angry boy who shouted, "Doc, if you've hurt her, I'll kill you!"

When she was through with her frantic crying and was quiet and ashamed, she was afraid of Doc Frail, who gripped her wrists as she lay on Ma Fisher's bed.

"What was it, Elizabeth?" he demanded. "Nothing is going to hurt you. What did you think you saw out there?"

"The Dry Flats," she whispered, knowing he would not believe it. "The glaring sun on the Dry Flats. And I was lost again and thirsty."

"It's thirty miles to the Dry Flats," he told her brusquely. "And the sun went down an hour ago. It's getting dark here in the gulch."

She shuddered.

"I'll give you something to make you sleep," he offered.

"I want Papa," she replied, beginning to cry again.

Back in his own cabin, Doc walked back and forth, back and forth across the rough floor boards, with Rune glaring at him from a corner.

Doc Frail was trying to remember a word and a mystery. Someone in France had reported something like this years ago. What was the word, and what could you do for the suffering patient?

He had three books in his private medical library, but they treated of physical ailments, not wounds of the mind. He could write to Philadelphia for advice, but—he calculated the weeks required for a letter to go East and a reply to come back to Skull Creek.

"Even if they know," he said angrily, "we'll be snowed in here before the answer comes. And maybe nobody knows, except in France, and he's probably dead now, whoever he was."

Rune spoke cuttingly. "You had to be in such a hurry to make her start back home!"

Doc said, "Shut your mouth."

What was the word for the mystery? Elizabeth remembered nothing about the runaway of the coach horses, nothing about the holdup that preceded it, only the horror that followed.

"Hysteria?" he said. "Is that the word? Hysteria? But if it is, what can you do for the patient?"

The lost lady would have to try again. She would have to cross the imaginary desert as well as the real one.

VI

I will not try to go out for a few days, Elizabeth told herself, comforted by the thought that nobody would expect her to try again after what had happened on her first attempt.

The desert was not outside the cabin, of course. It was only a dreadful illusion. She realized that, because she could look out and see that the street was in a ravine. Nothing like the Dry Flats.

Next time, she assured herself, it will be all right. I will not look up toward the tree where they—no, I will simply not think about the tree at all, nor about the Dry Flats. Other people go out by stage and nothing happens to them. But I can't go right away.

Doctor Frail did not understand at all. He came over the next morning, implacable and stern.

"I have a patient to see down at the diggings," he said, "but he can wait half an hour. First you will walk with me as far as Flaunce's store."

"Oh, I couldn't," she answered with gentle firmness. "In a few days, but not now. I'm not strong enough."

He put his hat on the table and sat on one of the two benches.

"You will go now, Elizabeth. You have got to do it now. I am going to sit here until you are ready to start."

She stared at him in hurt surprise. Of course he was a doctor, and he could be expected to be always right. He was a determined man, and strength came from him. It was good, really, not to make a decision but to have him make it, even though carrying it out would be painful. Like the time Papa made her go to a dentist to have a tooth pulled.

"Very well," she replied with dignity. She put her bonnet on, not caring that there was no mirror.

"You are only going for a walk to the store," he told her, offering his arm at the door. "You will want to tell your friends back home what a store in a gold camp is like. You will have a great many things to tell your friends."

She managed a laugh as she walked with her eyes down, feeling the men staring.

"They would not believe the things I could tell them," she agreed.

The sun was not yet high over the gulch and the morning was not warm but she was burning and thirsty and could not see anything for the glare and could not breathe because she had been running, but he would not let her fall. He was speaking rapidly and urgently, telling her she must go on. He was not Papa because Papa was never angry; Papa would never have let her be afraid and alone in the glare and thirsty and going to die here, now, if he would only let her give up and fall. . . .

She was lying down—where? On the bed in the cabin? And turning her head away from something, the sharp odor of something the doctor held under her nose to revive her.

The men had seen her fall, then, the staring men of Skull Creek, and she had fainted, and they must think she was insane and maybe she was.

She was screaming and Doc Frail was slapping her cheek, saying, "Elizabeth! Stop that!"

Then she was crying with relief, because surely now nobody would make her go out again until she was ready. The doctor was angry, a cruel man, a hateful stranger. Angry at a helpless girl who needed only to be let alone until she was stronger!

She said with tearful dignity, "Please go away."

He was sarcastic, too. He answered, "I do have other patients," and she heard the door close.

But she could not lie there and cry as she wanted to do, because she had to bar the door to keep out fear.

At noontime she was calmer and built a fire in the little stove and brewed some tea to eat with a cold biscuit of the kind Rune called bannock. Nobody came, and in the afternoon she slept for a while, exhausted, but restless because there was a great deal of racket from down the gulch.

Rune leaned against a building with his thumbs in his belt, watching two drunk miners trying to harness a mule that didn't want to be harnessed. Rune was amused, glad to have something to think about besides Doc Frail's cruelty to the lost lady.

"Leave her strictly alone till I tell you otherwise," Doc had commanded.

Rune was willing, for the time being. She had cold grub in the cabin and the water bucket was full. He didn't want to embarrass her by going there anyway. He had seen her stumble and struggle and fall. He had watched, from Doc's shack, as Doc carried her back to the cabin, had waited to be called and had been ignored.

The plunging mule kicked one of the miners over backward into the dust, while a scattering of grinning men gathered and cheered.

The other drunk man had a long stick, and as he struck out with it, the mule went bucking, tangled in the harness. A man standing beside Rune commented with awe and delight, "Right toward Ma Fisher's restaurant! Now I'd admire to see that mule tangle with her!"

He shouted, and Rune roared with him. A roar went up from all the onlookers as the far side of Ma Fisher's tent went down and Ma came running out on the near side, screaming. The mule emerged a few seconds behind her, but the drunk miner was still under the collapsed, smoke-stained canvas.

There was a frenzied yell of "Fire!" even before Rune saw the smoke curl up and ran to the nearest saloon to grab a bucket.

They kept the flames from spreading to any buildings, although the lean-to behind the tent was badly charred and most of the canvas burned.

Ma Fisher was not in sight by the time they got the fire out. Rune slouched away, grinning.

Ma Fisher made only one stop on the way from her ruined restaurant to the cabin. She beat with her fist on the locked door of the bank until Mr. Evans opened it a few inches and peered cautiously out.

"I want to withdraw all I've got on deposit," she demanded. "I'm going to my daughter's in Idaho."

He unfastened the chain on the inside and swung the door open.

"Leaving us, Mrs. Fisher?"

"Sink of iniquity," she growled. "Of course I'm leaving. They've burned my tent and ruined my stove, and now they can starve for all I care. I want to take out every dollar.

"But you needn't think I want to carry it with me on the stage," she warned. "I just want to make the arrangements now. Transfer it or whatever you do, so's I can draw on it in Idaho."

"Will you need some for travel expenses?" the banker asked, opening his ledger.

"I've got enough dust on hand for that. Just let me sign the papers and get started."

Rune, lounging in Doc's doorway, saw Ma Fisher jerk at her own door handle and then beat angrily with her fist, yelling, "Girl, you let me in! It's Ma Fisher."

She slammed the door behind her, and Rune grinned. He worried a little though, wondering how her anger would affect the gentle Miss Armistead. But he had his orders not to go over there. His own opinion was that the lost lady was being mighty stubborn, and maybe Doc Frail was right in prescribing the let-alone treatment till she got sensible.

Elizabeth listened with horror to Ma Fisher's description of the wrecking of her restaurant. Ma paced back and forth across the floor and she spat out the news.

"How dreadful!" Elizabeth sympathized. "What can I do to help you?"

Ma Fisher stopped pacing and stared at her. It was a long time since anyone had offered sympathy. Having had little of it from anyone else, she had none to give.

"I don't need nothing done for me," she growled. "I'm one to look after myself. Oh, laws, the cabin. I've got to sell this cabin."

"But then you'll have no place to live!" Elizabeth cried out.

"I'm going to Idaho. But I got to get my investment out of the cabin. You'll have to leave, Miss. I'm going tomorrow on the stage."

She was pacing again, not looking to see how Elizabeth was affected by the news, not caring, either.

"Man offered me five hundred dollars in clean dust for it not long ago, but I turned it down. Had to have a place to live, didn't I? Now who was that? Well, it won't be hard to find a buyer. . . . You've got your things all over the place. You better start packing. Could come on the same stage with me if you're a mind to."

Out into the open, away from refuge? Out across the Dry Flats—and before that, under the hanging tree? When she could not even go as far as Flaunce's store!

There was no one to help her, no one who cared what became of her. The doctor was angry, the boy Rune had deserted her, and this hag, this witch, thought only of her own interests. Papa had said, "We do what we must."

"I will give you five hundred dollars for the cabin," Elizabeth said coolly.

Doc Frail did not learn of the transaction until noon the next day. He had been called to a gulch ten miles away to care for a man who was beyond help, dying of a self-inflicted gunshot wound. Crippled with rheumatism, the man had pulled the trigger of his rifle with his foot.

Doc rode up to his own door and yelled, "Rune! Take care of my horse."

Rune came around from the back with the wood-chopping axe in his hand.

"Hell's broke loose," he reported. "Old lady Fisher left on the stage this morning, and the girl must be still in the cabin, because she didn't go when Ma did."

Doc sighed.

"Fellow that came by said she's bought Ma's cabin," Rune said, watching to see how Doc Frail would take that news.

Doc disappointed him by answering, "I don't care what she did," and went into his own building.

But while Rune was taking the mare to the livery stable, Doc decided he did care. He cared enough to cross the road in long strides and pound on the door, shouting, "Elizabeth, let me in this instant."

She had been waiting for hours for him to come, to tell her she had done the right thing, the only thing possible.

But he said, "If what I hear is true, you're a fool. What are you going to do in Skull Creek?"

She stepped back before the gale of his anger. She drew herself up very straight.

"Why, I am going to start a school for the children," she replied. "I have been making plans for it all morning."

"You can't. You can't stay here," Doc insisted.

"But I must, until I am stronger."

Doc glared. "You'd better get stronger in a hurry then. You've got to get out of this camp. You can start by walking up to the store. And I'll go with you. Right now."

Elizabeth was angry too. "I thank you for your courtesy," she said. "I must look out for myself now, of course." Looking straight into his eyes, she added, "I will pay your fee now if you will tell me what I owe."

Doc flinched as if she had struck him.

"There is no charge, madam. Call on me at any time."

He bowed and strode out.

He told Rune, "The order to leave her alone still stands," and told him nothing else.

Rune endured it for twenty-four hours. The door across the street did not open. There was no smoke from the chimney.

She's got just about nothing in the way of grub over there now, Rune fretted to himself. Ain't even building a fire to make a cup of tea.

But when Rune crossed the street, he did not go for pity. He had convinced himself that his only reason for visiting Elizabeth was that Doc had forbidden him to go there.

He knocked on the slab door but no answer came. He pounded harder, calling, "Miss Armistead!" There was no sound from within, but there was a waiting silence that made his skin crawl.

"It's Rune!" he shouted. "Let me in!"

A miner, passing by, grinned and remarked, "Good luck, boy. Introduce me sometime."

Rune said, "Shut your foul mouth," over his shoulder just as the door opened a crack.

Elizabeth said coolly, "What is it?" Then, with a quick-drawn breath like a sob, "Rune, come in, come in."

As she stepped away from the entrance, her skirt swung and he saw her right hand with a little derringer in it.

"The gun—where'd you get it?" he demanded.

"It was Papa's. They brought it to me with his things after—" Remembering that she must look after herself, not depending on anyone else, she stopped confiding. "Won't you sit down?" she invited formally.

"I just come to see—to see how everything is. Like if you needed something."

She shook her head, but her eyes flooded with tears. "Need something? Oh, no. I don't need a thing. Nobody can do anything for me!"

Then she was sobbing, sitting on a bench with her face hidden in her hands, and the little gun forgotten on the floor.

"Listen, you won't starve," he promised. "I'll bring your grub. But have you got money to live on?" He abased himself, admitting, "I ain't got anything. Doc don't pay me. If I had, I'd help you out."

"Oh, no. I will look after myself." She wiped her eyes and became very self-possessed. "Except that for a while I should appreciate it if you will go to the store for me. Until I am strong enough to walk so far by myself."

But Doc had said she was strong enough, and Doc Frail was no liar. Rune scowled at Elizabeth. He did not want to be bound to her by pity. It was bad enough to be bound to Doc by debt.

This tie, at least, he could cut loose before it became a serious burden.

"You got to get out of Skull Creek," he said harshly. "Unless you've got a lot of money."

"I have sufficient," she said.

Now she was playing the great lady, he thought. She was being elegant and scornful.

"Maybe where you come from, folks don't talk about such things," he burst out with bitterness. "It ain't nice, you think. Don't think I'm asking you how much you got. But you don't know nothing about prices here.

You ain't been paying full price for what you got, not by a long ways. You want to know?"

She was staring at him wide-eyed and shocked.

"Sugar's ninety cents a pound at Flaunce's," he told her. "It went down. Dried codfish—you're tired of it, I guess, and so's everybody—it's sixty cents. Dried apples—forty cents a pound last time they had any. Maybe you'd like a pound of tea? Two and a half, that costs you. Potatoes and eggs, there ain't been any in a long time. Fresh meat you can't get till another bunch of steers come in. Now how long will your money last you if you stay in Skull Creek?"

She had less than five hundred dollars left after buying the cabin. Stage fare—that was terribly high. She had never had to handle money, and only in the last year had she even had to be concerned about it, since Papa's affairs had gone so badly.

But she said coolly, "I have a substantial amount of money, thank you. And I am going to start a school. Now tell me, please, who paid for my supplies if I didn't?"

Rune gulped. "I can't tell you that."

"So it was Doctor Frail," Elizabeth said wearily. "I will pay him. Tell him that."

"He'd kill me," Rune said. "Remember, I never said it was him."

Between two dangers, the lesser one seemed to be telling Doc himself. He did so at the first opportunity.

Doc did not explode. He only sighed and remarked, "Now she hasn't even got her pride. How much money has she got to live on?"

"She didn't tell me. Won't tell you, either, I'll bet."

"And she thinks she can make a fortune teaching school!" Doc was thoughtful. "Maybe she can earn part of her living that way. How many children are there in camp, anyway?" He scrabbled for a sheet of paper and began writing the names of families, muttering to himself.

"Go to the livery stable," he said without looking up, "and get a string of bells. They've got some. Then figure out a way to hitch them over her door with a rope that she can pull from inside her cabin."

"What for?" Rune demanded.

"So she can signal for help next time somebody tries to break in," Doc explained with unusual patience.

And what will I do to protect her when the time comes? Doc Frail wondered. Look forbidding and let them see two guns holstered and ready? That will not always be enough.

The noted physician of Skull Creek can outshoot anyone within several hundred miles, but will he fire when the target is a man? Never again. Then his hand and his eye lose their cunning, and that is why Wonder Russell sleeps up on the hill. If I could not pull the trigger to save the life of my friend, how can I do it for Elizabeth? I must have a deputy.

Rune was on his way out when Doc asked, "Can you hit a target any better than you dodge bullets?"

Rune hesitated, torn between wanting to boast and wanting to be taught by a master. If he admitted he was no marksman, he was not a complete man. But a slave didn't have to be.

He answered humbly, "I never had much chance to try. Target practice costs money."

"Stop at the store and get a supply of ammunition," Doc ordered. "I'm going to give you the world's best chance to shoot me."

Rune shrugged and went out, admitting no excitement. He was going to have his chance to become the kind of man from whose path other men would quietly step aside.

Doc watched him go, thinking, Are you the one for whom I'll hang? Put a gun in your hand, and skill with it, and there's no telling. But your lessons start tomorrow.

"I wish the school didn't matter so much to her," Doc muttered. "I wish she wasn't so set on it."

He had made some calls early that morning and was back in his cabin, scowling across the street at Elizabeth's, with its door standing open to welcome the children of Skull Creek.

Her floor was scrubbed; the rough plank table was draped with an embroidered cloth, and her father's books were on it. She visualized the children: shy, adorable, anxious to learn. And their mothers: grateful for a school, full of admonitions about the little ones' welfare, but trusting the teacher.

Doc turned to Rune, saw the rifle across his knees.

"You planning to shoot the children when they come?" he demanded.

"Planning to shoot any miner that goes barging in there with her door open," Rune answered. "Because I don't think there's going to be any children coming to school."

Doc sighed. "I don't either. After all the notes she wrote their mothers, all the plans she made."

At eleven o'clock, they saw Elizabeth shut her door. No one had crossed the threshold.

Doc growled, "Bring my mare. I've got a patient up the gulch. Then go see about getting her dinner."

Rune muttered, "I'd rather be shot."

Elizabeth had the derringer in her hand, hidden in a fold of her skirt, when she unbarred the door. She did not look at him but simply stepped aside.

"I don't care for anything to eat," she said faintly.

"If you don't eat nothing, I don't either."

She sipped a cup of tea, but she set it down suddenly and began to cry. "Why didn't anybody come?" she wailed.

"Because they're fools," he told her sturdily.

But he knew why. He had guessed from the way the women acted when he delivered the notes. Elizabeth Armistead, the lost lady, was not respectable. She had come under strange circumstances, and the protection of Doc Frail was like a dark shadow upon her.

"I thought I would teach the children," she said hopelessly. "I thought it would be pleasant."

Rune drew a deep breath and offered her all he had—his ignorance and his pride.

"You can teach me," he said. "I ain't never learned to read."

The look of shock on her face did not hurt quite so much as he had supposed it would.

VII

Early cold came to Skull Creek, and early snow. Halfway through one gloomy, endless morning, someone knocked at Elizabeth's door, but she had learned caution. She called, "Who is it?"

A voice she did not know said something about books. When she unbarred the door, the derringer was in her hand, but she kept it decently hidden in the folds of her skirt.

He was a big man with a beard. He swept off a fur cap and was apologetic.

"I didn't mean to frighten you, ma'am. Please don't be afraid. I came to see if you would rent out some of your books."

Elizabeth blinked two or three times, considering the matter. "But one doesn't rent books!" she objected. "I have never heard of renting books. . . . It's cold, won't you come in so I can close the door?"

The man hesitated. "If you're sure you will let me come in, ma'am. I swear I'll do you no harm. It's only for books that I came. Some of the boys are about to go crazy for lack of reading matter. We drew straws, and I got the short one. To come and ask you."

It's my house, Elizabeth told herself. And surely no rascal would care for books.

This man happened not to be a rascal, though he acted so fidgety about being in there that Elizabeth wondered who he thought might be chasing him.

"They call me Tall John, ma'am," he said in introduction, cap in hand. "Any book would do, just about. We've worn out the newspapers from the States and we're tired of reading the labels on canned goods. And the winter's only just begun."

He paid five dollars apiece for the privilege of keeping three books for a month. (His listeners, when he read aloud in a hut of poles and earth, were a horse thief, a half-breed Arapaho Indian and the younger son of an English nobleman.)

Doc scolded Elizabeth for letting a stranger in, although he admitted that Tall John was a decent fellow.

"He was a perfect gentleman," she insisted. What bothered her was that she had accepted money for lending books.

Rune complained bitterly because his book supply was cut by three.

"Listen, boy," Doc said, "you can read like a house afire, but can you write? Your schooling isn't even well begun. Do you know arithmetic? If you sold me eight head of horses at seventy dollars a head, how much would I owe you?"

"I wouldn't trust nobody to owe me for 'em," Rune told him earnestly. "You'd pay cash on the barrel head, clean dust, or you wouldn't drive off no horses of mine."

But thereafter his daily lessons in Elizabeth's cabin included writing, spelling and arithmetic. When the only books she had left were readers through which he had already ploughed his impetuous way, he was reduced to sneaking a look at the three medical books in Doc's cabin—Doc's entire medical library.

When Rune boasted of how much he was learning in his classes at the lost lady's cabin, Doc listened and was pleased.

"Each week, you will take her a suitable amount of dust for tuition," Doc announced. "I will have to decide how much it's going to be."

"Dust? Where'm I going to get dust?" Rune was frantic; the only delight he had was being barred from him, as everything else was, by his poverty.

"From me, of course. I can properly pay for the education of my servant, surely?"

"The lady teaches me for nothing," Rune said in defense of his privilege. "She don't expect to get paid for it."

"She needs an income, and this will help a little." Doc felt lordly. He was doing a favor for both his charges, Rune and the pathetic girl across the street. "If you don't care to accept a favor from me," he told Rune, "you'd better get used to the idea." With a flash of insight, he explained, "It is necessary sometimes to let other people do something decent for you."

That is, he considered, it is necessary for everybody but me. And I have a sudden very excellent idea about the uses of gold.

He had an interest in several paying placer claims, which he visited often because the eye of the master fatteneth the cattle, and the eye of an experienced gold miner can make a shrewd guess about how many ounces there should be on the sluice riffles at the weekly cleanup. His various partners seldom tried to cheat him any more.

With the ground and the streams frozen, placer mining had come to a dead stop, but Dr. Frail's professional income had dwindled only a little, and there was so much dust to his credit with the bank that he had no financial problems anyway.

He strode up the street to visit Evans, the banker.

"Your dealings with your customers are strictly confidential, are they not?" he inquired.

"As confidential as yours," Evans replied stiffly.

"I want to make a withdrawal. The dust is to be put into leather pokes that can't be identified as the property of anyone around here. Old pokes, well worn."

"Very well," said Evans, as if it happened every day.

"Weigh it out in even pounds," Doc instructed, and Evans' eyebrows went up. "I want—oh, six of them. I'll be back for them this afternoon."

He sat with Elizabeth just before supper, drinking tea, listening to the sounds Rune made chopping firewood outside the back door. Rune had the bags of gold and orders to conceal them in the woodpile to be found accidentally.

"And remember, I know very well how much is in there," Doc had warned him. "I know how much she's supposed to find when she does find it."

Rune had glared at him in cold anger, replying, "Did you think I would steal from *her?*"

Tall John's shack burned when he built the fire too hot on a bitter cold day. The three men who shared it with him were away. He ran out, tried to smother the flames with snow, then ran back to save what he could, and the roof fell in on him.

When help came, he was shouting under the burning wreckage. His rescuers delivered him to Doc's office with a broken leg and serious burns on his shoulders and chest.

Doc grumbled, "You boys think I'm running a hospital?" and started to work on the patient.

"He's got no place to go; our wickiup burned," the horse thief apologized. "The rest of us, we can hole up someplace, but John can't hardly."

"He needs a roof over his head and conscientious nursing," Doc warned.

"I could sort of watch him," Rune suggested, wondering if they would sneer at the idea.

"Guess you'll have to," Doc agreed. "All right, he can have my bunk."

Then there was less company to help Elizabeth pass the time. Rune bought her supplies and carried in firewood, but he was always in a hurry. There were no more interesting evenings with Doc and Rune as her guests for supper, because Doc never stayed with her more than a few minutes.

Winter clamped down with teeth that did not let go. Elizabeth began to understand why Tall John had found it necessary to borrow books—she was reading her father's books over and over to pass the time. She began to understand, too, why a man of pride must pay for such borrowing.

She sewed and mended her own clothes until there was no more sewing to do. Doc commissioned her to make him a shirt and one for Rune. She finished them and was empty-handed again.

Then she peeled every sliver of bark from the logs that made her prison.

Rune came dutifully twice a day to bring supplies, and do her chores, but he no longer had lessons.

"Tall John's teaching me," he explained.

"And what are you studying?" she asked with some coolness.

"Latin. So I can figure out the big words in Doc's books."

"Now I wonder whether Papa brought his Latin grammar," she cried, running to look at the books she could not read.

"You ain't got one," Rune said. "I looked. We get along without. Sometimes we talk it."

"I didn't think anybody talked Latin," Elizabeth said doubtfully.

"Tall John can. He studied it in Rome. Told me where Rome is, too."

Elizabeth sighed. Her pupil had gone far beyond her.

She faced the bleak fact that nobody needed her at all any more. And Doc said there would be at least another month of winter.

"I don't want to impose on you, now that you're so busy," she told Rune with hurt dignity. "Hereafter I will bring in my own firewood and snow to melt for water. It will give me something to do."

"Don't hurt yourself," he cautioned. He didn't seem to see anything remarkable in her resolve to do hard physical labor. Elizabeth had never known any woman who carried water or cut wood. She felt like an adventurer when she undertook it.

Rune told Doc what she was planning, and Doc smiled.

"Good. Then you won't have to find what's in her woodpile. She can find it herself."

He visited her that evening, as he did once a day, briefly. She was a little sulky, he noticed, and he realized that she deserved an apology from him.

"I'm sorry not to spend more time in your company," he said abruptly. "There is no place I'd rather spend it. But for your own protection, to keep you from being talked about—do you understand why I'd rather not be here when Rune can't be here too?"

Elizabeth sniffed. "Have I any good name left to protect?"

The answer was No, but he would not say it.

"Rune says you're going to do your own chores," he remarked.

"Beginning tomorrow," she said proudly, expecting either a scolding or a compliment.

Doc disappointed her by saying heartily, "Good idea. You need some exercise."

Then he wondered why she was so unfriendly during the remainder of his visit.

Her venture into wood cutting lasted three days. Then, with a blister on one hand and a small axe cut in one shoe—harmless but frightening—she began to carry in wood that Rune had already chopped and piled earlier in the winter.

She was puzzled when she found a leather bag, very heavy for its size, and tightly tied. Unable to open the snow-wet drawstring with her mittened hands, she carried the bag into the house and teased the strings open with the point of a knife.

She glimpsed what was inside, ran to the shelf for a plate, and did not breathe again until the lovely yellow treasure was heaped upon it.

"Oh!" she said. "Oh, the pretty!" She ran her chilled fingers through the nuggets and the flakes that were like fish scales. "Maybe it belongs to

Ma Fisher," she said angrily to the emptiness of the cabin. "But I bought the place and it's mine now. And maybe there's more out there!"

She found them all, the six heavy little bags, and completely demolished the neat woodpile.

Then she ran to the rope of the warning bells and pulled it for the first time, pulled it again and again, laughing and crying, and was still pulling it when Rune came shouting.

She hugged him, although he had a cocked pistol in his hand. She did not even notice that.

"Look!" she screamed. "Look what I found in the woodpile!"

Doc came to admire, later in the day, and stayed for supper, but Elizabeth was too excited to eat—or to cook, for that matter. The table was crowded, because all the golden treasure was on display in plates or cups. She kept touching it lovingly, gasping with delight.

"Now you know," Doc guessed, "why men search for that. And why they kill for it."

"I know," she crooned. "Yes, I understand."

He leaned across the table. "Elizabeth, with all that for a stake, you needn't be afraid to go out next spring, go home."

She caressed a pile of yellow gold. "I suppose so," she answered, and he knew she was not convinced.

The woodpile was a symbol after that. She restored the scattered sticks to make a neat heap, but did not burn any of them. She went back to chopping wood each day for the fire.

She was hacking at a stubborn, knotty log one afternoon, her skirts soggy with snow, when a man's voice not far behind her startled her into dropping the axe.

He was on the far side of the frozen creek, an anonymous big man bundled up in a huge and shapeless coat of fur.

"It's me, Frenchy," he shouted jovially. "Looks like you're working too hard for a young lady!"

Elizabeth picked up the axe. When the man who once saved your life speaks to you, you must answer, she decided. Especially when you had nobody to talk to any more.

"I like to be in the fresh air," she called.

He waded through the snow. "Let me do that work for you, little lady."

Elizabeth clung to the axe, and he did not come too close.

"Sure having a cold spell," he commented. "Been a bad winter."

This is my own house, Elizabeth told herself. This man saved my life on the Dry Flats.

"Won't you come in and thaw out by the stove?" she suggested. "Perhaps you'd like a cup of tea."

Frenchy was obviously pleased. "Well, now, a day like this, a man can sure use something hot to drink."

Elizabeth felt guilty, ushering him into her cabin by the back way, as if trying to hide her doings from her guardians across the street. But he had come the back way, and not until later did it occur to her that his choice of routes had been because he wanted to avoid being seen.

He sat across the table from her, affable and sociable, waiting for the tea to steep. When his clothing got warmed, he smelled, but a lady could not tell a guest that he should go home and take a bath.

Frenchy had in mind to tell a fine big lie and perhaps to get himself a stake. The lost lady, he guessed, had brought lots of money with her. For her Rune bought the very best supplies available. She was strange, of course, about staying in her cabin all the time, and he had seen her almost fall down in a kind of struggling fit when she went outside. But she was very pretty, and she was nice to him. Doc Frail was her protector, but Frenchy had a strong suspicion that Doc Frail was frail indeed.

Frenchy went into his lie.

"Just can't hardly wait for a warm spell. I got the prettiest little claim you ever seen—colors galore. I'm going to be the rich Mr. Plante, sure enough. That is," he sighed, "if I can just keep eating till the ground thaws."

He blew politely into his tea to cool it.

"Yes, sir," mused Frenchy, "all I need is a grubstake. And whoever stakes me is going to be mighty lucky. That's how Doc Frail made his pile, you know. Grubstaking prospectors."

He did not ask her for anything. He did not suggest that she stake him. She thought of it all by herself.

"Tell me more, Mr. Plante," she said. "Maybe I will stake you."

He argued a little—couldn't possibly accept a stake from a lady. She argued—he must, because she owed him her life, and she would like to get rich. How much did he need?

Anything, anything—but with prices so high—and he'd have to hire labor, and that came high, too—

She calculated wildly. Six pokes of gold, a pound in each one. She had no basis for computing how much a prospector needed.

"I will give you half of what I have," she offered. "And you will give me half of the gold you find. I think we should have some sort of written contract, too."

Frenchy was dazzled. He had nothing to lose. He did not expect to have any gold to divide. His luck had been bad for months, and he intended to leave Skull Creek as soon as the weather permitted travel.

He dictated the contract as Elizabeth wrote in her prettiest penmanship, and both of them signed.

"The contract's yours to keep," he told her. It was a valid grubstake contract—if the holder could enforce it.

"I'll name the mine after you," he promised, vastly cheerful. "A few weeks from now—next summer anyway—you'll have to get gold scales to keep track of your take. When you see me again, you can call me Solid Gold Frenchy!"

At the Big Nugget, Frenchy took care to stand at the end of the bar nearest the table where Doc Frail was killing time in a card game.

The bartender was polite to Frenchy because business was poor, but his tone was firm as he warned, "Now, Frenchy, you know you ain't got no more credit here."

Frenchy was jovial and loud in his answer: "Did I say a word about credit this time? Just one drink, and I'll pay for it." He pulled out a poke.

Doc Frail was paying no attention to Frenchy and not much to the game. He took care to be seen in public most evenings, in the vain hope of weakening the camp's conviction that the lost lady was his property. He succeeded only in confusing the men, who felt he was treating her badly by leaving her in solitude.

Frenchy held up his glass and said with a grin, "Here's to the gold that's there for the finding, and here's to my grubstake partner."

Doc could not help glancing up. Frenchy had worn out three or four stakes already. Doc himself had refused him and did not know of a single man in camp who was willing to give him another start.

He looked up to see Frenchy grinning directly at him.

A challenge? Doc wondered. What's he been up to?

A suspicion of what Frenchy had been up to was like a burning coal in his mind.

Are you the man? he thought. Are you, Frenchy Plante, the man for whom I'll hang?

He stayed on for half an hour, until Frenchy had gone. He found Elizabeth in a cheerful mood, mending one of his shirts.

"The tea's been standing and it's strong," she apologized, getting a cup ready for him.

Drinking it, he waited for her to say that Frenchy had been there, but she only asked about Tall John's health.

Finally Doc remarked, "Frenchy Plante has suddenly come into comparative riches. He's got a grubstake from somewhere."

Elizabeth said mildly, "Is that so?"

"He said so when he bought a drink just now," Doc added, and Elizabeth was indignant.

"Is that what he's doing with it—drinking it up? I declare, I don't approve. I grubstaked him, if that's what you're trying to find out. But that was so he wouldn't starve and could go on mining when the weather moderates."

Doc said sadly, "Oh, Elizabeth!"

"It was mine," she maintained. "I simply invested some of it. Because I have plenty—and I want more."

Frenchy went on a prolonged, riotous and dangerous drinking spree. He was so violent that Madame Dewey, who kept the rooms above the Big Nugget, had him thrown out of there—at some expense, because two men were injured in removing him.

When he was almost broke, he really did go prospecting.

Doc and Rune treated Elizabeth with distant courtesy, mentioning casually the less scandalous highlights of Frenchy Plante's orgy. They did not scold, but their courtesy was painful. She had no friends any more, no alternately laughing and sarcastic friend named Joe Frail, no rude but faithful friend named Rune. They were only her physician and the boy who did her errands. She lived in a log-lined, lamplit cave, and sometimes wished she were dead.

There was a window by her front door; Rune had nailed stout wooden bars across it on the inside. For privacy, an old blanket was hung over the bars. She could peek through the small hole in the blanket for a narrow glimpse of the street, but nothing ever happened that was worth looking at. To let in daylight by taking the blanket off the window was to invite stares of men who happened to pass by—and sometimes the curious, yearning, snow-bound miners were too drunk to remember that Doc Frail was her protector, or if they remembered, too drunk to care.

One of them, who tried to get in one evening in mid-April, was cunning when he made his plans. He was sober enough to reconnoiter first.

He knew where Doc Frail was—playing cards at the Big Nugget, bored but not yet yawning. Rune was in Doc's cabin with a lamp on the table, bent over a book. Tall John was limping down the gulch with a lantern to visit friends. And Frenchy Plante, who had some right to the lady because he had found her, was somewhere out in the hills.

The intruder felt perfectly safe about the warning bells. If the lady pulled the rope, there would be no noise, because he had cut the rope.

Elizabeth was asleep on her bed, fully clothed—she slept a great deal, having nothing else to do—when knuckles rapped at the back door and a voice not quite like Doc's called, "Miss Armistead! Elizabeth!"

She sat up, frozen with fright. Then the pounding was louder, with the slow beats of an axe handle. She did not answer, and with senseless anger the man began to chop at the back door.

She ran and seized the bell rope. It slumped loose in her hands. She heard the dry wood crack and splinter. She did not even try to escape by the front door. She reached for the derringer that had been her father's, pointed it blindly and screamed as she pulled the trigger.

Then she was defenseless, but there was no more chopping, no sound at all, until she heard Rune's approaching shout. She was suddenly calm and guiltily triumphant. Making very sure that Rune was indeed Rune, she unbarred the front door and let him in.

"I fired the little gun!" she boasted.

"You didn't hurt anybody," Rune pointed out. The bullet had lodged in the splintered back door. "We'll just wait right here till Doc comes."

But Doc solved no problems when he came. He sat quietly and listened to Elizabeth's story.

"I don't know," Doc said hopelessly. "I don't know how to protect you." He motioned toward the shattered splintered door. "Rune, fix that. I'll repair the bell rope."

Rune nailed the back door solid again and was noisy outside at the woodpile for a few minutes. When he came back, he said briefly, "Nobody will try that entrance again tonight. I'm going to bring blankets and sleep on the woodpile."

In Doc Frail's cabin he bundled blankets together. He straightened up and blurted out a question: "How much time do I still owe you?"

"Time? That old nonsense. You don't owe me anything. I just wanted to cut you down to size."

"Maybe somebody will cut you down to size sometime," Rune said. "I suppose you were never licked in your life. The great Joe Frail, always on top of the heap. It's time you got off it."

Doc said, "Hey! What's this sudden insurrection?"

"All you do is boss Elizabeth around. Why don't you get down on your knees instead? Didn't it ever dawn on you that if you married her, you could take her out of here to some decent place?" Rune was working himself up to anger. "Sure, she'd say she couldn't go, but you could make her go—tie her up and take her out in a wagon if there's no other way. How do you know the only right way to get her out of Skull Creek is to make her decide it for herself? Do you know everything?"

Doc answered, "No, I don't know everything," with new humility. He was silent for a while. "Don't think the idea is new to me. I've considered it. But I don't think she'd have me."

Rune picked up his blankets. "That's what I mean," he said. "You won't gamble unless you're sure you'll win." He slammed the door behind him.

VIII

When Doc set out to court Elizabeth Armistead, he put his whole heart into it, since this was what he had been wanting to do for a long time anyway. He was deferential and suitably humble. He was gentle. He was kind. And Elizabeth, who had never had a suitor before (except old Mr. Ellerby, who had talked across her head to her father), understood at once what Doc's intentions were.

He crossed the street more often and stayed longer. He came at meal-time, uninvited, and said he enjoyed her cooking. He even cut and carried in firewood. He brought his socks to be mended. They sat in pleasant domesticity at the table, while Elizabeth sewed and sometimes glanced across at him.

In his own cabin, Rune studied with the patient, Tall John.

And fifteen miles away, Frenchy Plante panned gravel. The ground had thawed, and rain made his labors miserable, but Frenchy had a hunch. Ninety-nine times out of a hundred, his hunches didn't pan out, but he trusted them anyway.

On a slope by a stream there was a ragged old tree. Beside it he had a pit from which he had dug gravel that showed occasional colors. He groaned out of his blankets one gray dawn, in his ragged tent, to find that the tree was no longer visible. Its roots washed by rain, it had fallen headfirst into his pit.

Frenchy swore.

"A sign, that's what it is," he growled. "A sign there wasn't nothing there to dig for. Damn tree filled up my pit. Going to leave here, never go back to Skull Creek."

But he had left a bucket by the tree, and he went for the bucket. The tree's head was lower than its roots, and the roots were full of mud, slick with rain. Mud that shone, even in the gray light.

He tore at the mud with his hands. He shelled out chunks like peanuts, but peanuts never shone so richly yellow. He forgot breakfast, forgot to build a fire, scrabbled in the oozing mud among the roots.

He held in his hand a chunk the size of a small crabapple, but no crabapple was ever so heavy.

He stood in the pouring rain with a little golden apple in his muddy hands. He threw his head back so the rain came into his matted beard, and he howled like a wolf at the dripping sky.

He staked his claim and worked it from dawn to dusk for a week, until he was too exhausted by labor and starvation to wash gravel any more. He might have died there in the midst of his riches, because he was too weak to go back to Skull Creek for grub, but he shot an unwary deer and butchered it and fed. The discovery that even he could lose his strength— and thereby his life and his treasure—frightened him. He caught his horse, packed up, and plodded toward Skull Creek, grinning.

He slogged down the gulch at dusk, eager to break the news to Elizabeth Armistead, but he had another important plan. He shouted in front of a wickiup built into the side of the gulch: "Bill, you there? It's Frenchy."

The wickiup had been his until he sold it for two bottles of whiskey. Bill Scanlan looked out and said without enthusiasm, "Broke already? Well, we got beans."

A man known as Lame George, lying on a dirty blanket, grunted a greeting.

"Crowded here," he murmured. "But we can make room."

"Anything happening?" Frenchy asked, wolfing cold fried pork and boiled beans.

"Stages ain't running yet. This camp's played out. What'd you find?"

"Some good, some bad. Mostly bad." That was honest, not that honesty mattered much, and not that prospectors expected it even among friends. "I was thinking about that time the boys drove the mules through the old lady's tent. I bet there ain't been a funny joke like that for a long time."

Lame George said sadly, "There ain't, for a fact. Nothing much to do, nothing to laugh about. We been digging but couldn't raise a color."

"I got a good idea for a funny joke," Frenchy hinted. "On Doc Frail."

Lame George snorted. "Nobody jokes him."

"I'd make it worth a man's while," Frenchy said with great casualness, and Lame George sat up to demand, "What'll you do it with? You find something?"

"What you got, Frenchy?" Scanlan asked tensely.

"The joke," Frenchy reminded them. "What about the joke on Doc?"

"Hell, yes!" Lame George exploded. "Let us in on something good and we'll take our chances on Doc." He glanced at Scanlan, who nodded agreement.

"All I want," Frenchy explained, spreading his hands to show his innocent intentions, "is to make a social call on the lady, Miss Armistead, without getting my head blowed off. Is Tall John still living at Doc's?"

"He got better and moved to a shack. Rune still lives with Doc. But what," Lame George demanded with justifiable suspicion, "do you want with the lady?"

"Wouldn't hurt her for the world. Won't lay a hand on her. Just want to talk to her." Frenchy added with a grin, "Just want to show her something I found and brought back in my pocket."

They swarmed at him, grabbed his arms, their eyes eager. "You made a strike, Frenchy? Sure you did—and she grubstaked you!"

Elizabeth sat at the table, mending by lamplight. Doc was across from her, reading aloud to their mutual contentment. He sat in comfort, in his shirt sleeves, his coat and gun belt hanging on a nail by the front door. The fire in the cookstove crackled, and the teakettle purred.

Doc chose his reading carefully. In an hour and a half, he worked through portions of the works of Mr. Tennyson and Mr. Browning and, apparently by accident, looked into the love sonnets of William Shakespeare—exactly what he had been aiming at from the beginning.

"Why," Elizabeth asked, "are you suddenly so restless? Are you tired of reading to me?"

Doc discovered that he was no longer sitting. He was walking the floor, and the time had come to speak.

"My name," he said abruptly, "is not really Frail."

She was not shocked. "Why did you choose that one, then?"

"Because I was cynical. Because I thought it suited me. Elizabeth, I have to talk about myself. I have to tell you some things."

She said, "Yes, Joe."

"I killed a man once."

She looked relieved. "I heard it was four men!"

He frowned. "Does it seem to you that one does not matter? It matters to me."

She said gently, "I'm sorry, Joe. It matters to me, too. But one is better than four."

And even four killings, he realized, she would have forgiven me!

He bent across the table.

"Elizabeth, I enjoy your company. I would like to have it the rest of my life. I want to protect you and work for you and love you and—make you happy, if I can."

"I shouldn't have let you say that," she answered quietly. Her eyes were closed, and there were tears on her cheeks. "I am going to marry a man named Ellerby. And I expect I'll make his life miserable."

He said teasingly, "Does a girl shed tears when she mentions the name of a man she really plans to marry? I've made you cry many a time, but—"

He was beside her, and she clung as his arms went around her. He kissed her until she fought for breath.

"Not Ellerby, whoever he is, my darling. But me. Because I love you. When the roads are passable—soon, soon—I'll take you away and you'll not need to set foot on the ground or look at—anything."

"No, Joe, not you. Mr. Ellerby will come for me when I write him, and he will hate every mile of it. And I will marry him because he doesn't deserve any better."

"That's nonsense," Doc Frail said. "You will marry me."

Across the street, a man with a bad cold knocked at Doc's door. He kept a handkerchief to his face as he coughed out his message to Rune:

"Can Doc come, or you? Tall John's cut his leg with an axe, bleeding bad."

"I'll come," gasped Rune, and grabbed for Doc's bag. He knew pretty well what to do for an axe cut; he had been working with Doc all winter. "Tell Doc—he's right across the street."

"Go to Tall John's place," the coughing man managed to advise. As far as Rune knew, he went across the street to call Doc. Rune did not look back; he was running to save his patient.

When he was out of sight, another man who had been standing in the shadows pounded on Elizabeth's door, calling frantically, "Doc, come quick! That kid Rune's been stabbed at the Big Nugget!"

He was out of sight when Doc Frail barged out, hesitated a moment, decided he could send someone for his bag, and ran toward the saloon.

He tripped and, as he fell, something hit him on the back of the head.

He did not lie in the mud very long. Two men solicitously carried him back in the opposite direction and laid him in the slush at the far side of

Flaunce's store. They left him there and went stumbling down the street, obviously drunk.

Frenchy Plante did not use force in entering Elizabeth's cabin. He knocked and called out, "Miss Armistead, it's Frenchy." In a lower tone, he added, "I got good news for you!"

She opened the door and demanded, "Is Rune hurt badly? Oh, what happened?"

"The boy got hurt?" Frenchy was sympathetic.

"Someone called Dr. Frail to look after him—didn't you see him go?"

Frenchy said good-humoredly, "Miss, I'm too plumb damn excited. Listen, can I come in and show you what I brought?"

She hesitated, too concerned to care whether he came in or not.

"Remember," he whispered, "what I said once about Solid Gold Frenchy?"

She remembered and gasped. "Come in," she said.

Doc reeled along the street, cold, soaking wet, and with his head splitting. He would have stopped long enough to let his head stop spinning, but he was driven by cold fear that was like sickness.

What about Elizabeth alone in her cabin? Where was Rune and how badly was he hurt? Doc was bruised and aching, tricked and defeated. Who had conquered him was not very important. Skull Creek would know soon enough that someone had knocked the starch out of Doc Frail without a shot being fired.

Rune, wherever he was, would have to wait for help if he needed it.

At Elizabeth's door Doc listened and heard her voice between tears and laughter: "I don't believe it! I don't think it's really true!"

The door was not barred. He opened it and stood watching with narrowed eyes. Elizabeth was rolling something crookedly across the table, something yellow that looked like a small, misshapen apple. When it fell and boomed on the floor boards, he knew what it was.

He asked in a controlled voice, "Has the kid been here?"

Elizabeth glanced up and gasped. She ran to him, crying, "Joe, you're hurt—what happened? Come sit down. Oh, Joe!"

Frenchy Plante was all concern and sympathy. "My God, Doc, what hit you?"

Doc Frail brushed Elizabeth gently aside and repeated, "Has the kid been here?"

"Ain't seen him," Frenchy said earnestly. "Miss Armistead was saying you'd been called out, he was hurt, so we thought you was with him."

Doc turned away without answering. He ran, stumbling, toward the Big

Nugget. He stood in the doorway of the saloon, mud-stained, bloody and arrogant. He asked in a voice that did not need to be loud, "Is the kid in here?"

Nobody answered that, but someone asked, "Well, now, what happened to you?" in a tone of grandfatherly indulgence.

They were watching him, straight-faced, without concern, without much interest, the way they would look at any other man in camp. But not the way they should have looked at Doc Frail. There was nothing unusual in their attitudes, except that they were not surprised. And they should have been. They expected this, he understood.

"I was informed," Doc said, "that Rune had been knifed in a fight here."

The bartender answered, "Hell, there ain't been a fight here. And Rune ain't been in since he came for you two-three days ago."

Doc was at bay, as harmless as an unarmed baby. He turned to the door —and heard laughter, instantly choked.

Outside, he leaned against the wall, sagging, waiting for his head to stop spinning, waiting for his stomach to settle down.

There was danger in the laughter he had heard. And there was nothing he could do. Frail, Frail, Frail.

He realized that he was standing on the spot where Wonder Russell stood when Dusty Smith shot him, long ago.

He began to run, lurching, toward Elizabeth's cabin.

She was waiting in the doorway. She called anxiously, "Joe! Joe!"

Frenchy said, "I kept telling her you'd be all right, but I figured it was best to stay here with her in case anything else happened."

Doc did not answer but sat down, staring at him, and waited for Elizabeth to bring a pan of water and towels.

"Is Rune all right?" she demanded.

"I presume so. It was only a joke, I guess."

Golden peas and beans were on the table with the little golden apple. When Doc would not let Elizabeth help him clean the blood off his face, she turned toward the table slowly as if she could not help it.

"He named the mine for me," she whispered. "He calls it the Lucky Lady." Her face puckered, but she did not cry. She laughed instead, choking.

Rune came in at that moment, puzzled and furious, with Doc's bag.

"They said Tall John was hurt," he blurted out, and stopped at sight of Doc Frail.

"The way I heard it," Doc said across the towel, "you were knifed at the saloon. And somebody hit me over the head."

Rune seemed not to hear him. Rune was staring at the nuggets, moving toward them, pulled by the same force that had pulled Elizabeth.

Frenchy chortled, "Meet the Lucky Lady, kid. I got a strike, and half of it is hers. I'll be leaving now. No, the nuggets are yours, Miss, and there'll be more. Sure hope you get over that crack on the head all right, Doc."

Doc's farewell to Elizabeth was a brief warning: "Bar the door. From now on, there'll be trouble."

He did not explain. He left her to think about it.

She did not go to bed at all that night. She sat at the table, fondling the misshapen golden apple and the golden peas and beans, rolling them, counting them. She held them in her cupped hands, smiling, staring, but not dreaming yet. Their value was unknown to her; there would be plenty of time to get them weighed. They were only a token, anyway. There would be more, lots more.

She hunted out, in its hiding place, a letter she had written to Mr. Ellerby, read it through once, and burned it in the stove.

The golden lumps would build a wall of safety between her and Mr. Ellerby, between her and everything she didn't want.

She sat all night, or stood sometimes by the front window, smiling, hearing the sounds she recognized although she had never heard the like before: the endless racket of a gold rush. Horses' hoofs and the slogging feet of men, forever passing, voices earnest or anxious or angry, the creak of wagons. She listened eagerly with the golden apple cupped in her hand.

Even when someone pounded on her door, she was not afraid. The walls are made of gold, she thought. Nobody can break them down. A man called anxiously, "Lucky Lady, wish me luck! That's all I want, lady, all in the world I want."

Elizabeth answered, "I wish you luck, whoever you are," and laughed.

But when, toward morning, she heard an angry racket outside the back door, she was frightened for Rune. She ran to listen.

"I've got a gun on you," he was raging. "Git going, now!" And men's voices mumbled angrily away.

She spoke to him through the closed back door.

"Rune, go and get Doc. I have been making plans."

The three of them sat at the table before dawn. Coffee was in three cups, but only Rune drank his.

Doc listened to Elizabeth and thought, This is some other woman, not the lost lady, the helpless prisoner. This is the Lucky Lady, an imprisoned queen. This is royalty. This is power. She has suddenly learned to command.

"I would like to hire you, Rune, to be my guard," she began.

Rune glanced at Doc, who nodded. Rune did not answer. Elizabeth did not expect him to answer.

"I would like you to buy me a gold scale as soon as possible," she continued. "And please find out from Mr. Flaunce what would be the cost of freighting in a small piano from the States."

Doc said wearily, "Elizabeth, that's defeat. If you order a piano and wait for it to get here, that means you're not even thinking of leaving Skull Creek."

"When I thought of it, thinking did me no good," she answered, and dismissed the argument.

"Rune, please ask Mr. Flaunce to bring over whatever bolts of dress material he has—satin, in a light gray. I shall have a new dress."

Rune put down his coffee cup. "You could build a lean-to on the back here. I'd ought to stay pretty close, and I don't hanker to sleep on that woodpile often."

She nodded approval. "And another thing: grubstaking Frenchy brought me luck. Other miners will think of the same thing, and I will grubstake them, to keep my luck."

Rune growled, "Nonsense. Hand out a stake to every one that asks for it, and you'll be broke in no time. Set a limit—say every seventh man that asks. But don't let anybody know it's the seventh that gets it."

Elizabeth frowned, then nodded. "Seven is a lucky number."

Doc picked up his cup of cool coffee.

A handful of gold has changed us all, he thought. Elizabeth is the queen —the golden Queen Elizabeth. Rune is seventeen years old, but he is a man of sound judgment—and he is the second best shot in the territory. And I, I am a shadow.

Doc said gently, "Elizabeth, there may not be very much more gold for Frenchy to divide with you. You are planning too much grandeur."

"There will be a great deal more," she contradicted, serenely. "I am going to be very rich. I am the Lucky Lady."

IX

At the end of a single week, the fragility of the Skull Creek gold camp was plain. The town was collapsing, moving to the new strike at Plante Gulch.

The streets swarmed and boomed with strangers—but they were only passing through. Flaunce's store was open day and night to serve prospectors replenishing grub supplies and going on to the new riches. Flaunce was desperately trying to hire men to freight some of his stock on to diggings to set up another store before someone beat him to it.

Doc Frail lounged in his own doorway waiting for Rune to come from Elizabeth's cabin, and watched the stream of men passing by—bearded, ragged, determined men on foot or on horseback, leading donkeys or mules, driving bull teams with laden wagons, slogging along with packs on their shoulders. Almost all of them were strangers.

Let's see if I'm what I used to be, Doc thought, before Frenchy tricked me and got me hit over the head.

He stepped forward into the path of a pack-laden man, who was walking fast and looking earnestly ahead. When they collided, Doc glared at him with his old arrogance, and the man said angrily, "Damn you, stay out of the way," shoved with his elbow, and went on.

No, I am not what I used to be, Doc admitted silently. The old power, which had worked even on strangers, was gone, the challenge in the stare that asked, Do you amount to anything?

Rune came weaving through the crowd, and Doc saw in him power that was new. Rune looked taller. He wore new, clean clothing and good boots, although the gun in his holster was one Doc had given him months before. Rune was no longer sullen. He wore a worried frown, but he was sure of himself.

Doc pointed with his thumb to a vacant lot, and Rune nodded. It was time for his daily target practice, purposely public. In the vacant space where nobody would get hurt, Doc tossed an empty can, and Rune punctured it with three shots before it fell. The steady stream of passing men became a whirlpool, then stopped, and the crowd grew.

Someone shouted, "Hey, kid," and tossed another can. Doc's pistol and Rune's thundered a duet, and the crowd was pleased.

When Rune's gun was empty, Doc kept firing, still with his right hand but with his second gun, tossed with a flashing movement from his left hand as the first weapon dropped to the ground. No more duet, but solo now, by the old master. He heard admiration among the men around them, and that was all to the good. It was necessary that strangers should know the Lucky Lady was well protected. The border shift, the trick of tossing a loaded gun into the hand that released an empty one, was impressive, but Rune had not yet perfected it enough for public demonstration.

That was all there was to the show. The crowd moved on.

"Go take yourself a walk or something," Doc suggested. "I'll watch Elizabeth's place for a while."

"There's a crazy man in town," Rune said. "Did you see him?"

"There are hundreds of crazy men in town. Do you mean that fanatical preacher with red whiskers? I've been on the edge of his congregation three or four times but never stopped to listen. I wouldn't be surprised if the camp lynched him just to shut him up."

"He scares me," Rune admitted, frowning. "They don't like him, but he gets everybody mad and growling. He don't preach the love of God. It's all hell fire and damnation."

Doc asked, suddenly suspicious, "Has he been to Elizabeth's?"

"He was. I wouldn't let him in. But when I said he was a preacher, she made me give him some dust. She'd like to talk to him, figuring she'd get some comfort. He's not the kind of preacher that ever comforted anybody. Go listen to him when you have time."

"I have more time than I used to," Doc Frail admitted. Two new doctors had come through Skull Creek, both heading for the booming new settlement at Plante Gulch.

Doc had an opportunity to listen to the preacher the next afternoon. The piano player at a dance hall far down the street threw his back out of kilter while trying to move the piano. Doc went down to his shack, gave him some pain killer and with a straight face prescribed bed rest and hot bricks.

The man squalled, "Who'll heat the bricks? And I can't stay in bed— we're moving this shebang to Plante Gulch soon as they finish laying a floor."

"They need a piano player when they get there," Doc reminded him. "I'll tell the boss to see to it you get the hot bricks. You are an important fellow, professor."

"Say, guess I am," the man agreed. "Unless they get a better piano player."

Doc left the proprietor tearing his hair because of the threatened delay, then went out to the street. It was crowded with men whose movement had been slowed by curiosity, for across the street on a packing box the red-haired man was preaching.

His eyes were wild, and so were his gestures, and his sermon was a disconnected series of uncompleted threats. He yelled and choked.

"Oh, ye of little faith! Behold I say unto you! Behold a pale horse: and his name that sat on him was Death, and Hell followed with him! Verily, brethren, do not forget hell—the eternal torment, the fire that never dieth. And I heard a great voice out of the temple saying to the seven angels, go your ways, and pour out the vials of the wrath of God upon the earth.

"Lo, there is a dragon that gives power unto the beast, and you worship the dragon and the beast, saying, 'Who is like unto the beast?' And the dragon is gold and the beast is gold, and lo, ye are eternally damned that seek the dragon or the beast."

The preacher was quoting snatches of Revelation, Doc realized, with changes of his own that were not exactly improvements. But gold may be a dragon and a beast, indeed.

A man in the crowd shouted, "Aw, shut up and go dig yourself some beast!" and there was a roar of approving laughter.

"Remember Sodom and Gomorrah!" screamed the red-haired man. "For their wickedness they were burned—yea, for their sin and evil! Lo, this camp is wicked like unto those two!"

Doc Frail was caught in an impatient eddy in the moving crowd, and someone growled, "Give that horse a lick or we'll never get out of Sodom and on to Gomorrah by dark!"

The preacher's ranting stirred a kind of futile anger in Joe Frail. What makes him think he's so much better than his congregation? Doc wondered. There's a kind of hatred in him.

"A sinful nation," shouted the preacher. "A people laden with iniquity, the seed of evildoers, children that are corrupters. Hear the word of the Lord, ye rulers of Sodom; give ear unto the law of our God, ye people of Gomorrah!"

The Book of the Prophet Isaiah, reflected Joe Frail, who was the son of a minister's daughter. Immediately the red-haired man returned to Revelation:

"There is given unto me a mouth speaking great things, and power is given unto me to continue forty and two months!"

A man behind Joe Frail shouted, "We ain't going to listen that long."

"If any man have an ear, let him hear! He that leadeth into captivity shall go into captivity; he that killeth with the sword must be killed with the sword."

Joe Frail shivered in spite of himself, thinking, And he that killeth with a pistol?

In that moment a man's voice said behind him, *"That is the man,"* and Doc went tense as if frozen, staring at the red-haired madman.

"That's the man I told you about," the voice went on, moving past him. "Crazy as a loon. His name is Grubb."

How could it be? Doc wondered. How could that be the man for whom I'll hang?

After a few days, the madman went on to Plante Gulch.

By August, Elizabeth Armistead was rich and getting richer. The interior log walls of her cabin were draped with yards of white muslin, her furniture was the finest that could be bought in Skull Creek, her piano had been ordered from the East, and she dressed in satin. But only a few men ever saw her, only every seventh man who came to beg a grubstake from the Lucky Lady, and Frenchy Plante when he came to bring her half the cleanup from the mine.

This is Saturday, Doc Frail remembered. Cleanup day at the sluices. Frenchy will be in with the gold. And I will spend the evening with Elizabeth, waiting for him to come. The Lucky Lady hides behind a golden wall.

He found Elizabeth indignantly arguing with Rune.

"Frenchy sent a man to say they have a big cleanup this time," she told Doc. "And they want a man with a reputation to help guard it on the way in. But Rune refuses to go!"

"I don't get paid to guard gold," Rune said. "I hired out to guard you."

"Half of it's mine," she argued.

"And half of it's Frenchy's. He'll look after it. The bank's going to open up whenever he comes. But I'm going to be right here."

Doc said without a smile, "Young lady, you seem to have a sensible fellow on your payroll," and was pleased to see Rune blush.

By George, he thought, that's probably the first decent thing I ever said to him!

"I'll be here, too," Doc promised. "Just making a social call."

He was too restless to sit down and wait. He stood in the doorway, looking out, thinking aloud: "The month is August, Elizabeth. The day is lovely, even in this barren cleft between barren hills. And you are young, and I am not decrepit. But you're a prisoner." He turned toward her and asked gently, "Come for a walk with me, Elizabeth?"

"No!" she whispered instantly. "Oh, no!"

He shrugged and turned away. "There was a time when you couldn't go because you didn't have any place to go or enough money. Now you can afford to go anywhere, but you've got a pile of nuggets to hide behind."

"Joe, that's not it at all! I can't go now for the same reason I couldn't go before."

"Have you tried, Elizabeth?"

She would not answer.

He saw that Rune was watching him with slitted eyes and cold anger in the set of his mouth.

"Maybe your partner will bring you some new and unusual nuggets," Doc remarked. "I wonder where he gets them from."

"From his mine, of course," Elizabeth answered. Her special nuggets were not in sight, but Doc knew they were in the covered sugar bowl on the table.

"Madam, I beg to differ. The Lucky Lady is a placer operation. Water is used to wash gold out of dirt and gravel. Most of your nuggets came from there, all right. But—spread them out and I'll show you."

Unwillingly, she tipped the sugar bowl. It was packed with gold; she had to pry it out with a spoon. And this was not her treasure, but her hobby, the private collection she kept just because it was so beautiful.

Doc touched a golden snarl of rigid strands. "That's wire gold, hardened when it cooled. It squeezed through crevices in rock. Rock, Elizabeth. That's hard-rock gold, not placer, and it never came from diggings within a couple of hundred miles from here. Neither did those sharp-edged nuggets with bits of quartz still on them. That gold never came from the mine Frenchy named for you."

Elizabeth stared, fascinated and frightened. "It was in with some other lumps he brought. Where did he get it?"

"He sent for it, to give you. Some men go courting with flowers. Frenchy gives his chosen one imported gold nuggets."

"Don't talk that way! I don't like it."

"I didn't suppose you would, but it was time to tell you."

Frenchy was cleverly succeeding in two purposes: to please Elizabeth and to taunt Joe Frail.

And we are harmless doves, both of us, Doc thought.

"I wish you'd keep those grubstake contracts at the bank," Doc remarked. Four of them were paying off, and some of the others might. "Why keep them in that red box right here in your cabin?"

"Because I like to look at them sometimes," she said stubbornly. "They're perfectly safe. I have Rune to guard me."

Doc smiled with one corner of his mouth, and she hastened to add, "And I have you, too."

"As long as I live, Elizabeth," he said gently.

Rune tried to clear the air by changing the subject. "I hear the preacher, Grubb, is back."

"Then I would like to talk to him," said Elizabeth. "If he comes to the door, please let him in."

"No!" Doc said quite loudly. "Rune, do not let him in. He's a lunatic."

Elizabeth said coolly, "Rune will let him in. Because I want to talk to him. And because I say so!"

Doc said, "Why, Elizabeth!" and looked at her in astonishment. She sat stiff-backed with her chin high, pale with anger, imperious—the queen behind the golden wall, the Lucky Lady, who had forgotten how vulnerable she was. Doc Frail, newly vulnerable, and afraid since the great joke Frenchy had played on him, could not stare her down.

"Rune," he began, but she interrupted, "Rune will let him in because I say so."

Rune looked down at them both. "I will not let him in, and not because Doc says to keep him out. I won't let him in—because he shouldn't get in. And that's how it is."

Doc smiled. "The world has changed, Elizabeth. That's how it is. Rune holds all the winning cards—and nobody needs to tell him how to play them."

Rune guessed dimly in that moment that, no matter how long he lived or what he accomplished to win honor among men, he would never be paid any finer compliment.

"Guess I'll go see what's doing around town," he said, embarrassed.

"Both of you can go!" Elizabeth cried in fury.

To her surprise, Doc answered mildly, "All right," and she was left alone. The nuggets from the sugar bowl were scattered on the table. She touched them, fondled them, sorted them into heaps according to size and shape. She began to forget anger and imprisonment. She began to forget that she was young and far from home.

Doc Frail was only a hundred yards away from the cabin when a messenger on a mule hailed him: "Hey, Doc! My partner Frank's hurt up at

our mine. There's three men trying to get him out, or hold up the timber-
ing anyway."

He flung himself off the mule and Doc, who had his satchel, leaped into
the saddle. He knew where the mine was.

"Send some more men up there," he urged, and started for it.

Rune, strolling, saw him go and turned at once back to the Lucky
Lady's cabin. He did not go in. He hunkered down by the front door and
began to whittle.

Down beyond the Big Nugget, the red-haired man was preaching a new
sermon, lashing himself to fury—and attracting a more favorably inclined
audience than usual. His topic was the Lucky Lady. There was no more
fascinating topic in Skull Creek, for she was young and desirable and
mysterious, and she represented untold riches, even to men who had never
seen her, who knew her only as a legend.

"Lo, there is sin in this camp, great sin!" Grubb was intoning. "The sin
that locketh the door on deliverance, that keepeth a young woman prisoner against her will. There is a wicked man who shutteth her up in a
cabin, that she escape not, and putteth a guard before her door that
righteousness may not enter!"

His listeners were strangers. They believed him, because why not?

One nudged another and murmured, "Say, did you know that?" The
other shook his head, frowning.

"She cannot be delivered from evil," intoned Grubb, "because evil
encompasseth her round about. She has no comfort within those walls
because the servant of the Lord is forbidden to enter."

Someone asked, "Did you try?"

Grubb had tried just once, weeks earlier. But he remembered it as
today, and anger was renewed in him. He began to yell.

"Verily, the servant of the Lord tried to enter, to pray with her for
deliverance, to win her from evil. But the guard at the door turned him
away and bribed him with nuggets. Lo, the guard is as evil as the master,
and both of them are damned!"

His audience saw what he saw, the arrogant doctor who would not let
the Lucky Lady go, and the young man who idled at her doorway to keep
rescuers away. His audience stirred and murmured, and someone said, "By
damn, that's a bad thing!" His audience increased, and Grubb, for once
delivering a message to which men listened without reviling him, went on
screaming words that he convinced himself were true.

One man on the edge of the crowd walked away—the horse thief who
was a friend of Tall John, and of Doc who had cured him, and of Rune

who had nursed him. The horse thief passed the barbershop and observed that Frenchy Plante was inside, getting his hair cut. Frenchy's mule was hitched in front, and the gold from the weekly cleanup was no doubt in the pack on the mule. But Frenchy was watching from the barber chair with a rifle across his knees, so the horse thief did not linger.

Walking fast, but not running, he paused in front of the Lucky Lady's cabin and spoke quietly to Rune:

"The red-haired fellow is raising hell, working the men up. Saying the girl could get away if it wasn't Doc pays you to keep her locked up. Don't act excited, kid. We're just talking about the weather. I think there's going to be hell to pay, and I'll go tell Tall John. Where's Doc?"

"Went on a call, on Tim Morrison's mule—to Tim's mine, I guess. Thanks."

Unhurried, Rune entered the Lucky Lady's cabin and sat down.

The horse thief, who did not happen to possess a horse just then, went to the livery stable and rented one. At a trot, he rode to the place where Tall John was washing gravel. Tall John dropped his pick and said, "Go look for Doc." He himself started back toward Elizabeth's cabin at a brisk limp.

Tall John observed that a fairly large crowd had gathered down beyond the Big Nugget, and occasionally a shout came from it.

If they ever get into her cabin, he told himself, they'll have to kill the boy first—and if that happens, she won't care to live either. He and I, between us, will have to keep Frenchy out. Heaven forbid that he should be her rescuer!

Tall John knocked on Elizabeth's door and after he identified himself, Rune let him in. He sat down to chat as if he had come only for a friendly visit.

The horse thief met Doc Frail walking. The man trapped in the cave-in had died. He was still trapped.

"There's trouble," the horse thief said bluntly, and told him what the trouble was.

"I'll take that horse, please," Doc replied. He rode at a trot; he did not dare attract attention by going faster. And he did not know what he was going to do when he got to the cabin—if he got there.

It is too late to try to take her out of Skull Creek now, he realized. I wonder how much ammunition Rune has. I haven't much—and what can I do with it anyway, except to shoot through the roof and make a noise?

He heard Frenchy shout "Hey Doc!" from down the street, but he did not turn.

The crowd beyond the Big Nugget was beginning to stir and to scatter on the edges. Rune, watching from a peephole in the blanket on the window, let Doc in before he had a chance to knock.

The three inside the cabin were still as statues. Elizabeth said, "They've just told me. Joe, I'll go out when they come in and I'll tell Grubb it isn't so."

"You'll stay right here," Doc answered. "I hope you will not think I am being melodramatic, but I have to do something that I have been putting off for too long. Tall John, can I make a legal will by telling it to you? There's not time to write it. I want to watch that window."

Elizabeth gasped.

Tall John said, "Tell me. I will not forget."

"My name is Joseph Alberts. I am better known as Joseph Frail. I am of sound mind but in imminent danger of death. I bequeath two thousand dollars in clean gulch gold to—Rune, what's your name?"

Rune answered quietly, "Leonard Henderson."

"To Leonard Henderson, better known as Rune, to enable him to get a medical education if he wants it. Everything else I leave to Elizabeth Armistead, called the Lucky Lady."

"Oh, so lucky!" she choked.

He did not say that he wanted Rune to take her away from Skull Creek. It was not necessary.

"That mob is getting noisier," Doc commented. "Tall John, you'd better go out by the back door."

"I will not forget," Tall John promised. He left the cabin, not stopping even to shake hands.

Just outside the window, Frenchy shouted, "Lucky Lady! I got gold for you! Open the door for Frenchy, Lucky Lady."

No one inside the cabin moved. No one outside could see in.

Frenchy hiccuped and said, "Aw, hell, she ain't home." He rode on, then shouted, "But she's always home, ain't she?"

Doc spoke rapidly. "If I go out this door, both of you stay inside—and bar it. Do you understand?"

"I get it," Rune replied. Elizabeth was crying quietly.

Frenchy's voice came back. "Doc, you in there? Hey, Doc Frail! Come on out. You ain't scared, are you?"

Joe Frail went tense and relaxed with an effort of will.

"You wouldn't shoot me, would you, Doc?" Frenchy teased. "You wouldn't shoot nobody, would you, Doc?" He laughed uproariously, and Doc Frail did not move a muscle.

He heard the muttering mob now, the deep, disturbed murmur that he had heard from the hill on the day the road agent swung from a bough of the great tree.

He heard a shrill scream from Grubb, who saw Frenchy coaxing at the window and had seen Frenchy enter the cabin before.

Grubb's topic did not change, but his theme did, as he led his congregation. His ranting voice reached them:

"Wicked woman! Wicked and damned! Will all your gold save you from hell fire? Wanton and damned—"

Doc forgot he was a coward. He forgot a man lying dead in Utah. He forgot Wonder Russell, sleeping in a grave on the hill. He slammed the bar upward from the door and stepped into the street.

His voice was thunder: "Grubb, get down on your knees!"

Grubb was blind to danger. He did not even recognize Doc Frail as an obstacle. Clawing the air, he came on, screaming, "Babylon and the wicked woman—"

Doc Frail gasped and shot him.

He did not see Grubb fall, for the mob's wrath downed him. The last thing he heard as he went down under the deluge was the sound he wanted to hear: the bar falling shut inside the cabin door.

X

The rabble. The rabble. The first emotion he felt was contempt. Fear would come later. But no; fear had come. His mouth was cotton-dry.

He was bruised and battered, had been unconscious. He could not see the men he heard and despised. He lay face down on dirty boards and could see the ground through a crack. On a platform? No, his legs were bent and cramped. He was in a cart. He could not move his arms. They were bound to his body with rope.

The rabble shouted and jeered, but not all the jeering was for him— they could not agree among themselves. He knew where he was; under the hanging tree.

A voice cried furiously, "A trial! You've got to give the man a trial!"

Another shout mounted: "Sure, try him—he shot the preacher!"

This is the place and this is the tree, Joe Frail understood, and the rope must be almost ready. Grubb was the man, and I hardly knew he existed.

There was nothing that required doing. Someone else would do it all. There was something monstrous to be concerned about—but not for long.

And there was Elizabeth.

Joe Frail groaned and strained at the rope that bound him, and he heard Frenchy laugh.

"Let the boys see you, Doc," Frenchy urged. "Let 'em have a last good look!"

Someone heaved him to his feet and he blinked through his hair, fallen down over his eyes. The mob turned quiet, staring at a man who was as good as dead.

There was no need for dignity now, no need for anything. If he swayed, someone supported him. If he fell, they would stand him on his feet again. Everything that was to be done would be done by someone else. Joe Frail had no responsibilities any more. (Except—Elizabeth? Elizabeth?)

"Hell, that's no decent way to do it," someone argued with authority, not asking for justice but only for a proper execution. "The end of the cart will catch his feet that way. Put a plank across it. Then he'll get a good drop."

There was a busy delay while men streamed down the hill to get planks.

Joe Frail threw back his head with the old arrogant gesture and could see better with his hair tossed away from his eyes. He could see Skull Creek better than he wanted to, as clearly as when he first walked under the tree with Wonder Russell.

Elizabeth, Elizabeth. He was shaken with anger. When a man is at his own hanging, he should not have to think of anyone but himself.

And still, he understood, even now Joe Frail must fret helplessly about Elizabeth. Who ever really died at peace except those who had nothing to live for?

Men were coming with planks—four or five men, four or five planks. They busied themselves laying planks across the cart to make a platform so they could take satisfaction in having hanged him decently and with compassion. And from the side, Frenchy was bringing up a team of horses to pull the cart away.

Someone behind him slipped a noose down over his head, then took it off again, testing the length of the rope. Above, someone climbed along the out-thrust bough of the tree to tie it shorter. Joe Frail stood steady, not looking up, not glancing sideways at the horses being urged into position.

The crowd was quieter now, waiting.

Just as the team came into position in front of the cart, he saw movement down in the street of Skull Creek and strained forward.

Elizabeth's door had opened and Rune had come out of her cabin.

No! No! You damn young fool, stay in there and do what you can to save her! By tomorrow, they'll slink off like dogs and you can get her away safely. You fool! You utter fool!

What's he carrying? A red box.

No, Elizabeth! Oh, God, not Elizabeth! Stay in the cabin! Stay out of sight!

But the Lucky Lady had emerged from her refuge and was walking beside Rune. Walking fast, half running, with her head bent. Don't look, Elizabeth! My darling, don't look up! Turn back, turn back to the cabin. Tomorrow you can leave it.

A man behind Doc remarked, "Well, would you look at that!" but nobody else seemed to notice.

Doc said sharply, "What the hell are you waiting for?" Suddenly he was in a hurry. If they finished this fast enough, she would go back—Rune would see to it.

She was leaning forward against the wind of the desert that was thirty miles away. She was stumbling. But she did not fall. She had got past Flaunce's store.

The red box Rune is carrying? The box she keeps her gold in. Go back. Go back.

Someone slipped the noose down over his head again and he groaned and was ashamed.

She was struggling up the first slope of the barren hill, fighting the desert. Her right arm was across her eyes. But Doc could see Rune's face. Rune was carrying the heavy box and could not help the Lucky Lady, but the look on his face was one Doc had seen there seldom. It was pity.

The team was ready, the platform was prepared, the noose was around the condemned man's neck. The Lucky Lady stopped halfway up the hill.

There was almost no sound from the rabble except their breathing. Some of them were watching Elizabeth. She lifted her right hand and fired a shot from the derringer into the air.

Then they all watched her. The silence was complete and vast. The men stared and waited.

Rune put the red box on the ground and opened it, handed something to Elizabeth—a poke, Doc thought. She emptied it into her hand and threw nuggets toward the silent mob.

No one moved. No one spoke or even murmured.

Why, Rune has no gun, Doc saw. It is a long time since I have seen him with no holster on his hip. And Elizabeth has fired into the air the one shot her pistol will hold. They are unarmed, helpless. As helpless as I am.

The voice he heard was his own, screaming, "Go back! Go back!"

A man behind him rested a hand on his shoulder without roughness, as if to say, Hush, hush, this is a time for silence.

Elizabeth stooped again to the box and took out something white—the sugar bowl. She flung the great, shining nuggets of her golden treasure, two and three at a time, toward the motionless men on the slope. Then they were not quite motionless, there was jerky movement among them, instantly ceasing, as they yearned toward the scattered treasure but would not yield.

Elizabeth stood for a while with her head bent and her hands hanging empty. Joe Frail saw her shoulders move as she gulped in great breaths of air. Rune stood watching her with that look of pity twisting his mouth.

She bent once more and took out a folded paper, held it high, and gave it to the wind. It sailed a little distance before it reached the ground. She waited with her head bowed, and the mob waited, stirring with the restless motion of puzzled men.

She tossed another paper and another. Someone asked the air a question: "Contracts? Grubstake contracts?"

And someone else said, "But which ones?"

Most of the contracts had no meaning any more, but a very few of them commanded for the Lucky Lady half the golden treasure that sifted out of paying mines.

Frenchy's voice roared with glee: "She's buying Doc Frail! The Lucky Lady is buying her man!"

Joe Frail quivered, thinking, This is the last indignity. She has gambled everything, and there will be nothing for her to remember except my shame.

All the contracts, one at a time, she offered to the mob, and the wind claimed each paper for a brief time. All the nuggets in the sugar bowl. All the pale dust in the little leather bags that made the red box heavy.

Elizabeth stood at last with her hands empty. She touched the box with her foot and Rune lifted it, turned it upside down to show that it held nothing more, and let it fall.

Frenchy's shout and Frenchy's forward rush broke the mob's indecision. He yelled, "Come and git it, boys! Git your share of the price she's paying for Doc Frail!"

Frenchy ran for the scattered papers, tossed away one after another, then held one up, roaring, and kissed it.

The rabble broke. Shouting and howling, the mob scattered, the men scrabbled for gold in the dust. They swarmed like vicious ants, fighting for the treasure.

A jeering voice behind Doc said, "Hell, if she wants you that bad!" and cut the rope that bound him. The knife slashed his wrist and he felt blood run.

The Lucky Lady was running up the slope to him, not stumbling, not hesitating, free of fear and treasure, up toward the hanging tree. Her face was pale, but her eyes were shining.

The Third reel West

Portville Free Library
Portville, New York 14770